No Time to Explain

Read more Kate Angell

Sweet Spot (Richmond Rogues)

No Tan Lines (Barefoot William)

Unwrapped (Anthology)

He's the One (Anthology)

No Strings Attached (Barefoot William)

No Sunshine When She's Gone (Barefoot William)

The Sugar Cookie Sweethearts Swap (Anthology)

No One Like You (Barefoot William)

No Breaking My Heart (Barefoot William)

No Time to Explain

KATE ANGELL

KENSINGTON PUBLISHING CORP.
www.kensingtonbooks.com

KENSINGTON BOOKS are published by

Kensington Publishing Corp.
119 West 40th Street
New York, NY 10018

All Kensington titles, imprints, and distributed lines are available at special quantity discounts for bulk purchases for sales promotions, premiums, fund-raising, educational, or institutional use.

Special book excerpts or customized printings can also be created to fit specific needs. For details, write or phone the office of the Kensington sales manager: Kensington Publishing Corp., 119 West 40th Street, New York, NY 10018, attn: Sales Department; phone 1-800-221-2647.

KENSINGTON and the K logo are Reg. U.S. Pat. & TM Off.

ISBN-13: 978-1-4967-0368-2
ISBN-10: 1-4967-0368-5

First Kensington trade paperback printing: October 2017

10 9 8 7 6 5 4 3 2 1

Printed in the United States of America

First electronic edition: October 2017

ISBN-13: 978-1-4967-0369-9
ISBN-10: 1-4967-0369-3

Thanks, always, to Alicia Condon, Editorial Director.
Arthur Maisel, production editor, you are appreciated.
Debbie Jarodsky Roome, for all our years of friendship.
(In memory of) Jody Jarodsky Denison. I appreciated your
doggy day care stories, featuring your Goldendoodle, Murphy.
TK, my favorite Triple-A player.
My longtime readers, thank you for sticking by me. You are
the best. Welcome to my new readers. Enjoy Barefoot William
and the Rogues.
Play ball!

No Time to Explain

RICHMOND ROGUES
Starting Lineup

28 – RF – Halo Todd
19 – C – Hank Jacoby
13 – 3B – Landon Kane
22 – CF – Rylan Cates
6 – SS – Brody Jones
17 – 1B – Jake Packer
45 – LF – Joe Zooker
3 – 2B – Sam Matthews
55 – P – Will Ridgeway

One

"*Here comes the bride.*"

The wedding march echoed down the Barefoot William Boardwalk. The annual Southwest Florida bridal event brought both engaged and expectant women to the beach. It was a sea of sexy, sweet, and everything in between. Joe "Zoo" Zooker took it all in. The idea of marriage made him sweat. It triggered his gag reflex. He could, however, admire the ladies planning their weddings, as long as they didn't involve him. He was a bachelor. For life.

"Does Crabby Abby's General Store sell condoms?" asked his Richmond Rogues teammate Jake Packer. Better known as Pax.

Joe and Pax presently leaned against the blue metallic railing that separated the boardwalk from the beach. Joe knew where the condoms were shelved. He'd stocked up earlier in the week. "They're back by the pharmacy, bottom shelf, next to the douches and the K-Y lubes."

"You need anything, bro?"

Joe shook his head. He had six Magnum XLs in his wallet to get him through the night.

"Be right back, then." Pax pushed off the railing. He walked the short distance to purchase his protection. He planned to get lucky. So did Joe.

The team was in town for spring training, with an entire weekend to kill. Booze, babes, and sex would definitely come into play. Monday, and they'd turn serious. They'd live and breathe baseball. The entire team would assemble for workouts and scrimmages. Nine Roanoke Rebels would also hit the field. Affiliate Triple-A players participating in preseason practices and an exhibition game. Showcasing their talent and hoping for the call to suit up in the majors.

Joe hated squad competition. Dean Jensen in particular got under his skin. The minor leaguer played left field. Joe's position. Joe had refused him, four years running. Under Rule 5 draft, Dean had one final year to either make the club's expanded forty-man roster or be passed over. The guy kept coming after Joe, harder and faster each season. He just wouldn't let up. But then, Joe wouldn't have, either, if the situation had been reversed.

He rolled his shoulders now. Cracked his knuckles. It was too nice of a day to dwell on the asshat. He turned and stared out over the Gulf. Clear skies. Turquoise water. White sugar sand. Sunbathers. Sand castles. Carnival rides, an amusement arcade, and a long fishing pier stretched south. Paradise. He would retire here. Years from now. Following his last bat.

Joe waited patiently on Pax—for all of five minutes, before restlessness claimed him. He wasn't good at standing still. He was in continuous motion. A few brave men mingled with the wedding-minded ladies. He tugged down the bill on his black baseball cap. His mirrored Maui Jim aviators allowed him to stare, and not be caught doing so. He stepped into the crowd. Pax would find him. Unless he found a hot babe first.

So many women. Blondes, brunettes, redheads. A chick with purple hair. The multicolored storefronts on the beachside shops were all open, welcoming the stirring breeze and the aroma of salty air. The scent of freshly popped popcorn wafted, along with the aroma of chocolate fudge, cheesy nachos, cotton candy, and women's perfume.

Ladies came on to him. He was recognized by many. Flirted with by most. Inviting glances and promising smiles. His navy T-shirt scripted with *I've Broken All the Rules Today, So You'll Have to Make New Ones* drew whispered suggestions. Half-naked women appealed. Kink tempted. He liked the attention. A lot.

Space was tight. Whether intentional or by accident, female bodies pressed against him. Some snugged as close as skin. He didn't mind the touching. Although a few hands got downright personal. Arousal heightened his senses. He was looking for a weekend lover, but no one fully caught his eye. So he kept on walking, sex foremost on his mind.

Long decorated tables lined both sides of the boardwalk. Signs were visible. Bridal banners arched overhead. Women clustered, checking out the area's best photographers, florists, engraved invitations, caterers, bakers, wedding and reception venues, entertainment, hairstylists, makeup artists, prenuptial consultants, and other important services. Mannequins exhibited wedding gowns. Assorted accessories, from veils, crystal tiaras, rhinestone headbands, and sashes to every type of jewelry exhibit came next. Along with the garters.

Garters. Worn on a bride's thigh. A total turn-on. He scanned the ruffled, pearled, lacy, feathered, monogrammed, brooched, and rhinestoned collections. Foreplay. He might buy one for the pure pleasure of slipping it up his next conquest's leg, then slowly sliding it down. Sexy.

"Something blue," he heard a woman say, softly and wistfully.

He glanced toward where her voice had come from. Stopped, and got an eyeful. A slender blonde stood in profile, alone at the end of the table, toying with a pale blue satin garter with a silver heart charm. He was a sucker for long hair. The sun had run its fingers through this woman's strands, leaving them streaked and shiny. The ends touched her waist. He openly stared as she bent, her shoulders curving, her ass jutting out. Sweet cheeks were outlined beneath her short skirt. Gently stretching the elastic, she worked the garter over a sandaled foot—her toenails painted silver—then up her calf and onto her thigh. She had nice legs. Freckled knees. She straightened, admired the garter. She had yet to notice him. He appreciated her further.

Her smile came slowly, on a sigh. "Perfect, don't you think, Lori?"

He shifted his stance. Cast her in his shadow. Then removed his aviators for a better look. Twirled them by an arm. He wasn't Lori, but that didn't stop him from saying, "Hot, sweetheart."

She jerked up, and he took the opportunity to check her out. Wide eyes, deep and dark as midnight. A sharp contrast to her fairness. Tip-tilted nose. Full glossed lips, slightly parted. She wore a navy tank top; her denim skirt had a gold side zipper. Zippers made for a quick strip. Diamond studs sparkled at her ears. A collection of thin gold bracelets circled her wrist. A pearl ring on her forefinger. She was pretty, he mused, but not nearly as attractive as the babes in his nightly party posse. Those he chose for getting it on. Still, he'd give her five minutes.

She didn't ignore him, but neither did she invite conversation. He initiated, "Nice assortment of garters."

"See one you like? Try it on."

Was she serious or playing him? "None in my size."

"Elastic stretches."

She had him there.

"The pink garter with the red hearts and white feathers looks like you."

Looks like me? Was that how she saw him? Hearts and feathers? Her polite expression gave nothing away. He crossed his arms over his chest, hooked his thumbs in his armpits. Widened his stance. Questioned, "Having a good time?"

"Not as good as you." Dry-toned.

"I don't follow."

"This is a female event."

Predominantly female, but open to the public. He'd noted five guys on the boardwalk. Seven, counting him and Pax. "Your point?" he asked.

She told him. "Men don't always attend bridal affairs for the right reasons. You shouldn't be here unless you're hearing wedding bells."

No ringing. None whatsoever.

"There are hundreds of hopeful ladies over there on the boardwalk," she added. "Vulnerable, emotional, and seeking their happily-ever-afters, while you men are opportunists." Pause. "You're not here to score, are you?" she innocently inquired.

He wasn't taking advantage of anyone. He set her straight. "I'm not hitting on you, hon."

"Talk to me, not to my garter."

Busted. She was on to him, had caught him eyeing her legs. He liked her thigh gap. "I've got integrity." On a good day.

She glanced toward the beach. "There's an amateur volleyball tournament going on near the lifeguard station. A Frisbee contest by the ice cream stand. Kite flying on the pier. Sand-castle sculpting by the shore. Yet you've chosen the bridal event."

"I'm tapping in to my feminine side."

Her gaze returned to his. "There's nothing feminine about you."

He had a hard face, or so he'd been told. Dangerous. Intimidating. He played his features to his advantage. Several scars. A twice-broken nose. A death stare. "I like to browse." Not necessarily through the bridal items for sale, but cruising for women gave him pleasure.

"Browsing often leads to buying." She tilted her head, thoughtful. Observed, "You'd need to shave before trying on any bridal veils, otherwise your whiskers will catch on the delicate lace. And you'd have to tie back your hair for both the Swarovski two-tiered circlet and the vintage chandelier birdcage."

Birdcage? That blew his mind.

A few more thoughts emerged. "When it comes to wedding gowns, large men should stay away from ruffles and layers. I can picture you in plain silk. Ivory, maybe. Or blush. Go full-length, to cover the roll at your waist. Flabby thighs. Better choose low heels. You're plenty tall."

Lastly, "You might also consider a manicure. Your nails look rough. Manscaping would clean you up."

Shave his chest and his pubic hair? Not happening. Lady was a fusion of sarcasm and sweet smiles. He didn't know how to take her. Her suggestions sucked. Along with her attitude. She confused the hell out of him.

No female had ever described him in a dress before. He had no words. She saw him as fat, when he was actually fit. He'd nearly killed himself off-season with endurance and weight training. He had single-digit body fat.

She rose up on tiptoe, looked over his shoulder. "I need to locate my friend Lori." She strained to look over the crowd. "I don't see her."

"It's just you, me, and the garters."

She flat-footed. "Lori wouldn't walk off and leave me."

"You have a fear of being alone?" Rather disturbing.

"I prefer alone," she informed him. "My car's with the mechanic, in need of repairs. Lori's my ride."

Made sense. His day was open. He had free time. He foolishly found himself saying, "I could drive you."

"Drive me *where*?"

"Wherever you need to go."

"California." She was testing him.

Farther than anticipated. He wasn't crossing state lines or changing time zones for her. "Anywhere local?"

"I don't get into cars with strangers."

Stranger danger? Him? She had to be joking. He introduced himself, "I'm Joe." His teammates and bar squad all called him Zoo. "You?"

She scanned his T-shirt. "Not sure we need a name exchange. I play by the rules. You break them. I'd rather take a taxi."

A cab over him? He had a classic Jaguar XKE convertible in the parking lot. Mint condition. A chick magnet. Leather seats that molded to his body like a lover. A phallic long bonnet. Big engine. Top speed. Ground-hugging. Raring to go.

Somehow she'd failed to recognize him. That bothered him. A little. He was high-profile. Rogues fans filled the stadium during spring training. The players were a significant part of the community. Available for interviews, charitable appearances, and bachelor auctions. He usually couldn't cross the street without someone requesting an autograph. Without a woman asking him out.

"Do you know who I am?" He needed his ego stroked.

"I don't watch cartoons." Smile or smirk, he couldn't tell.

Harsh. He'd yet to figure her out. Women had numerous ways of catching his attention. Most were sweet, sexy, and feisty. But never this sarcastic. He racked his brain.

They hadn't met, as far as he could remember. She didn't look the bar type. The Lusty Oyster and the Blue Coconut were his second homes.

He'd tried to be nice, friendly, appear to have no ulterior motive. She was challenging, though, for no apparent reason. Their conversation was going nowhere. He gave her one last shot. "What's with you?" he asked.

"Ask yourself the same question."

Question himself? He was his own answer.

She wrapped up with, "Leaving now." Dismissing him.

He had her blocked between the table and his body, and before he could step back, she squeezed by him sideways. Her foot ground down on his booted toe. Her raised knee came close to his boys. He sucked in air, inhaled her scent—light and as warm as sunshine. He smelled citrus, and he had the questionable urge to sniff her hair. Dumbass. Not cool.

He tried to take in what had just happened. He honestly didn't get it. She'd showed no interest in him. Not even a hint. "That's it?" he called after her.

"You expected more?" she tossed over her shoulder. "No time."

He had no idea what he'd expected. What he wanted. The fact that she'd left him standing there irritated the hell out of him. He'd complimented her garter in passing. She'd cut him off permanently. Her aversion to him was unsettling. Her tight smile disconcerting.

He held back, refusing to go after her. Her loss. He needed to move on. He had a line of women waiting to date him. Less snark, more seduction. He was ready for a willing woman to have her way with him. To take him slowly and sinfully. All night long.

"Shoplifter!" an older woman monitoring the accessories table shouted. She rounded the table, elbowing him and others aside, as she stormed after the person who'd just ripped her off. He'd been standing at the table, yet somehow he'd missed the five-finger discount. Boardwalk security joined the chase. Two men in khaki uniforms. Chaos ensued.

Gutsy thief, Joe thought. Stealing in broad daylight, then fading into the foot traffic. He followed the charge at a distance. Curious. He stood a wide-shouldered six-foot-four, and his height gave him an advantage. He could easily track the action. He glimpsed the unfriendly blonde a few yards ahead. She was alone one second, then surrounded by security the next. Trapped. The taller guard gripped her upper arm. Detaining her. Nasty accusations flew. Loudly.

Attentive, he took it all in. He hadn't seen her lift anything. But then, he'd been staring at her legs. He might've missed something. Perhaps she'd taken an item prior to his arrival. Stuck it in her purse. He'd blocked her from the proprietor's view. Until she could slip into the throng.

He watched as the shorter of the guards drew a notepad from the pocket of his slacks. He flipped it open, went on to request the shop owner's name. Joe had hearing loss in his left ear, thanks to his old man cuffing him as a kid. He strained to hear. Apparently Giselle was the accuser. Stewie was the blonde, from what he could detect. Odd name. She didn't look like a Stewie. More like a Summer, Shayla, or Sienna. Skylar.

Giselle pointed to the blonde's thigh. Her hand shook, all righteous indignation. "She stole the garter. It's under her skirt."

Stewie paled. She placed her hand over her heart, then said, "Not on purpose, I swear."

Giselle huffed. "Customers look, but they don't touch.

You not only handled the merchandise, you tried on the garter, and then you snuck off. Outright theft."

"She didn't get far." The taller guard appeared proud of his takedown. "I'll radio for a squad car."

Stewie's eyes widened in panic. She scanned the crowd, searching for someone she might know. Someone to vouch for her character. To save her. Apparently her friend Lori was nowhere in sight. Her gaze glanced off him. Swung back. Relief, uncertainty, doom, all flickered over her features. She frowned. All hope faded. She expected him to turn on her. To walk away. As well she should. He could be a dick on occasion. Far more badass than good guy. That's who he was. No shame. No remorse. His own man.

She'd flipped him off without any thought of further consequence. That consequence was now. Karma had returned her to him. She was in trouble, and he could help. He smiled to himself. She would owe him for saving her. Owe him big-time.

Game face on, he stiff-armed his way through the crowd. Glared people back. They gave him space. He eyed Stewie. Her lips parted. Her breath caught. She had no idea what he would do, what he might say, but then, neither did he. He went with the obvious. Women came and went in his life. He seldom went on a date with the same girl twice. But he made Stewie his date-for-the-day. Despite her sucky attitude.

Once he reached her, he draped his arm about her shoulders and drew her to his side. Tucked her in tight. She fit nicely. Her shuddered resistance appeared to be shivery compliance to those looking on. They gave the impression of a couple. He dipped his head, nuzzled her cheek, then spoke low near her ear, "Time for me now, babe?"

She blushed. Deeply. Perhaps embarrassed by her previous snub or merely at the fact that their bodies were touching so intimately. "No need for an arrest, Roy," Joe read the security guard's name stitched over the pocket on his khaki shirt. "I can explain the garter heist."

"Joe Zooker." Roy recognized him. He grinned broadly. "Shed some light, my man. I'm listening." He released his hold on Stewie. She shook out her arm. A purple thumbprint showed above her elbow. Joe's body tensed. He hated that she'd been manhandled. That she'd been bruised. Son of a bitch.

A protective growl rose deep in Joe's throat. A warning. Dark. Animalistic. He tamped it down. Now was not the time for further confrontation. He needed to get Stewie off the hook and away from the security guards. He was good at stretching the truth, always had been. White lies were as much a part of his life as baseball, booze, and sex.

He went with, "We were browsing the bridal event, and we stopped at Giselle's table. My woman here"—he claimed her—"found a garter that she liked, and I asked her to try it on. She did so—for me." He stroked Stewie's hip, fingered the denim, then suddenly hiked her skirt three inches up her thigh, until the accessory was visible. He nudged Roy. "Sweet mercy, don't you think?"

The guard eyed Stewie's gartered thigh along with the other onlookers. There were nods of approval, and a low whistle rose from one man in the back. Comments ensued. Everyone agreed with Joe: Pale blue was her color. The heart charm, romantic. It was the perfect wedding accessory.

Stewie shifted beside him. She dug her nails into his wrist, pushed his hand off her hip. Her attempt to step back failed. He tightened his hold. She huffed her annoyance. The lady was unappreciative.

Joe clarified to Roy, "She asked me to purchase the garter while she moved on to the next table. Cake toppers. She walked away, and I was reaching for my wallet, just as Giselle shot past me. There was no one to pay." Short pause. "She's no thief. It was an innocent mistake. I went after Giselle ready to pay, but she'd already sounded the alarm."

Roy accepted Joe's account without question. "Thanks for clearing it up, Joe." He nodded to Stewie. "Purchase it or return the garter, so we can close the incident."

Robbery dismissed. Accountability upheld. No one was headed to jail. Interest waned. The crowd thinned. There was no price tag on the garter. "How much?" the blonde asked Giselle.

"Sixty dollars."

Joe raised an eyebrow. Apparently elastic didn't come cheap.

"The charm is sterling silver," the shop owner said in defense of the cost.

Stewie dipped one shoulder, rolled down the garter. "I don't have sixty—"

"I do." Joe bent, placed his hand over hers, then skimmed the garter back up. Higher, this time. Denim brushed the backs of his knuckles. His thumb met her thigh gap. Satin against smooth skin. Their secret. He and Stewie knew she wore the garter, yet it was no longer visible to the casual observer. He squeezed her freckled knee. Straightened. She tried to pass under his arm, to wiggle free. He refused to let her go. Not until he was ready.

Payment came next. He removed three twenties from his wallet. Giselle snatched the money from his hand. Hurried back to her unsupervised table.

A new disturbance drew security down the boardwalk. Two women were arguing over a wedding veil. It was about to get ripped in half. The area cleared. Passersby skirted them. Joe and Stewie were left alone. He and his supposed date.

He stared down at her. She stared up at him. Her sigh was heavy. Her expression questioning. "Do you think I stole the garter?" His response seemed important to her.

He shook his head. "There's not a criminal bone in your body. You were blamed—"

"It was all your fault."

He stopped short. "How do you figure that?"

"You cornered me by the accessories table. Came on to me."

Get real. "No more than a passing comment."

"You stared at my garter."

"I'm a leg man, babe."

"You made me uncomfortable."

"I tend to fluster women."

"Not in a good way."

"Good for most."

"Don't flatter yourself. I couldn't get away from you fast enough."

"Fast got you into trouble," he reminded her. "You walked off without paying for the garter."

She stuck out her chin. Stubborn. "I would've eventually noticed it, gone back, and paid."

"Giselle was quick. She accused you of shoplifting. I saved your ass. Kept you out of jail."

Her dark eyes flashed. "I could've managed just fine without you." The lady was short on gratitude.

"Keep telling yourself that, hon. Your booking was seconds away."

She huffed. Her breasts rose, inches from his chest. Her nipples nearly flicked him. "I would have been entitled to a phone call. Someone would've bailed me out."

"Not Lori, she deserted you."

"I have other friends."

"You'd have sat in Holding until your ride arrived. Paperwork takes time. Cops eat doughnuts. Cells are nasty. You'd never have survived."

"And you would have?"

"I have."

She didn't seem all that surprised by his comment. Pretty accepting, actually. She obviously didn't think much of him. So be it. He had a juvenile record, having been the fall guy when he took the rap for a stolen car for his younger brother. He'd never regretted his decision.

She swallowed, said, "I'll pay you for the garter once I get my paycheck."

He offhandedly wondered where she worked. He decided not to ask. It wasn't important. "No need. Keep your money."

"I hate owing people."

Especially him. He could see it in her eyes. "Trade-off, then," he proposed. "What do you have that I might want?" He had something in mind. He lowered his gaze to her mouth.

Her lips thinned. "You've got to be kidding."

"Not joking."

"Jerk."

He'd been called worse.

She breathed in deeply. "You're insane."

"I'm so mental I'd follow you around all day for that kiss."

"You have way too much time on your hands."

He never gave up. Never gave in. "One kiss, then I'm gone. I've got other obligations." He had a professional commitment at the Beachside Memorial Hospital Children's Ward. Legendary superheroes Batman, Captain America, and Super Zooker were scheduled to entertain the young patients for an hour. He didn't want to be late. Didn't want to disappoint the kids. He used his super-powers for good. Smiles were contagious. Healing came through laughter and happiness.

His attention centered on Stewie. She was growing on him, in a smart-mouthed sort of way. Which he didn't fully understand. She wasn't someone he would ever date. That she would ever even be his friend was questionable. Companionship was a two-way street. She hadn't taken to him—at all.

He preferred a warm, willing woman. Sexual experience mattered to him. Stewie might not be a virgin, but he'd bet his first home run of the preseason that she was all missionary position and snuggling. He liked X-rated.

He eyed her now; her expression hadn't changed. It was sullen, disapproving. No visible softness. A first for him. He reconsidered his request for a kiss. He'd never forced himself on a female before, and he wasn't about to start now. If they kissed, fine; if not, that was okay, too. There were lots of kissable lips there today on the boardwalk.

A beach babe in a skimpy sundress passed by within a foot of him. Ignoring Stewie, she arched an eyebrow, lightly touched his arm, signaling her availability. Definitely a hot prospect for the night. He winked, but didn't commit. She blew him a kiss, moved on.

"Kiss her instead of me," Stewie suggested. Hopeful.

"I plan to kiss you now. Her, possibly later."

"You're such a hound."

What if he was? No big deal. "I'm single. I like the la-dies. I've been known to howl at the moon—"

"Chase your tail?" Spoken with a straight face.

"I don't do circles."

She gave a single-shoulder shrug. Not caring.

Applause rose from the beach. He glanced over the blue metal railing. A volleyball game had ended. Cheers for the winners. Congratulations from the losers.

A Frisbee sailed high and fast and far too close. It looked like a flying saucer. Someone had a strong arm.

His attention returned to her. "Ready for me?" he asked.

"Hurry up and get it over with."

"I've never hurried a kiss."

He eased toward her, allowing their bodies to meet. His male heat and muscle pressed against her slender curves. He slid his hands into her hair. Summery silk. His thumbs traced the frown lines at the corners of her mouth. Creamy skin, despite the creases. He waited for her to warm up to him. She shivered instead.

Pulsing seconds passed as he gave her time to push him away. Amazingly, she did not. The lady was paying her debt, albeit reluctantly. He was tempted to take her mouth fully. To lightly scrape her lip with his teeth. To slip her his tongue. He lowered his head. Her eyelids shuttered. She appeared a martyr.

He gentled. Calm and persuasive. An airbrush of warm breath over her mouth, in hopes of parting her lips. But she remained tight-lipped. He nipped one corner; she scrunched her nose. Not a pretty face. He hated second-guessing himself. He held back, unsure. Then he changed his mind at the last minute. Leaning back, he kissed her on the forehead. Quick, light. Uneventful. Then he withdrew. She blinked. Confused.

He lowered his gaze to her legs. "Wear our garter and think of me."

"The garter comes off shortly, and it stays off. No thoughts of you." Snippy woman.

"Believe what you will."

"You know different?"

He looked up. "Wait and see." Her indifference amused him. It was too forced. He'd bet she would wear the garter to bed. They were about to part ways. He gave her one final chance to be cordial. "We didn't get off on the best foot, did we?" he asked. Definitely not.

"I stomped on yours earlier." When she'd edged around him at the accessories table.

"You're heavier than you look," he said, tongue in cheek.

"Are you trying to be funny, or are you saying I'm fat?"

"Funny."

"You're not."

There was no winning with her. Pride pushed him in the opposite direction. "'Bye, Stewie." He took his leave, all jock strut and arrogance.

"*Stewie?*" Her voice hit him between the shoulder blades. Damn if she didn't come after him. All flushed and offended. Breasts heaving. Fire in her eyes. A woman wanting the last word.

They faced off near Goody Gumdrops, a penny candy store. Joe could go for a jawbreaker about now. Or bubble-gum baseball cards. He was still a kid at heart. He kept his cool despite her outburst. "Isn't that your name?" he asked. Had his ears deceived him?

"No, it's not."

"You look like a Stewie."

"Insulting me again?"

"Being truthful." Not really.

"I'm Stevie, short for Steven."

"A guy's name?" Puzzling.

"After my father. My parents wanted a boy."

"Anyone ever call you Junior?"

"Don't be the first."

"Steven what?" he tried.

"Last names are for relationships."

"No sweat. I'm not that into you."

"I can live without you, too."

He had to ask, "Do you dislike all men, or is it just me?"

Her silence said it was *him.*

"Because you see me as an opportunist."

"Pretty much."

Fine by him. He glanced at his watch. A Genesis X1, Advertised for the man who wouldn't be told what to do. It fit him. He'd spent thirty minutes with her. He'd planned on five. Time he'd never get back. He flicked his wrist, waved her off. "Hope your day improves."

"It has to—you're leaving."

They parted ways. His day could only get better, too. It immediately upgraded. A hottie in a bikini top and Boom Boom shorts bumped into him. On purpose. Barely covered breasts and peekaboo butt cheeks. There'd been room for her to walk around, but she'd cut his corner. Close. She tapped the front of his shirt with a finger, near his nipple. Grinning, she read his T-shirt, "Rules are meant to be broken."

She was a sex pack of wild, curly hair, phenomenal tits, narrow waist, and long legs. A *Take Me Home Tonight* tattoo curved over her left breast. He wondered where else she might be inked. He'd bet that her inner thigh had sexy script on it. *Lick Me,* maybe.

She could keep him hard for the entire weekend. No doubt about it. He was tempted to invite her to meet him at the Driftwood Hotel later that night. Apartment housing for the players. Many of his teammates had purchased homes in town, but Joe hadn't gotten around to it yet. Maybe this season. He'd enlist a Realtor.

His hesitation had the dark-haired babe rolling her eyes and moving on. Had he missed out? More likely than not. He didn't feel all that bad. He was more partial to blondes.

He glanced back at Stevie one final time. She gazed back. A long stare. They blinked simultaneously. She looked away first, took in the boardwalk. Something felt *off.* The fight seemed to have left her. She relaxed against the metal railing now, her sudden change in mood confusing him. Her features had softened. She nodded to passersby, both women and the infrequent man. Her eyes were bright and smiling. She appeared happy. Away from him. He frowned.

He sensed she was about to leave. Perhaps she was going to go in search of her friend Lori. Stevie needed a ride home, he remembered. Before he knew it, she'd slipped into the crowd, swallowed up by the masses of wedding consumers. Gone.

His heart gave an unexpected squeeze. The tightness in his chest annoyed him. Why should he care where she went? Whom she was with? What she did? The reason was simple, though utterly ridiculous. *Because she was wearing his garter.* That gave him every right to go after her. And so he did. Keeping his distance.

"He's following me," Stevie Reynolds whispered to her best friend, Lori Rafferty, once they'd connected at the wedding cake table. Three local bakers offered samplers. Small confectionary squares of traditional vanilla and buttercream, along with new takes on flavor profiles. Stevie moaned over the whipped-orange chiffon laced with strawberry schnapps. She would've enjoyed another piece, if seconds were allowed. The crowd nudged her aside before she could grab a napkin.

Lori finished off her last bite of cherry-glazed mocha. "Who's *he?*" she asked, peering at Stevie over the rim of her red heart-shaped sunglasses. Her green gaze was curious.

"Joe."

"Joe who?"

Indrawn breath. "Zooker."

Lori gaped. "Not 'the Zoo'?" She finger-quoted.

"One and the same."

"I wasn't aware you knew him."

"Chance meeting earlier." It was hard to confess. She'd been mindful of him for several years. Her cousin DJ spoke often of Joe. He envied the Rogue, imitated the left fielder's drive and focus. Right down to Joe's swagger and smugness.

"Must have been some meeting," Lori speculated. She glanced down the boardwalk. "Something must've gone right for Joe to come after you like that. I'm impressed."

I'm wearing his garter. That thought gave her goose bumps. She'd told him that she would be slipping it off immediately, yet it remained high on her thigh. She didn't need a public restroom to remove it. She could slide the garter off at any time. Yet she had not. Joe was enough of a hound to sniff out that fact. To track her down. To grin his satisfaction.

"We had words," Stevie admitted.

"Flirty, suggestive words?"

Not even close. "I called him an opportunist." She'd started it.

Lori was shocked. "Whatever for?"

"He's just here this afternoon to score."

"Not a big deal." Lori glanced in his direction. "Can't condemn a man for checking out the ladies. He's not forcing himself on anyone. If anything, the women are all over him." Pause. "I think he's a genius. The dating possibilities here are endless."

Leave it to Lori to side with Joe. Despite their closeness, the two women were as different as night and day. Lori was a guy's girl. She preferred hanging with men over women. She loved sports, she watched action flicks, she was opinionated and strong-willed, and she didn't give a damn what others thought. She presently wore an over-sized white button-down and boyfriend-style jeans.

Stevie, on the other hand, was a girl's girl. She liked sisterhood, romantic comedies, feminine clothing, delicate jewelry, and gourmet cooking. She shied away from relationships, preferring to concentrate on herself and get her life in order. A personal choice.

"How close is Joe?" she questioned.

"He just passed Denim Dolphin, the children's store."

Stevie stood before Waves, a women's swimsuit shop, three doors down. He was close. Too close. She cut him a quick look.

He dominated the boardwalk. Big man. Bigger entourage. The lustful female crowd swept him along. Unrestrained touching, kisses, and deep sighs. Joe responded, spreading himself around. Slowing to sign autographs. Posing for photos. Making everyone feel special.

"He's one dangerous-looking dude," said Lori. "His body's built from a kit."

Stevie's heart agreed, skipping a beat. Athletes weren't new to her. Some of her closest guy friends played sports, including her cousin DJ. Joe had an undeniable presence. Roughly handsome. Lawless blue eyes. Slicing cheekbones. A slightly crooked nose. A mouth that invited kissing. Square jaw. Strong neck. Powerful shoulders. Muscled chest. Long legs. A total alpha.

Lori moistened her mouth with the tip of her tongue. She eyed the ballplayer with interest. "Should he stop and chat, introduce me. I'd like to meet him."

Stevie blanched. "I'm trying to avoid him, not take up where we left off." They'd parted poorly.

"I'd never run from that man."

Stevie wished she wore track shoes. "Join his party posse, then."

"His posse is renowned," said Lori. Stevie had heard the same rumors that her friend had heard. "Beach babes gone wild. They're all hot, sexy, the stuff of wet dreams. They wear next to nothing and do tequila shots off of their bellies. They take the night by the balls and squeeze." She grew thoughtful. "I'd never qualify. One beer is my limit. I'm in bed by eleven."

Stevie didn't qualify, either. Her favorite bar drink was a virgin piña colada. Lights-out by ten. "You could always talk to him about sports."

"Joe's a Rogue. He gets his sports talk at the ballpark. He'd find better uses for a woman's mouth than reciting his stats."

Stevie took a step away from Lori. "Are you coming or not? I'm gone."

"Not sure you can avoid him. He's here."

There, and facing her. His entourage pushed Lori back. Rather rudely. They then stepped on Stevie's sandaled feet. Painful. Joe blocked them from fully shoving her aside. Their gazes locked, and, in that instant, she saw only him. His unsettling eyes. The quirk of his mouth as he looked down at her legs. The faint line of the garter was visible beneath her skirt, for anyone who knew it was there. For everybody else, it appeared to be only a wrinkle in the denim. Joe grinned. A big old *gotcha* grin. For some reason, her still wearing the garter brought him amusement. Aggravation curled her fingers. She had the urge to wipe the smile right off his face.

He caught her clenched fist, and had the balls to laugh. A deep, rough laugh. Heat scored her cheeks in the silence that followed. Those around them stared. Confusion and curiosity gathered, thickening in the crowd. She was as cornered now as she'd been with the security guards. Her heart slammed against her ribs.

Joe leaned toward her. She gave him the cold shoulder.

He made her hot. Inappropriately warming her nipples. Her belly. Her thighs. Leaving her panties damp.

She had no escape. He fronted her. Women hovered behind her like a human wall. Eyeing her lips, he lowered his voice, then said, for her ears only, "You have cake crumbs on the corner of your mouth." He reached around her, snagged a napkin from the corner of the cake table. Handed it to her. Then left.

Left her standing there with her mouth wide open. Women pushed past her, rushing to catch up with him. Stevie and Lori could only stare after them.

Lori was the first to speak. "That was an interesting exchange."

"Obnoxious man," Stevie muttered. She turned to Lori, piqued. "Why didn't you tell me that I had crumbs on my mouth?"

"You were turned away from me. I never saw them."

Stevie's napkin had dissolved within her sweaty palm. Lori passed her a second. "*He* saw them." She hurriedly wiped them away.

"That he did," said Lori. "He had hungry eyes. I thought he was going to lick the crumbs right off of your lips when he bent over toward you."

Thank goodness he hadn't. His earlier kiss on her forehead had left her on edge. His second appearance moments ago had rattled her completely. She hoped she wouldn't see him again. Not today, anyway.

She scanned the nearby event tables. The security guard named Roy protected a glassed-in display of engagement rings and wedding bands. The diamonds sparkled in the sunlight. Roy recognized her and waved. "Stevie, sign up for the drawing. Lux Jewelers is giving away bridal sets. Your choice, if your name is picked."

Lori headed over to the table. Stevie was more hesitant. She dragged her feet. What was the point of entering the drawing? There was no man in her life. An unrequited love held Lori's heart. She'd cared for DJ, for as long as Stevie could remember. Her cousin hadn't a clue. Despite Lori's countless hints and propositions, the dude was oblivious.

Trailing Lori to the table, Stevie filled out the square piece of paper. She could always pass the win to her friend if her name was drawn. She folded the form, dropped it in the padlocked wooden box. Subsequently admired the rings. Unique, beautiful, and incredibly expensive. A starburst engagement ring winked at her. Stevie couldn't help but wink back.

"Where's Joe?" the security guard asked her as she worked her way down the table.

What to say? That she wasn't his keeper? That they'd gone their separate ways right after the garter fiasco? That she had no desire to see him again? She drew in a short breath, said, "He's—"

"Right behind you, babe." Joe appeared, a human boomerang. He slipped his arms about her waist and drew her back against him. His hands spanned her abdomen with the familiarity of a lover. Her bottom wedged against his groin. "I had an errand, but I'm back now."

She wished he'd stayed away. His *errand* had included flirting with dozens of women during a walk down the boardwalk. "You didn't have to return." She attempted to pry his fingers off her stomach. He had big hands. He covered her hip bone to hip bone.

He spoke near her ear. "You got rid of the crumbs."

Her mouth compressed. "Did you think otherwise?"

"I came to be sure."

"You've checked, so good-bye."

"Chill," he whispered. "I heard Roy ask about me. I didn't want to blow our cover as a couple. We don't want security to reinvestigate your case."

"It wasn't a 'case.'"

"It was documented. Roy wrote it all out in his notepad."

"With pencil, not pen. Erasable."

"But remembered."

"I was released."

"Into my care."

"I never heard the words *'your care.'*"

"I did."

The man was impossible. She had needed him for all of ten minutes. He was well-known in town. His word was respected. She was newly arrived. Not trusted. The situation had resolved itself. Over and done with—or so she'd thought. Yet he was starting things up again.

The security guard cleared his throat, requested, "Ladies, once you've filled out your information cards, drop them in the box and move along. You're blocking others from signing up. The next three tables have additional prizes."

Joe was forced to release Stevie. A slow slide of his hands over her stomach and hips. She jumped when he patted her bottom. "You're pretty free with your hands," she accused.

"I like to touch." He pressed his palm to her lower back, nudged her along. "Just keeping up appearances until we pass Roy."

They were well beyond the guard, and deep into the crowd when he let her go. The heated imprint of his hand remained, like a permanent tattoo.

Lori was eyeing her now. A smile played impishly over her mouth. "Who's your little friend, Stevie?" she asked.

"*Little friend*?" Joe was larger than life. He towered over her. "Lori, meet Joey."

Lori extended her hand, and Joe stretched to shake it. He frowned. "No one's ever called me Joey before."

No one would dare. "First time for everything, *Joey*," Stevie purposely repeated.

"Fine, *Stewie*."

Lori raised an eyebrow. "Pet names for each other already? What have I missed?"

"Private joke," said Stevie. She chose not to explain her earlier encounter with Joe.

Lori didn't press. The friends proceeded to check out the next table. A professional photographer offered a wedding video and photo album package. They filled out individual cards, then entered additional drawings for a five-course, sit-down dinner and open bar reception. A travel agency offered a ten-day honeymoon to Saint Thomas. All lavish and luxurious. Lastly, a drawing offered a spectacular centerfold spread in *I Do* bridal magazine. The potential bride's choice of locale. Winners would be announced on Sunday.

Security appeared shortly thereafter. The guards parted the crowd to make room for a fashion show. Models in designer wedding gowns took to the boardwalk, looking like walking fairy tales in satin, silk, and lace. Lori and Stevie both sighed over an off-the-shoulder dress comprised of sparkling crystals. Glass slippers peeked from beneath the hem.

A flower girl followed. She carried a white wicker basket filled with miniature bridal bouquets. The young girl tossed clusters of pale pink tea roses and baby's breath to hopeful women. She aimed one at Stevie, and Stevie sidestepped. Lori reached out, snagged it.

Her friend breathed in the fragrance, murmured, "This bouquet is the closest I'll ever get to planning an actual wedding."

"Don't sell your love life short."

"Your cousin has known me since middle school, and he's never acknowledged my existence."

"DJ's life revolves around sports."

"He hangs up his jock at the end of the day. His down-time includes his buddies, but not me."

"Not you or any other woman. He doesn't date much."

"I'm relieved by that."

"Get him to the beach and wear your new bikini."

"It shows a lot of skin."

"He'd have to be dead not to notice you."

"We'll see." Lori looked over her shoulder, noted, "Your man, Joey, isn't keeping up with us."

He was not "*her man.*" Still, Stevie glanced his way. He'd distanced himself from them, and was leaning against the blue metal railing. Surprisingly, he was alone. He removed his baseball cap, slapped it against his thigh. His hair was nonconformist long. The breeze lifted it, mussed it up. He ran one hand down his face, and the color drained. He appeared pale beneath his tan. He rubbed his throat, as if he was having trouble swallowing. Then he rolled his shoulders. He looked down. Shifted his weight. Shuffled his feet. He was visibly ill at ease.

Realization came with her stare. She nearly laughed out loud. She'd been right about him. Joe Zooker was a fraud. Far from marriage-minded, he'd come to the bridal event to flirt, charm, and find a new lover. He'd attracted many women. His choices were numerous. Yet his pained expression said it all. Rings, receptions, and all things wedding gave him cold feet.

The parade of gowns had pushed him to the edge. He'd momentarily removed himself from the event. Her plans to draw him back in would ultimately distance him further. From her. She had no immediate desire to get married. Obviously neither did he.

She finger-waved, called to him, "Joey, join us. I want your opinion on a gown."

Had his eyes just crossed? He settled his cap low on

his head and pushed off the railing. Then he crossed to her slowly, slipping between a model with a bustled train and a second flower girl, who was tossing red rose petals. Several petals landed on his shoulder. He brushed them off. He looked out of place, a rugged man amid goddess gowns.

"Which dress?" He gave a long-suffering sigh. "I can't stay long. I've got other commitments."

"Do those commitments have breasts?" Snarky-sweet.

"You the jealous type?"

"Not when it comes to you." A white lie. A man with a huge female following would drive her nuts. He'd never narrow his choice down to just one woman. Not that she cared.

The fashion show continued. Lori pointed to a model in a vanilla-cream satin gown with a sweetheart neckline and a mermaid skirt. The bride floated toward them. "Whatcha think, big guy?" she asked Joe. "The perfect gown?" The back showcased a long row of pearl buttons.

He shrugged. "Good enough, I guess."

Lori contemplated, "It would take a groom half the night to undo the closures."

"No man wastes that much time on his wedding night. I'd pop those pearls while I ripped it off of her."

Lori's eyes dilated, her expression dreamy.

Stevie shivered. No man had ever wanted her badly enough to tear off her clothes. The word *thrilling* came to mind. She dismissed the thought outright. Joe had plans for the afternoon, and so did she. She cut him loose. "Lori and I want to check out the music venue. The harpist, pianist, accordion player."

"I'm outta here." Which she'd expected. He nodded to Lori, then touched his hand to Stevie's thigh. A slow burn tucked beneath her skirt. Then it shot high. "I don't need X-ray vision to picture your garter under your skirt."

"X-ray vision is for superheroes."
"I could be a superhero."
"Only if you used your powers for good."
"Trust me, babe, I'd be very, very good."
She believed him.

Two

Three superheroes pushing wheelchairs raced around the central nurses' station. Twelve circling laps, then a final straightaway down the sixth-floor pediatric hallway of Beachside Memorial Hospital. The finish line was marked by a stream of toilet paper stretched between the drinking fountain and the door handle to the linen room. Easy to break.

In compliance with the motto of "safety first," the kids were strapped to their chairs with physical therapy belts. They pumped their arms, shouted, urging Jake Packer, costumed as Captain America, Sam Matthews as Batman, and Joe as Super Zooker to go faster. Running was not allowed. A hospital regulation. So Super Z took giant steps. No rules broken. The galactic bounty hunter edged out the lead.

"Victory is ours!" Super Zooker shouted as his chair turned the corner. One of the RNs winked at him. He winked back. He liked a woman in scrubs. Accessible sex. Drawstring pants were easy to untie. Fast to drop around the ankles. A female physician in nothing but a white lab coat turned him on, too. A fantasy recently satisfied. She'd given him one hell of a physical.

"We're going to win!" His nine-year-old patient

squealed her excitement. Ashley's face was flushed. Her thinning hair broke from her ponytail. Hanging limp and loose at her shoulders. Chemo had been rough on her. Her happiness meant everything to him. He'd known her for a year, from her initial diagnosis. Lymphoma. She was finally in remission. He gently wobbled her chair, making it more like an amusement park ride and drawing further giggles. She'd be going home soon. A second chance at life. Ashley was one of the lucky ones.

The bounty hunter pressed forward. A challenge was a challenge. The superheroes took winning seriously, even when it came to a walking wheelchair race. His chief competitor was Batman. The caped crusader rode his heels, all heavy-booted steps and flapping cape.

Batman purposely bumped the back of his calves. Super Zooker sneered over his shoulder. Batman bared his teeth. Captain America's athletic lunges were close to catching up to them.

"*Kapow! Wham! Zoom!*" Bat-fight words. "Point your toes!" he encouraged the boy in his wheelchair. David had a broken leg. His plaster cast was elevated on the foot plate. The two could easily take the win, a big toe ahead of everyone else.

Super Z carefully weaved his wheelchair from side to side so that Batman didn't have room to sneak by. But the caped crusader cheated. He ducked through the nurses' station, a diagonal shortcut that immediately put him ahead. David pumped his arm.

Super Zooker and Captain America booed him. Loudly. Batman grinned triumphantly.

A small crowd had gathered. A dozen children emerged from their rooms, assisted by medical staff. It was slow going for most. Several leaned on walkers. Others clutched tall IV poles, supporting medical solutions and health monitors. All wanted to catch the outcome. Only three laps around the station left to go.

Captain America came on strong. He zigged right, zagged left, trying to pass Super Z. The Cap championed Drew, a twelve-year-old boy with a dislocated shoulder, set in a temporary sling. He faced surgery the next day.

Authentically costumed in his patriotic jumpsuit, Captain America embodied justice. He entrusted Drew to hold his disc-shaped shield with a five-pointed star design in its center. The boy strained against his therapy strap, leaning as far forward as his chest would allow. He reached out his good arm, held the shield high. A hand's advantage at the finish line.

Tension grew as Super Zooker gained on Batman. Soon side by side, they exchanged a short, but significant look. Message received. A silent understanding. Super Z and the caped crusader gave ground, and allowed Captain America to squeeze in between them. A tight fit. The wheels on the chairs rubbed. They walked abreast the last twenty feet down the hallway, keeping perfect pace. The race ended in a three-way tie. Cheers rose. Everyone was a winner.

"Victory lap," directed Super Z. The champions wound around the nurses' station one final time to a round of applause.

An elevator door *swoosh*ed open, and Carla, a nutritionist, stepped off, pushing a snack cart. She regarded the kids in the wheelchairs. Their eyes were bright. Their smiles broad. Exhilaration pulsed as rapidly as their heartbeats.

"Superhero races," she noted. "Lucky you. The best day ever. I bet you've worked up a hearty appetite."

"Starving," said Drew.

David nodded. "Super hungry."

Sweet Ashley patted her tummy in agreement.

"Let's get you back to your rooms, then," she said. "I've got apples and PowerBars today."

Food was motivation. The kids wiggled on their cushioned seats, excited to return. Captain America allowed David to keep his shield. A cool souvenir. Aides came to assist them back to bed. High fives and hugs all around, and the superheroes took their leave. Carla tossed each of them a nutty-fruity health bar. Captain America ate his on the spot. Super Zooker and Batman saved theirs for later.

Dr. Daniels was making his rounds, clipboard in hand. He motioned to the heroes. A tall man with white hair and glasses, he struck up a conversation. "Visitation day?"

Super Z nodded. "Visits and a race."

Daniels was appreciative. "Your attention to our patients boosts their spirits. I personally want to thank you."

"We enjoy spending time with the kids," Batman said.

"Are you in a hurry to leave, or can you spare a few extra minutes?" the pediatrician inquired.

Super Z rolled back the cuff of his black shirt and looked at his watch. Late afternoon. Happy Hour at the Lusty Oyster called his name. Loudly. He wanted to get out of his costume and have a cold beer. The sooner the better. Instead, he asked, "What do you need?"

"The annual Kuts for Kids is taking place on the first floor, near the administrative offices," Daniels told them. "The event is for children who have cancer or who have lost their hair due to a medical condition call alopecia areata. The nonprofit organization provides hairpieces to financially disadvantaged children who are suffering from long-term medical hair loss from any diagnosis. We have five volunteer stylists set up in the east wing executive conference room. Out with the table, in with the salon chairs. There's a long line of women wanting to donate today. There's also a representative from a hair prosthetics manufacturer on-site."

"Wigs," Super Z muttered. Sweet Ashley was hoping for one before she left the hospital.

"The prostheses restore self-esteem and confidence," added the doctor, "enabling a child to face the world and her peers."

Captain America scratched the stubble on his chin. "My hair's not long enough to donate."

Super Zooker pulled back his brown hair with a leather strip. He ran his hand along the back of his neck, and was about to offer four inches, when the doctor stated, "No haircuts for any of you. Twelve inches are needed for the wigs. Just take a few minutes on your way out to mingle with the donors. I have cafeteria workers passing out iced tea and cookies. Superhero gratitude would go a long way with the ladies."

Batman widened his stance. He thumped his buff and bulked-up armored chest. "I'm in."

"Me, too," agreed Captain America. "I need to make an adjustment first. My rented jumpsuit isn't sized correctly. It's too damn tight—"

"You gained weight in the off-season," Batman razzed.

"—and the material's pinching my balls, chafing my thighs," Cap finished. He headed to the men's room.

Super Zooker nodded to the doctor. "We're good, as soon as Captain America gets his boys in order."

The doctor appeared pleased. "Boardwalk photographer Eden Cates-Kane is taking pictures for the local paper. You can get duplicates for the Richmond Rogues newsletter and website."

Eden was married to third baseman Landon Kane. She owned Old Tyme Portraits, a lucrative shop on the boardwalk. The vintage photos showcased men and women standing behind life-sized cutouts, their faces pictured above vintage swimwear, Roaring Twenties attire, and numerous other frames. She was often called on to shoot events and activities around Barefoot William.

Captain America returned, and the physician said, "Have a good spring training. I have tickets to your weekend games. We'll see you again soon." A nurse flagged him down. He left the superheroes at the elevator bank.

Two doors slid open simultaneously. Batman and Captain America charged into one. "Race you to the lobby," Cap called to Super Z as he hit the DOWN button, and the elevator doors began to close.

Joe shook his head. Men would be boys. The three ballplayers were always in competition, for one thing or another. He punched the outer wall button with his thumb. The doors to their elevator slowly opened once again, which gave him time to dive into the second lift and begin his own descent. He smiled to himself. He'd won this one.

Alone in the elevator, he took a moment to straighten his costume. He tucked his black shirt back into his black leather pants. Then patted down his brown suede duster. He tipped his crown-shaped bounty hunter hat with a braided band over his masked eyes. Went on to skim back his hair and retie the leather strip.

The elevator soon reached the lobby. He exited and looked around as he waited for his teammates. He noticed that their car stopped on every floor, picking up passengers.

Beachside Memorial was aesthetically healing. The entrance appeared more hotel than hospital. Tinted bronze glass curved around the wide, circular lobby. The Gulf view was both peaceful and soothing. The three-story atrium created adjacent to the reception area was spacious and airy. Members of a music ministry played the grand piano several times a week. Calming entertainment for both visitors and patients alike. The air smelled clean and fresh, not antiseptic.

Balloons and flowers brightened the windows of the gift shop. Soft, overstuffed seating eased a person's bones. The chairs were so comfortable that a patient or visitor could actually fall asleep. An art display of inspirational sayings was on permanent display on the terrazzo floor. He crossed over to look more closely at the one word that stood out to him: *heal.* Life was all about recovery, whether from illness or from difficult challenges.

The scent of coffee drew his attention to a wide staircase that led to a small balcony café. Murals on both sides of the steps depicted the deep roots of the community. A polished wooden plaque gave an abbreviated history on local founding father William Cates.

Cates had left Frostbite, Minnesota, in early nineteen hundred, a farmer broken by poor crops and a harsh early winter. He'd sold his farm, hand-cranked his Model-T, and driven south, until Florida sunshine thawed him out. On an uninhabited stretch of beach, he'd rolled up his pants legs, shucked his socks and work boots, and walked into the Gulf. He immediately put down roots and called Barefoot William home. He later married. A family was born. The once sleepy fishing village slowly grew into a popular and prosperous resort town.

The Rogues team captain Rylan Cates was a direct descendent of William. Generations of Cateses still owned and operated boardwalk businesses. Heritage and family were all-important to them. They shared a closeness Joe had never known. He'd grown up with a father who cheated on his mother and who disciplined his kids with fists. His mom got even with his dad's affairs by having her own. She used the grocery money to buy clothes. The cupboards and refrigerator were often bare. Not a healthy environment.

The free breakfast and lunch programs at school had fed Joe and his brother. No snacks or supper. He'd worked a part-time job at age sixteen, taking tickets at a movie theater. Minimum wage and buckets of popcorn. He'd filled his belly with cheesy corn. He scored a nightly box of Milk Duds for his brother.

Physically, he resembled his father. Both were big men with trigger tempers. That's where the similarity ended. His father was a cheater. Joe was not. He'd fast-talked women into his bed. French-kissed them to drop their panties. For him, sex was sex, and relationships were short-lived. No commitments. Every lover was aware that he was hers for only one night. Sunrise showed him the door. He was then free to date someone new the next night. No consequences. No deception. Simple and straightforward. No tears or outbursts.

The shuffle of feet brought Sam Matthews up behind him. "Man, that elevator was slow," he complained. "I thought we'd never get to the lobby." His Batman cape drooped, the ends dusting the floor. He tightened the cords at his shoulders, hiked it up.

Pax came next. He bent and tugged his sagging red Captain America boots up his calves. They fell short. He rolled over the leather. "Fat knees," he grunted. "I need to start jogging."

"You could run back to the hotel," suggested Sam.

Voice lowered, Pax said, "Not in this costume. This skintight jumpsuit sucks. I'm tucked and taped. My boys can't breathe."

"You'll air it all out shortly," said Sam.

Pax grunted. "The sooner, the better." He eyed Joe. "Where are we headed?"

"The administrative wing. Down the hallway past the gift shop." Joe led the way.

The three superheroes crossed the lobby, rounded the corner, and found themselves in a wide hallway, crowded with women. All sizes, all shapes, all with long hair. Five orderly lines led to the executive conference room. A woman in a navy suit, holding a clipboard, passed out release forms to the donors for the haircuts.

The men were immediately recognized. "Batman!" "Captain America!" "Super Zooker!" echoed all around them. The ballplayers moved up the line. The ladies smiled, accepting appreciative hugs and light kisses on the cheek from the heroes.

Cafeteria workers, carrying trays, served raspberry iced tea and snickerdoodles. Joe's favorite cookie. He took two. He and his teammates chatted with the ladies. Complimenting their big hearts and willingness to support sick kids.

They worked their way into the conference room. Their final stop before heading out. Salon chairs spread the width of the room. Joe took in each of the five immediate donors. Three brunettes, a redhead, and . . . a blonde.

His heart stuttered. *Stevie.* She flipped her sunshine hair over her shoulder and settled on the far chair, nearest the wall. The stylist draped a blue nylon cape over her shoulders, then briefly stepped aside to speak to one of the other beauticians. Stevie sat with her hands clutched in her lap, her gaze lowered. Pensive or praying. He wasn't sure which.

Joe held back. The simple fact that she was about to cut her hair gave him pause, despite the worthy cause.

For some reason, her pose aroused him. Absurd notion; still, his imagination took hold. An erotic teasing. Fantasy unfolding.

He visualized his fingers in the shiny length, as he drew her to him. Slowly. Suggestively. Expectant. Deep kisses and discovering hands. Desire. Need. Readiness. Clothes disappearing. A quick strip. A naked oneness. She'd straddle his thighs. Her hair fanning her body. The strands splitting over her breasts. Peek-a-boo nipples. Topping the hollow of her abdomen. A hint of her belly button. A suggestion of her sex. A natural blonde. So damn hot.

His palms began to sweat. His dick stirred. He mentally shook himself. Returned to reality. Stevie sat in the stylist chair, no longer nude, no longer atop his thighs. She had yet to see him. She stared into a narrow standing mirror, calmly awaiting her cut.

Joe crossed to her, while Sam and Pax divided their time among the other ladies. He leaned over her shoulder, startling her. The mirror reflected his grin and her frown. His superhero outfit made her blink.

"Who—*Joe?*" Recognition flashed in her dark eyes. Up came her chin, and her words had bite. "Not again. What are you doing here?"

"Being a superhero."

"I thought you were a ballplayer."

"That's my true identity."

"You're into pretend?"

"I like to fantasize."

The stylist returned with a wink and a smile. Joe recognized her from the Blue Coconut. She'd bought him a beer. They'd slow-danced. Nothing more. "Super Zooker, how's my favorite bounty hunter?"

"Hunting cosmic criminals is hard work, Capri."

She lowered her gaze. "You look good doing it, my man. Nice leather pants."

His lingering thoughts of Stevie had left him hard. There was no hiding the bulge beneath his zipper, despite shaking out his legs and shuffling his feet. He mentally talked his dick down. His dick was not a good listener.

"Are you here for support or just for show?" Capri inquired.

"Dr. Daniels requested we make an appearance."

"Women love superheroes."

"Not every woman," he muttered, eyeing Stevie. She glared back.

"Step aside, Super Z," the hairdresser requested. "You're welcome to stay and watch, but I need room to get around the chair."

Joe spoke to Stevie before retreating. He gently skimmed her hair behind her left ear, lowered his voice, asked, "Are you sure you want to cut your hair?"

"You're questioning my decision?"

"You'll look—"

She sat up straighter on the chair. "What? Like a boy?"

"No one would ever mistake you for a guy." Truth.

"So, what's your problem?"

He liked women with long hair. Plain and simple. Pretty selfish on his part. He wasn't dating or involved with Stevie. They'd just met, and weren't even close to being friends. Why should he care? A total puzzler. He thought of sweet Ashley and her chemo treatments. The loss of her hair, and her need for a wig. "No concerns. Your call," he managed.

"Thanks, since it's my hair."

"Have you ever worn it short?"

"Not since the day I was born."

"Hair grows back," said Capri, as she nudged Joe aside, making room for photographer Eden Cates-Kane.

Eden of the frizzy hair, freckles, and easy smile arrived with her Nikon. "Stevie, I'm Eden," she greeted. "I have a proposition for you. We've got an ideal photo op if we have Joe pose with you, combining two community events. The pictures could be used by the hospital, local newspaper, and the Rogues website and newsletter. What do you think?"

"Love the idea," Capri approved.

Joe nodded. "Fine by me, too."

Stevie was slower to agree. She side-eyed him; scrunched her nose. Indecisive. Her dislike of him was evident. Silence held. Tension built, until she finally sighed, gave in. "Okay."

"Excellent." Eden was pleased. "Let me check out the angles and frame my shots. We'll get started shortly."

In the ensuing seconds, Batman Sam and Captain America Pax made their way to Joe. "Super Z, what's happening?" asked Pax.

"Eden's about to photograph Stevie and me," he told them.

The ballplayers hugged Eden, then turned their attention to the seated woman with the waist-length hair. "Stevie?" Pax and Sam questioned at the same time. She nodded. They introduced themselves, then eyed her with interest. Their attention annoyed Joe. For some unknown reason.

He hadn't planned on presenting his teammates to Stevie, but the men bookended her now. They were at their most charming. Stevie was all smiles, which irritated Joe even more. She praised their superhero costumes and admired their dedication to the children. Sam and Pax ate it all up. Joe swore Sam even smacked his lips. There'd be no prying them off her.

Excluded from the conversation, Joe leaned against

the wall. Frustration had him scuffing his boot on the polished gray tiles. He left a mark—the only smudge on the pristine floor. He hunkered down and rubbed it clean with his thumb.

Pax had the plums to take off his gloves and stroke Stevie's hair. She didn't flinch. Didn't dissuade him. The strands slipped through his fingers like rays of sunshine. Annoyance slid bone-deep. He'd never resented his teammates until that moment. But Joe couldn't call them out; he had no valid reason. He clenched his fists instead. So tight that his knuckles hurt.

Possessiveness was the death of a man. He had no designs on her, although she did wear his garter. He wasn't looking for a girlfriend or forever lover. Yet despite his lone-wolf status, he didn't appreciate the guys' disruption. He felt left out. Difficult for a man used to being the center of attention.

Eden was professional, precise in her shots. There was no hurrying her. He'd wanted her to take the photo before the guys arrived. Too damn late. He was stuck on the outside, looking in. He felt like a Triple-A player.

Eden circled the stylist chair, came to him. Helped him hold up the wall. She studied him with her narrowed photographer's eyes. "Scowls scare people off. You won't photograph well."

"I'm not scowling."

"Your death stare and the tic in your jaw muscle say otherwise. You're grinding your teeth." Amusement curved her lips. "If I didn't know better, I'd think you were jealous."

"Not a chance."

She shrugged. "What do I know?"

"You know nothing, Eden."

"Not one thing." Her tone was teasing. "I'm here to take photos, not make observations. I want to take a few shots of Stevie and Capri during the cutting process. Then the superheroes and Stevie."

"*All* the heroes?"

"Groups are always nice."

"What about—" He had a hard time finishing the thought.

"Pairs?" she guessed.

A sharp nod.

She gave him a long look. "I was about to suggest just that. You have a good eye for composition, Joe."

Composition? He knew nothing about photography. His pictures chopped off heads and cut his subjects in half. Eden was being kind. But she'd relaxed him. "Thanks," he muttered.

"Welcome." She grew thoughtful. "I'll shoot you and Stevie last, after her haircut. The final impression of the day. Work for you?"

"Works for me."

Relieved, he released a breath he hadn't realized he'd been holding. He'd never had his photo taken with just one woman before. He'd always been surrounded by beach and boardwalk babes. His party posse. However, singling out Stevie for the final photo felt right. Just one shot like that wouldn't hurt. Wouldn't crimp his reputation as a "ladies' man." At the end of the day, it was all about the promo, not the girl. Or so he tried to convince himself.

"Let's do it," Eden announced. She crossed over to the chair. "Stand up a second, Stevie. I want to capture the full length of your hair."

Stevie complied, rising and shaking out her hair. The strands shimmered, sleek and shiny, skimming her waist. Pax whistled. Sam moaned low in his throat. Joe shifted his stance. Eden focused her Nikon, then did what she did best. She captured the moment on film.

Stevie turned in a full circle before sitting back down. Eden gave her a thumbs-up. Next she instructed, "Superheroes surround her." Pax stood to the right, Sam to the left, and Joe moved behind the chair. Eden crouched, took in all angles, and clicked away. Soon she straightened. "Fantastic. Now, heroes, please move aside." They did so, and Eden then motioned to Capri. "Your turn."

The stylist selected a thin scrunchie from her collection of bands, then slipped into the camera frame. Joe listened closely as Capri explained the process to Stevie. "I'll be putting your hair up into a ponytail, then cutting it off one inch above the band. I'm going with a braid, because it's so long. Makes it much easier to handle. The length of your hair can be processed for two, maybe even three wigs. You'll make several little girls very happy."

Joe cleared his throat, then asked, "Can I make a request for one of the wigs? There's a young girl, Ashley Hammond, on the sixth floor. She's a cancer survivor and soon to be released. She's in need of a hair prosthetic. She's blond, too. I'd like her to be a recipient of Stevie's hair."

Stevie twisted, faced him. Their gazes locked. She softened to him, compassion showing in her eyes for all of a second. "I'd like that, too," she said, then turned away.

Capri pointed to a stack of forms on a nearby table. "Fill one of these out," she told Joe. "Speak privately with the manufacturer on-site." She scanned the room. "The man in the blue suit by the cookie table is David Harkness. He works closely with Dr. Daniels and the children's parents. I'm sure a superhero would have some pull."

Joe could use his powers for good. The image of Ashley in a shoulder-length wig warmed his heart. It was a cause worth investigating. He crossed his arms over his chest and watched as Capri finished braiding Stevie's hair. Eden continued taking photos. Every second was documented.

Capri then picked up a pair of scissors and air-snapped the blades together. *Snip, snip.* Stevie's shoulders tensed slightly. Pax and Sam gave involuntary jerks. Both men covered their groins with their palms. Joe grinned at them. "It's a haircut." His teammates protected their balls.

"We still good to go?" Capri asked Stevie, giving the donor an opportunity to back out, not wanting her to have any regrets.

Stevie was ready. "Go ahead."

With a swift, concise snip, Capri cut off the ponytail. The stylist then put the braid into a sealed plastic bag with rubber bands at both ends. She set the bag aside, eyed Stevie, then said, "Give me ten minutes, and I'll give you a free trim." She returned the scissors to a sectional case on a rolling stand and withdrew a smaller pair. "Bangs, a little feathering. A new you," she predicted.

Joe glanced at his watch. Ten minutes edged toward fifteen, and a crowd began to gather. People gaped, eyes wide, at Stevie's transformation. Even the custodian, sweeping the floor, now leaned on his broom handle and stared. Stevie's profile was facing Joe, and it wasn't until Capri unfastened her cape and turned Stevie directly toward him that he got the full effect. The change was so startling, so stunning, he sucked in air. Dry mouth, tight throat, constricted chest. Sweaty palms.

Gone was the woman with the long hair. Its length had been weighing down her delicate features. Her shortened hair brought out her dark eyes, sharpened her cheekbones, and emphasized her full lips. She was a total knockout.

Capri held up a hand mirror, allowing Stevie a close-up view. "Sunlit, flirty, pretty," she complimented.

"Damn," from Pax.

"Babe . . ." Sam muttered.

Joe had no words.

The crowd began to clap, and the applause only grew louder as Stevie dipped her head, and color crept up her now-visible, very pale neck. Being the center of attention embarrassed her, but her modesty only endeared her more to the packed room.

A steadying breath, and Stevie Reynolds glanced up, meeting Joe's gaze. Seeking reassurance. His face was closed, his expression hard to read. Those gathered approved her cut, but he'd remained quiet. Too silent for a man who'd come on to her on the boardwalk, and again crossed her path at Kuts for Kids.

She heard the *click* of the camera, and realized that Eden was still shooting. "I'd like a superhero to be in the final photo, too. Super Z, close in," she said to Joe.

A surreal freeze-frame. Stevie watched him approach, all slow swagger and sex appeal. Yet his gaze was straight-forward. One corner of his mouth lifted. A flash of teeth. Then, lowering his voice, he approved. "Nice, Stewie."

She shouldn't have cared what he thought, but she did. Her heart skipped a beat. "I don't look like a boy? Peter Pan?"

"You look more feminine now than you did before."

His compliment deepened her blush. She heated from the inside out. Her skin had never felt so warm. She fanned herself with her hand.

"Make this last photo memorable," Eden called over to them.

"What do you mean?" asked Stevie.

Eden gave them a small, almost secretive smile. "I'm sure Super Z can come up with something."

That "*something*" made Stevie nervous.

Eden sensed her apprehension, and added, "PG rating, dude."

Stevie stilled as he leaned in. He kept his hands to himself, but his nearness intimidated her with its sexual charge. His kiss was familiar, warm and whisper-soft on her brow. Identical to the earlier kiss on the boardwalk, when he'd saved her from Security. His reward.

"Excellent," Eden praised them, winding down. "Super-hero, super cut. Thanks, everyone." She waved on her way out.

"My chair is open." Capri motioned to the next donor in line. "We've a lot of cuts yet to go before we close the doors."

Stevie shouldered her hobo bag, then looked toward the door.

"I'll walk you to the entrance," Joe offered.

"I can find my own way."

"Big hospital, you could get lost."

"There are plenty of signs and staff members around to guide me."

He shrugged, stepped back, and let her go. She moved on.

Pax pushed past Joe. "Done here. I'll follow you out."

"Behind you, too," said Sam. "Time to get out of my costume. I'm itching in places I didn't know could itch."

"I'll catch up with you guys later," came from Joe. "I need to speak to the hair prosthetic manufacturer on Ashley's behalf."

"Happy hour?" asked Sam.

"The Lusty Oyster."

"Catch you there," said Pax.

The glass door seized Joe's reflection as Stevie left the conference room. He stood alone. Tall, built, and danger-ous. His gaze narrowed on their departure. She watched him watch her as she and his buddies started down the hall. Distracted, she bumped into the door frame as she made her escape. She staggered back a step. Pax curved his hand over her shoulder, steadied her. She intuitively knew without looking that Joe had just smiled. Jerk.

They reached the foyer, passed through the automatic doors, then stood beneath the wide awning. She rummaged through her hobo bag for her cell phone. Once she found it, she texted Lori for a ride. There was no immediate response from her friend. A cement bench provided a place for her to wait. She sat down.

Sam took off his Batman cowl and mask. He ran his hands through his hair, mussing it up. Went on to ask, "Need a lift?"

"Thanks, but I'm good," she said—or so she hoped. Stevie was always punctual, often arriving five or ten minutes early. But time meant little to Lori. She was known to get easily sidetracked. Forgivable, yet annoying at times.

Pax removed his Captain America cap, untied his mask. Questioned, "You free tonight?"

She had no immediate plans. But partying with the Rogues went against her promise to her cousin. DJ was in town for several weeks, and he'd asked her not to associate with the ballplayers. He had his reasons, which she understood and accepted. She would abide by his wishes.

She'd been sharp and sarcastic with Joe from the moment they'd met. Totally disagreeable. It was her only defense against her attraction to the man. She'd expected him to back off, to drop his pursuit of her. But instead he continued to pull her in. She would redouble her efforts. Strengthen her mind-set.

She passed now. "Sorry, I'm busy." She would spend time with her aunt instead.

"I figured you'd have a date," said Pax. "Never hurts to ask, though. We're in the moment, and it's pretty last-minute. Stop by the Oyster if your schedule changes. We'd show you a good time."

She bet they would. Both handsome guys, full of themselves, and out to party. Women would go wild for them. "I'll keep you in mind," she assured him.

Each man gave her a smile meant to entice. Pax arched an eyebrow, flashed his dimples. Sam's boyish good looks, crooked grin, and amazing blue-violet eyes were hard to resist. The hue should've been effeminate, but instead it only enhanced his contrasting masculinity.

They left her then, crossing the street to the parking garage. Disappearing into the darkened lot, all stealth, strut, and a flapping bat cape.

Stevie folded her hands in her lap and sat quietly. A sturdy seawall separated the hospital from the beach. The coastline was deserted. The day was winding down, the sun less intense. It was now low tide, and the surf gave way to the sand.

Hunger crept up on her. She should've had a snickerdoodle when the tray was passed. She texted Lori a second time. Then a third. Sighed. She didn't have the money to hail a cab. Walking seemed to be her only other option.

"You waiting for me?" Male voice, warm breath on her neck, and Joe appeared behind her.

"Waiting on Lori."

"Your friend seems to disappear a lot."

"She'll show," Stevie said with conviction.

"When?"

"Soon enough." Her stomach growled.

"You hungry?"

"I missed lunch."

"I have a health bar we can share." He reached into the side pocket of his suede duster, scored the nutty-fruity snack. He circled the bench, came around to sit down beside her, purposely close. He bumped her hip, brushed her thigh. He split the bar, giving her the smaller half. She peeled back the wrapper, ate it in two bites. She wanted more.

She noticed Joe had yet to finish. He was a slow chewer. He held a decent-sized piece between his fingers. He sensed her stare, cut her a look. "You're drooling."

She touched her fingers to the corners of her mouth. "Am not."

"You checked."

She'd already had crumbs on her lips earlier in the day. She would hate to drool in front of him now.

"You want the last piece?" he offered.

She nodded. Lips parting. He fed her. His gloved thumb lingered, gently pressing her bottom lip. Raw leather. Soft mouth. Mesmerizing. Seductive.

Lost in the moment, she swallowed hard. The piece of health bar went down whole. Lodged in her throat. She coughed, choked.

Joe thumped her on the back. Hard.

She recovered, squeaked, "I'm fine."

He hovered over her, concern in his eyes. The bar settled heavily in her stomach, yet his nearness bothered her more. She rose, began to pace. A stiff breeze off the Gulf blew her skirt between her legs. Up her thighs. She tugged it down. Where was Lori?

Joe's, "You still wearing my garter?" stopped her in her tracks.

Obnoxious question, but one she was forced to answer. She was wearing the same clothes she'd had on earlier in the day. There hadn't been time following the bridal event for her to return home and change. To remove the garter. Kuts for Kids took priority. Lori had dropped her off—then disappeared.

"No garter."

"I saw a flash of blue."

"In your dreams."

"Prove me wrong."

"Take my word for it."

He grinned, knowing she lied. He relaxed on the bench, tilted back his head, squinted through his mask, and looked at the sky. His out-of-the-blue comment—"You don't like me much"—was more statement than question.

"Life isn't a popularity contest," she returned. "Not everyone has to like everyone else."

"Whom do you like?"

"Why do you care?"

"Just trying to figure you out."

"I'm not complicated. What you see is what you get."

"Play with me."

"Play *what* with you?"

"A favorite game of mine. How Well Do You Know Me?"

"We only met this morning."

"Doesn't matter. Some things you can intuitively recognize in a person."

What did he know about her? Curiosity got the better of her. "Who plays your game? Women you date, lovers?"

"It started as a bar game and worked its way into my bed," he said matter-of-factly.

She wouldn't be sleeping with him. Ever. But she did have time to kill. She slowly walked back toward him. "The rules?"

"We make assumptions about each other. The person being asked answers either 'true' or 'false.' But you have to be completely honest."

She could handle that. "How many assumptions in this game?"

"Twelve."

Too many. "Less."

"Ten, then. The winner scores the most points."

"What do I win?"

"That's yet to be determined," he said. "Don't get ahead of yourself, sweetheart. You haven't won yet."

He removed his bounty hunter hat and hooked it over his knee. Off came his mask, revealing rugged features. His hard stare homed in on her. She settled on the bench, a significant distance from him. Her skirt rode up slightly. The cement warmed the backs of her thighs. She started with, "You play professional baseball."

He shook his head. "Too obvious. Dig deeper."

"You're sexually active—"

"Common knowledge. Still doesn't count."

She bristled. "You're impossible."

"I'm so possible."

She went back in time, imagined him in elementary school. A kid who was often in trouble. Tattered blue jeans. Torn T-shirt. Fights and mouthing off. A holy terror. "By fifth grade, you'd spent more time in the principal's office than you did in the classroom."

"True. Discipline and I never got along. I had a permanently assigned desk in detention. I called the principal by his first name behind his back."

"One to zero." She was pleased with herself. "I'm ahead."

"Barely." He curbed her excitement. "We just got started. You were always the teacher's pet. Goodie Two-Shoes."

"True. I was helpful. Respectful." One-one.

"I'd have pulled your ponytail on the playground."

"Why?" she asked, curious.

"To remind you that not everyone's as perfect as you."

"My cousin DJ would've punched you for me."

"Brave, huh?"

"My best guy friend. He's always had my back."

"I'd rather have your front."

Never. She side-eyed him, then resumed their game. "Your high school yearbook? You were most likely to have scored with half the girls in your senior class."

"Not really a category." He chuckled. "But still true. Although it was closer to sixty percent."

She believed him.

His brow creased. "Your yearbook? You were most likely to succeed."

She couldn't help but sigh. "Yes, but I haven't been all that successful."

He surprised her with, "Success isn't always measured in high profiles and salaries. Personal growth counts, too." Insightful.

Two to two.

"Most time in the locker room," she assumed.

"Most time in the library," from him.

They both nodded. Three all.

"I loved to read. To learn," she disclosed.

"You look brainy."

His observation surprised her. "You seem street-smart."

"I've known gutters."

General remarks. No points.

"Most organized," he continued.

She liked an orderly life. "Most competitive."

"I go after what I want."

She bet he did. Four to four. "Biggest—"

"What?" He had the nerve to grin.

"Ego."

He threw back his head and laughed. "The world revolves around me, right?"

"So you think."

"Biggest ballbuster."

"Who, me?" Snarky innocence.

"Yeah, you."

"No way."

"Way, sweetheart. I'm taking the point. Five-five." He lowered his gaze to her chest. Lingered on her breasts. "You follow your heart."

Her gaze touched on his leather pants. "You lead with your—" The word *dick* caught in her throat.

"Yeah, I do."

"Six all," she updated the score.

He ran one hand down his face. Rubbed the back of his neck. "No tattoos for you."

"You're right." Rogues had tats. Lori had shared that fact. Inked at their groin. Team tradition. Third baseman Landon Kane had a sword with the word *Invincible* scrawled along the blade. Right fielder Halo Todd went with *Caution: Hard and Hot. Who's on First?* reflected first baseman Jake Packer's position. Joe, rumor had it, went with a hellhound, a mythical black dog with red eyes. Tenacious and vicious. A testimony to his baseball skills.

His hellhound was renowned. Publicly visible among his fans, party posse, lovers. She refused to admit that she knew about his ink. She purposely lost a point by saying, "Daffy Duck on your butt?"

His expression called her crazy. "No ass duck."

Six to seven, his favor.

He knuckled his chin. Scruff shadowed his jawline. "Bet you karaoke."

"I . . . have. But not well. I choose easy songs that make me look good."

"'Happy' by Pharrell Williams?"

How did he know? She nodded.

He calculated, "There are about eighty words in the lyrics but they feel like ten. Minimal effort, maximum crowd-pleaser."

"Bet you can't recite a nursery rhyme."

"Name one," he challenged.

"I'm a Little Teapot" was the first to come to mind. "You can stand up and do the movements, too, if you'd like." That would be entertaining.

"No dancing," he muttered under his breath before he lowered his voice, sing-songed, "I'm a little teapot, short and stout, here is my handle, here is my snout. When—"

"'*Snout*'?" she burst out. Was he serious? "Try 'spout.' It's a teapot, not a pig."

He shrugged. "I lost the hearing in my ear as a kid. Some words aren't always clear."

"No one corrected you?"

"My teacher thought I was being a smart-ass."

That made sense to her. He'd mistaken her name in the noisy crowd on the boardwalk. "Stevie" had sounded like "Stewie" to him. She cut him some slack. "'Wheels on the Bus' might be easier for you."

"'Go 'round and 'round.'"

"I'll let you slide. Seven-eight, you lead."

"Around your house," he presumed. "You shout at appliances."

She blinked. Wanted to deny his assumption, but could not. "Once or twice, and only when the timer on the microwave sticks and burns my bag of popcorn."

"I have a toaster that makes its own decisions," he admitted. "All selections brown too dark. It hates bagels. I've raised my voice, too."

"Watching TV, you call out referees."

"That I do," he confessed. "Refs miss calls. I set them straight."

Eight to nine. She gave great thought to her tenth and final assumption. She studied his face. Rough, with several scars. His nose . . . "You broke your nose in a fistfight," she presumed. "Twice."

He touched his forefinger to the bumps on his nose.

Grew silent. She wasn't sure he would even answer. He finally did. "One fistfight, defending my younger brother against a neighborhood bully. The second was a door slammed in my face."

"You were slow in moving out of the way?"

"My dad was faster."

"Oh . . ." She felt awful, but doubted that he would accept her sympathy. Saying nothing seemed better than saying something that might offend him. She kept it light. "Do I get a half a point for the fistfight? It was a two-part assumption."

"I'm easy. Take it." He took his sweet time with his own last impression of her. "You like me more than you're willing to admit."

That gave her pause. "We barely know each other. I don't dislike you, but I do find you annoying."

"Annoying, tolerable, close enough. I find you a challenge."

"I'm not a game or a competition."

"If you were, I'd already have won." Arrogant man.

"Don't bet on it."

"I'm a sure thing, Stewie."

"I'm not, Joey. You lost the point."

"I won overall. Nine to eight-point-five. My prize?"

"That I played the game with you."

"That's it? I was hoping for more."

"Less is often more."

He pulled a face. Snorted.

The hardness of the cement bench forced her to her feet. Her bottom felt numb. She needed to stretch. She strolled to the curb, searched the road for approaching vehicles. One came her way, but it wasn't Lori. She'd spent far too much time in Joe's company. His game had been interesting and fun, but it had tipped the scales in his favor. She found she liked him—a little. She needed her friend—now. Before she liked him—a lot.

"You leaving me?" he called to her.

"Shortly." Or so she hoped. On foot if she had to. The weather wasn't in her favor, though. Clouds had confiscated the sun. The sky was now overcast. "Looks like rain," she noted.

"I'll need to put the top up on my convertible."

She wondered what kind of car he drove, but didn't give him the satisfaction of asking. Most likely something sporty and fast. A thrill ride. Just like the man himself.

"I could give you a lift," he offered for the second time that day.

She'd declined on the boardwalk. She hedged now. "Maybe, if Lori doesn't show. Or if there's lightning and thunder and I'm feeling desperate."

"I've never been any woman's last resort."

"I'll give her five more minutes."

Joe glanced at his watch, tracking the time. "Four minutes, forty-five seconds . . . Four minutes, thirty seconds . . ." Irritating man.

Distant thunder humbled her. She might have to relent and accept his ride. *Hurry up, Lori.*

The entrance doors *swoosh*ed open behind them, distracting him from his countdown. A male transporter pushed an elderly patient in a wheelchair toward a waiting car at the curb. The aide assisted the man onto the passenger seat, shut the door, and the vehicle drove off.

The hospital employee waved and called to Joe, "Big season ahead, dude." He recognized the Rogue.

"Planning on it," Joe agreed.

"I checked out the spring training schedule, and your first game is against your Triple-A affiliate."

Joe's shoulders tensed. "The Rebels. I'm aware."

"Rivalry never hurts. It keeps players sharp." The transporter pushed the wheelchair back through the automatic doors.

Thunderheads bulked up. A storm crouched on the shoreline. The quiet before the storm hung heavily between them. Joe sat as still as stone, his breathing shallow. Lowering his gaze, he stared down at the sidewalk, his expression closed. A muscle ticced in his cheek. Something the transporter had said left him unresponsive. Spring training, their upcoming schedule, Triple-A? She hadn't a clue. The man was complex. "Umm . . ." was all she had.

"Nothing to talk about." He ended their conversation.

A sputtering engine claimed her attention, as an orange and white 1966 Volkswagen bus crawled down the road toward her. *Unleashed Dog Day Care*, the address and phone number, stood out in bold, block letters on both sides of the vehicle, along with painted images of numerous breeds of dogs. Her friend had arrived.

The VW slowed, stopped, backfired at the curb. "Wow, cool haircut," Lori admired. She peered around Stevie, eyed Joe on the bench. "You're looking Zoo-posse-hot."

"No posse," Stevie was quick to say. "It was superhero day for Joe. He and two other Rogues passed through Kuts for Kids."

"Sorry I'm late," Lori apologized.

"You're here now—that's all that matters." Her friend had saved her from riding with Joe.

"Blame Otis," Lori explained, referring to the bus. "I left Unleashed an hour ago. Transported a cocker spaniel, a collie, and a Doberman to their designated homes. Then stopped to get gas and add oil. *Chug-chug*. AC went out, and I opened the front Safari split-windows. Felt like a fan in my face. A police officer pulled me over for driving too slow. Couldn't be helped. No ticket, I got off with a warning. Otis is on his last set of tires."

Stevie understood the delay. "I tried to call you."

"I forgot my iPhone in my hurry to load the dogs."

The back of Stevie's neck prickled, and she realized that Joe had joined them at the curb. He slapped his bounty hunter hat against his thigh, eyed the bus. "Unleashed? I'm in need of dog care. Is that where you work?" he included both women.

Stevie shot Lori a *no-info* look, which her friend ignored. "Stevie's aunt Twyla owns Unleashed. Twyla recently broke her leg, and we're in town to help out. The dog care is on Outer Drive. A big old Florida Victorian set on twenty acres."

"My aunt may have a full house," Stevie discouraged. "What kind of dog do you have?"

"A two-year-old Rottweiler, Turbo."

The middle linebacker of dogs. "Obedience school?" she asked.

"Homeschooled."

Which meant the dog was as unruly as Joe.

"I'm sure Turbo will fit in just fine," said Lori. "Twyla prefers pets over people, and she always manages to squeeze in one more. You'd need to call ahead, though, to fill out an application and be interviewed. Twyla's available on Sundays."

Joe took it all in. "I'll phone Twyla this evening, and set up an appointment for tomorrow."

"Morning is best for her," Stevie put in. "If you're able to rise and shine."

He grinned then, slow and sexy. "I'm up early. I'm never one to waste a morning—"

Erection. She heard the word without his saying it.

"Jog." He winked, waved, left them.

"Mmm-hmm." Lori watched him round the front of

the VW bus and cross the street, all confidence and swagger. "He brings new meaning to leather pants."

Stevie silently agreed. Nice fit. Soft leather on a hard body. He was one fine superhero, about to hit the bars and use his powers for sex.

Three

Sunday early, Twyla Lawrence sat behind her office desk, her broken leg elevated on a footstool. Stevie admired her aunt. She defied age, looking more fifty than sixty with her silver-blond hair, clear hazel eyes behind teal reading glasses, and a smile that felt like a hug.

Sunshine spirited through the bay window of her office, trying to warm up the sixty-degree morning. Two red pottery mugs and matching plates offered up breakfast. A strong Colombia brew laced with cream, and slices of cinnamon-raisin toast.

"Ruler," her aunt requested of Stevie. It lay inches beyond her reach. Stevie passed it to her. Her aunt hiked up one side of her baggy sweatpants, revealing her plaster cast, which stretched from knee to ankle. "Itchy," she muttered, carefully sliding the plastic ruler inside. She scratched, then soon sighed her relief.

Setting the ruler aside, Twyla shifted her weight, straightened. She then flipped open her daily planner and scanned her appointments. "Interview with Joe Zooker and his Rottweiler, Turbo, at eight," she noted. "Lori mentioned you've met the Rogue. I'd like you to sit in on our meeting."

Stevie inwardly cringed. She wished Lori hadn't shared about their encounters. She wanted to decline, but she couldn't deny her aunt's request. Twyla was family. A triplet. Stevie's mother was her younger sister by sixty seconds. DJ's mom, third youngest by two minutes. All close-knit.

She took a sip of coffee, evaded. "You're certain?" Hoping her aunt might change her mind. She and Joe had crossed paths three times on Saturday. Twice on the boardwalk and once at the hospital. She wasn't ready to see him again today. Too soon.

"I want your input, sweetie," Twyla assured her. "You're managing Unleashed during my recovery. We can take up to twenty dogs at the day care, and we presently have four openings. You'll make the final decision. I want you to be comfortable with the dogs we choose."

Comfortable? Joe made her crazy. He was too rugged, sexual, raw. Should she accept his application, she'd be facing him at both the morning drop-off and the evening pickup. Twice a day was twice too much. Chances were good that he'd also board his dog when the team went on the road. Turbo would be a four-footed reminder of the man even when he was gone.

She had yet to confide in her aunt that her cousin disliked Joe. It would serve no purpose—it was just a guy thing. She and Lori resided in two of the four bedrooms on the second floor of the old Florida Victorian. Twyla had occupied the master suite until her fall. Since navigating the stairs on crutches had become daunting, she'd temporarily moved to the guesthouse, located behind the garage at the back of the property. It was quiet and convenient for her healing. She'd discussed renting out the third bedroom, but she hadn't advertised or acted on it. It would take a special person to live at a dog care.

Having Joe's dog on the premises would irritate DJ. Big-time. Her cousin dropped by often. DJ was focused on his future, and a possible transition in his career. A huge advancement that would require skill and a lot of luck. He didn't need any distractions. Or a confrontation with Joe. She would try to find a reason for rejection in Turbo's paperwork, a nice way to politely decline him for the day care. To keep peace within the family.

"More coffee?" Stevie offered her aunt.

Twyla held up her mug. "Top it off, please." Stevie poured from the Mr. Coffee. Her aunt glanced at her watch, went on to suggest, "Why not set out a cup for Joe? He'll be arriving shortly."

Twyla had stacked guest mugs on a bookshelf. Stevie added a third. Less than a minute later, a sleek convertible Jaguar XKE turned down the circular driveway. Navy, classic, phallic. The driver parked, opened his door, and his dog climbed over him, beating him out of the sports car. Stevie and her aunt watched through the window as Joe Zooker attempted to bring Turbo under control. There was tugging, chewing on the leash, then more tugging.

"A muscle dog," Twyla murmured.

Stevie checked out Joe and the tensing and flex of his body as he brought the Rottweiler to heel. "A handful."

Her aunt's eyes twinkled. "The man or his dog?"

Heat crept up Stevie's neck. "Turbo, of course."

"That's who I thought you meant."

The two crossed the wraparound porch and soon faced the door. A thumb-punch to the doorbell, and it barked. A deep *woof-woof-woof.*

Stevie didn't move.

"You might want to get that," Twyla nudged.

"I could . . ."

"You should."

Stevie slowly rose. She caught her reflection in a wall mirror next to a filing cabinet. With a hint of bed head, her short hair appeared more spiky than feathery. Her expression was drawn, her lips flat against her teeth. She'd dressed casually in a soft yellow polo with *Unleashed* scripted over the pocket. Brown shorts and sandals. No garter. She dragged her feet to the front door. Slowly opened it. Not looking forward to their meeting.

Taken in by Joe's grin, she missed Turbo's lunge. His front paws hit her square in the chest, and she lost her balance. Went down. Turbo stood over her. Licked her face with sloppy kisses.

"He likes you." Joe seemed pleased.

Turbo nuzzled her chest.

"*Really* likes you."

Her jaw clenched. "No manners."

"You look good flat on your back."

She struggled to sit up. "Get him off me."

"Better him on you than me."

Had he really just said that? Unbelievable. She glared.

"Sit, Turbo," he commanded.

The big dog parked on her thighs. Squashed her hips.

"Stand," from Joe.

"He's not listening."

"He listens when he wants to."

"Make him listen now."

"I'm working on it. Up, dude."

Turbo wagged the stub of his tail. "Not a good first impression, *Joey*."

"We already know each other, *Stewie*."

"You're here for an interview. Best foot forward."

"I'm meeting with Twyla."

"And me," she said flatly. "The decision is mine."

His grin turned to a grimace. "Seriously?"

"As a judge."

"Give us a chance, woman."

"I could say no right now," she threatened.

"But she won't." Twyla's voice of reason reached them.

Her aunt stood in the doorway to her office, leaning on one crutch. She patted her good leg, said, "Come, Turbo. Let's get acquainted."

The Rottweiler obeyed. He rolled off Stevie and trotted over to Twyla, stubby tail wagging. He allowed Twyla one pat on his head before darting into her office. To explore. Stevie exhaled sharply. She accepted Joe's hand, held out to her. Strong grasp. Callused palm. He pulled her up so fast, she fell against him. His body caught her. His arms wrapped her tight.

She lost all sense of self. Her concentration was solely on the man who held her. She looked up. Wide shoulders, jawline scruff, the slight quirk to his lips, the flare of his nostrils. His gaze was narrowed, dangerously dark. His thoughts impossible to read.

He widened his stance, and she found her legs between his own. His faded blue cotton T-shirt brushed her breasts. His male heat escaped his torn and laddered jeans, warming her thighs.

She couldn't breathe. Couldn't move. Could only mock. "Sunday best?" she asked of his clothes. "Hardly presentable."

"The appointment's all about Turbo. He's had a recent bath."

"You should've showered. You smell doggy."

He pulled out the front of his shirt, sniffed. "Downy, not doggy. Careful, babe. Insulted, I bite."

She hadn't meant to be mean. It went against her nature. But Joe had pushed her buttons. On purpose. Words slipped out that she couldn't recall. She breathed him in. An inconspicuous sniff. His scent, musk and masculine. Fabric fresh. Dominant and desirable.

"How bad could you bite?" she wondered. *Aloud.* Kicking herself afterward. Did she really want to know?

She'd provoked, and he responded. Her shorter haircut

left her neck bare, vulnerable. He tucked his chin against her pale throat. Her tender skin. His whiskers scraped. Abrasive. He nipped her. Grazing teeth and sucking. A love bite. The Rogue had marked her—his.

Awareness shivered through her body. Arousal stoked. Her belly felt fluttery. Sexual thoughts invaded. Flustering her. She couldn't think straight with him so close. He overpowered her.

She jerked back, as mad at him as she was at herself. She touched her neck. Felt the warm moistness of his mouth. The slightly raised flesh, certain to bruise. "No, no, no," she gasped. "What have you done?"

Nonchalant. "I bit you."

"I don't believe it," she sputtered.

"Never ask how I do anything if you don't want to be shown."

Her hands shook as she turned up the collar of her polo. She couldn't face Twyla with a fresh hickey. Too embarrassing. Adjustment made, she nodded toward the office and said stiffly, "We'll see you now."

He followed her so closely that if she'd stopped, he would've humped her backside. She sped up, and so did he. The toe of his boot lightly scraped her heel as she walked into the office. The wall mirror captured her flushed, breathless, and wild-eyed image. Joe's reflection flashed, too, looking devious and wicked.

No greeting from Turbo. He sat beside her aunt's chair, his big head resting on her thigh. He didn't move a muscle when they entered. Her aunt motioned them to take a seat. They did so. The office was small, the man large. His presence took over the room. He squeezed into one of the two chairs. The wingback arms of the two overlapped. They rubbed elbows. Thighs. Ankles.

"You could move over," she muttered.

"Could." But he didn't.

Idiot. Stevie scooted her chair away, distancing herself by inches. He sat in profile to her now. His hard face appeared even harder at a side angle. Chiseled granite.

Twyla eyed Stevie with interest. "Everything okay, hon?" she asked.

Stevie fingered her collar, making sure it stood up. Her love bite was momentarily hidden. "I'm fine," she responded, her voice shaky.

"Very well, then." Twyla next turned to Joe. "I'm Twyla Lawrence. Welcome to Unleashed."

"Joe Zooker," he returned, reaching across the desk and shaking her hand. "I appreciate your seeing me so quickly."

"Dire circumstances, from what you've indicated," Twyla said. "Let's talk before you fill out the registration forms. Spring training starts tomorrow, and Turbo needs day care."

"That's right," from Joe. "I'm looking for immediate placement."

Stevie was curious. "Where has he been staying?"

"With me at the Driftwood Hotel."

"He's not happy there?"

"He's . . . bored."

Twyla nodded, sympathetic. "A bored dog gets restless."

"Destructive," Joe admitted.

"How much damage?" Stevie asked.

Joe hesitated. Twyla eased his way. "I've dealt with dogs for forty years, son. Nothing you can say will surprise me. It's important we know his personality, should we accept his application."

"Honest dialogue," Stevie stressed.

Turbo lifted his head off Twyla's thigh, looked at Joe, as if dreading his bad habits coming to light. He whined, begging Joe to go easy on him.

Joe exhaled. Stated, "He acts out when I leave him alone."

"Lonesome," Twyla noted. "Separation anxiety."

"I purchased sturdy toys to distract him. A solid wood shaped bone, a tire-tread Tuffzilla, and a chicken-flavored Nylabone, manufacturer guaranteed to withstand the strongest chewer. My boy defied the dog toy companies. They all bit the dust."

He ran one hand through his hair. Sweeping it off his face. Revealing a strong forehead and a bold arch to his brows. "Turbo didn't stop with the toys. He went on to rip up a corner of the carpet, gnaw a leg on the dresser, remove and splinter a baseboard near the door."

"Your boy was busy," Twyla calmly remarked.

"Unfortunately, Turbo also growled at two maids from Housekeeping. They notified the office of the damage. No sympathy from the manager. He handed me a bill for the repairs and replacements, then requested that Turbo and I vacate the premises. Within the week." He shrugged, admitted, "A justifiable demand, but it still sucks. It's high season. Snowbirds are in town, filling hotel rooms and rental properties. *No Vacancy* signs all along the coastline."

Sympathy registered in Twyla's gaze. Stevie felt a moment of compassion, as well. It didn't last long. The Rogue knew a lot of people in town. He could crash somewhere. Hire a pet sitter.

Joe shouldered the blame for his dog's actions. "I'm aware of his temperament, and I should've been more attentive," he explained. "I broke my bond with Turbo. We've been joined at the hip during the off-season. Being alone for several hours flipped his destroyer switch, which was totally my fault. I had places to be and people to see on Saturday. I lost track of time, got caught up—"

"In the bridal event," Stevie reminded.

"That, and the hospital appearance. The superhero gig was scheduled before I arrived in town. I'd never break my word to those kids."

Twyla nodded supportively. She scratched the rottie's ears. The dog sank against her side. Calm. Content. "You need a safe place for Turbo to stay when you have obligations."

Stevie hardly considered the bridal event to be an *obligation*, but she let it go. Joe had been looking for a lover. She wondered whether he'd found one. Who'd warmed his bed last night?

"Was Turbo left alone yesterday evening, as well?" slipped out.

He side-eyed her. "Application conversation or curiosity?" he baited. "Asking whether I had a date, babe?"

She sniffed. "My concern was for your dog."

"I'm not irresponsible," he defended. "My boy and I both crashed early."

"Oh . . ." A weight lifted off her chest. Had she sighed? She hoped it wasn't noticeable. Too late.

Her aunt raised a brow, eyes wide.

Joe's grin annoyed her most. Slow, sexy, significant.

Twyla came to her rescue. "Coffee?" She held up the glass carafe. Joe accepted a cup. She poured. He drank half, in one sip.

"Traditional commands?" Stevie returned to asking the appropriate questions to please her aunt.

"The basics. He's restless, like me, and responds best following a morning run. A release of excess energy."

"You'll have exercised Turbo before you drop him off?" Very important to Stevie. "I don't want a repeat of this morning's greeting."

"We'll jog early," Joe assured her. "He'll listen afterward."

"How do *you* respond following your run?" Snarky undertone.

"Depends on what I'm asked to do," he returned. "What did you have in mind, babe?"

Twyla cleared her throat, intervened. "We don't ask much of anyone. Our staff is competent. Amazing. All animal lovers. Unleashed is more than a job to them. They treat the dogs like kids. Nurturers providing a safe and secure environment. My employees are also all knowledgeable about behavior modification. They are certified in first aid and animal CPR. We have a veterinarian on call, and the emergency center is less than a mile south. Are Turbo's shots updated?"

"I can have his records faxed from the clinic in Richmond."

"No hurry," Stevie waved it off. "We're interviewing, not accepting at this point."

Turbo made a guttural noise in his throat. "He's already found his place with Twyla," Joe noted.

"My aunt won't be around much of the days when Turbo's here," Stevie specified. "She's to rest, doctor's orders."

"You'll be dealing mostly with my niece, and, on occasion, with her friend Lori. Is that agreeable to you?" Twyla asked him.

Agreeable to him? What about to her? Stevie nearly blurted out. She held her tongue.

"Fine, Twyla, but I'll miss seeing you," Joe responded in an obvious bid to charm her aunt.

Twyla appreciated his compliment. Her eyes sparkled. "I'll hobble in and out," she promised. "Make sure the dogs don't take the staff members hostage."

"Turbo looks like a ringleader," said Stevie.

Joe grinned. "I'd pay your ransom."

Stevie wasn't as enchanted as her aunt. "Why Unleashed? There are three other canine care facilities in town. BarkTastic?"

"I drove by," he told her. "Outdoor runs and dog walkers. No freedom."

"We're off-leash," Twyla informed him. "The dogs

have the run of six lower rooms on the first floor, plus two
fenced-off acres. We have a monitored treadmill. There's
also canine playground equipment."

"A doggy crawl tunnel?" His tone was hopeful. "It's
Turbo's favorite whenever we go to the dog park."

Twyla nodded. "A twenty-foot plastic tunnel, extra-
wide, with spy holes for visibility. A Rover Jump Over,
two King of the Hill piles of dirt, deck rest platforms, and
a small pool. Lifeguard on duty."

"Nice," from Joe. He stretched out his legs, leaned
back in the chair. He casually slid his foot toward Stevie.
Rubbed his boot against her sandals. She kicked his ankle.

She leaned as far away from him on her own chair as
she could manage. Standing up was next. "Did you try
Smoochie Poochie?" she persisted.

"Sounded . . . pink. Too girly."

"Paws 'R Us?"

"They prefer small dogs, under forty pounds."

Turbo was a tank. "Socialization?" she inquired. "Does
he get along with other dogs?"

Joe rolled his tongue in his cheek. "Pretty much so. Several of my teammates recommended your place. Turbo's
met Rylan Cates's Great Dane, Atlas; Halo Todd's pug,
Quigley; Will Ridgeway's Chihuahua, Cutie Patootie."

"There will be sixteen to twenty dogs here, daily," Stevie stated. "Will he need one-on-one handling, or will he
take to the group?"

"No hands-on. He'll fit in."

"You're certain?" Hard to believe.

"So sure, I'll pay a month in advance."

"No need," Twyla inserted. "Daily or weekly rates depend on the owner. Turnover disrupts our routine. We
like consistency. Most of our dogs are regulars. We have
all sizes and ages, from rambunctious puppies and active
adults to mellow seniors and special-needs dogs."

Joe's brow creased. "Special needs?"

"Triple Threat, or Triple to his pals." Stevie spoke fondly of the dog. "A miniature pinscher born with a birth defect, only three legs. Triple runs with the pack at playtime. He keeps up well."

Conversation slowed. Twyla finished off her coffee, awkwardly rose. Turbo moved aside, giving her room to collect her crutches. "I want you to be as satisfied with us as we are with you," she said. "Stevie can give you the tour of the house and the yard. There are no other dogs around just now. Turbo can run free. Explore. See if he'd be happy here."

The big dog wagged his tail.

Joe stood, moved the chairs out of Twyla's way, nearly unseating Stevie. Her aunt now had a clear path to the door. She smiled cordially. "I'll be in the kitchen, and will see you before you leave."

Joe winked at her aunt. "I'd like that."

Her smile turned serious. "Stevie has the final word on all new applicants," Twyla reminded him. "I'm sure she'll come to the right decision." She disappeared down the hallway. Turbo took off after her.

Stevie drew a breath from deep in her belly. Exhaled slowly. She was about to walk Joe around the house. A waste of time, as far as she was concerned. She planned to stand her ground, decline his application. That was her intention, anyway.

She pushed off her chair, turned, and came breast to chest with the man. She'd been deep in thought, and hadn't realized how he'd invaded her space. Yet there he was, leaning over her, hot-bodied and breathing her air. She hoped he'd step back. He did not. She sucked in her stomach, pulled back as far as possible, and eased around him. Still, their bodies brushed. Intimately. Her nipples grazed his arm. Her hip skimmed his groin.

He had the balls to grin. "You feel good."

So did he. Solid and strong. He affected her. Light-headed, her legs shaky, she managed to reach the door. She wanted to send him packing, but she would never disrespect her aunt. Twyla trusted her with the business, so Stevie went through the motions.

"This way." She began the tour, pointing to a plaque near the front door. *Pets Welcome. Owners Tolerated.* "My aunt's motto."

"Twyla seemed to like Turbo," said Joe. "And me."

"She's polite to everyone."

"Shame you don't take after her."

"I'm nice," she objected.

"Define 'nice.'"

"Giving you a tour of our facility."

He rolled his eyes.

They walked together. The hallway was wide, yet he walked adjacent to her. There was contact. Purposeful on his part. Their hands and arms brushed, their hips bumped, and he nearly tromped on her foot.

She sidestepped. "Must you crowd me?"

"I hadn't realized—"

"You're aware," she insisted. "You've touched me eight times."

"Nine, hon."

She'd only counted eight. He was off by one. His ninth came seconds later. Taking the collar of her polo in hand, he hiked it up her neck. "You're flashing my hickey."

She blushed. She was so hot, Joe's fingertips heated before he lowered his hand. He teasingly blew on his fingers to cool them. Her heartbeat was visible at the base of her throat. Accelerated by his nearness. He liked throwing her off balance, and he would continue to do so. Repeatedly. "Keep moving. You're holding up the tour."

She glared.

He grinned.

The thick-padded rubber floors muffled their footsteps. The padding was soft on the dogs' joints and paws. Bone-shaped wooden benches offered seating. Photos of boarders covered the walls. "Atlas." He noticed a picture of team captain Rylan Cates's Great Dane. The big dog lay on the floor, surrounded by playful Dalmatian puppies. One puppy had climbed onto Atlas's back, biting the Dane's floppy ear. Atlas's expression was happy, goofy. Accepting.

"Does Turbo like puppies?" Stevie asked him.

"He's never been around them."

"We have a special Puppy Room," she said. "Atlas is the only bigger dog we trust to play nice. No roughhousing."

"Do you favor him?" He didn't want Turbo to be left out.

"No favorites. All dogs are treated equally."

Sounded fair. "Has the Victorian ever been a family home, or was it always a dog care facility?"

"My aunt considers the dogs her family."

He understood. He and Turbo were tight. His dog was similar to a child, working through his terrible twos. His destructive tendencies weren't any worse than a kid throwing a temper tantrum. "Has Twyla lived here long?"

"Thirty-five years. The Victorian was run-down and needed a face-lift when she first purchased it. Once it was authenticated and preserved, the house became eligible for the National Register of Historic Places, and it could have become a tourist attraction."

Joe smiled. "Instead it went to the dogs."

She nodded. "My aunt's preference. She's never regretted her decision. Animals are her life."

Joe admired the wide central staircase that rose to the second floor. A balcony overlooked the main hallway below. "Bedrooms?" he asked.

"Four total, along with a small sitting room for watching TV or reading. The third-story turret is a library," Stevie told him. "Dogs aren't allowed up there. That's our personal space. We stretch an expandable lattice gate across the bottom of the staircase, so the dogs don't climb. Running and playing on steps can be dangerous for them anyway."

No gate today. A shadowed streak ran out of one bedroom and into another. Turbo? Joe hoped his boy wasn't already getting into trouble.

"There's also a narrow back staircase off the kitchen. It was once used by servants to serve breakfast to residents still in bed," she added.

"Breakfast in bed is nice," he said. "Although most mornings I'm hungrier for a woman than food."

"More than I needed to know."

"I like to share."

"Please don't."

He took in the high ceiling beams, intricate carved-wood medallions, crown molding, and wainscot paneling. No dust or cobwebs. "Big place. Lots of upkeep, I imagine."

"More than my aunt can handle alone. A cleaning crew comes in each evening. Lawn maintenance cuts the grass twice a month."

Joe liked what he'd seen and heard so far.

They passed a small boutique area filled with high-fashion collars and leashes, seasonal pet attire and accessories, toys, and organic treats. Lights out, it was closed for the day, yet Joe peered inside. His brow creased. "Why do people dress up their pets?"

"They treat them like kids."

"On Halloween, Turbo could wear camouflage."

"Guerrilla warfare," she muttered.

Stevie didn't hold back. He liked a gutsy woman. Feisty.

He still didn't understand her constantly putting him down, though. But for now he let her comments drift, not stick. He wasn't taking them personally anymore—or at least not too seriously.

The Toy Room came next. The floor was clear; all the toys had been piled into big plastic bins. "Turbo likes tennis balls and sock toys," he let her know. Both were visible in the bins.

They neared the back door. Two cameras were mounted on either side. "Webcams?" he assumed.

"Six total, running whenever dogs are on the premises. Pet owners are given passwords, and they can click onto our website throughout the day. Track the action."

"I could watch you, too."

"I'll be sure to wave." Caustic.

"I'll wave back."

"There's no return signal feed."

"Still, you'll know."

Her sigh was heavy. Long-suffering. He flattened his palm on her lower back, nudging her forward. She allowed his touch for two steps, then picked up her pace, walking ahead of him. He'd had her for *two* entire steps. Not bad. He was wearing her down.

She pointed to a small area at the rear of the house, informed him, "The mudroom, converted to Time-Out. Quiet space separate from other activities. Exuberant and overactive dogs often need a few minutes to calm down, same as a child. Time-out gives them that opportunity."

Joe's chest tightened at the thought of Turbo being reprimanded. Inside the Time-Out area, there was a big bowl for water and a rectangular plaid-covered dog bed. However comfortable, though, he would hate to see the rottie boxed in.

He brought up the fact, slowly saying, "Turbo doesn't take to tight spaces. Time-out won't benefit him."

"It's helped with other dogs."

"You need to understand Turbo's history," he admitted. Pain hit him whenever he discussed the dog's past. "Abused. I adopted him from the local no-kill shelter before the Annual Barefoot William Dog Jog last year. The charity event promotes forever homes. Players showcased adoptable dogs during the race. I chose Turbo."

He swallowed hard. "According to his file, he'd been living outside, chained to a tree. There are deep scars beneath his collar. His owner moved, left him behind. The neighbors reported his barking for food. He'd been starved."

Stevie's face turned pale, her expression sad. She placed a hand over her heart. "I'm sorry."

"I've spoiled him rotten ever since." Truth. "Turbo has no restrictions. He often gets the better of me. I'm fine with that. No regrets. It is what it is."

Stevie nodded. "I understand. But freedom is one thing; free-for-all, quite another. My aunt refers to our dog day care as 'controlled chaos.' She's never had a dogfight. Never an escapee. We want to keep it that way."

"Be kind to my boy."

"Should Turbo be accepted, he will be handled with great care. We don't want to break his spirit. I prefer a spray bottle. A light mist to the face stops misbehavior pretty quickly."

His dog's face would be wet the entire day. Still, it was a gentler method of discipline than many others he'd heard of. "Thank you."

"Don't thank me yet."

He was still being screened.

She cracked the back door so he could peer out. He was impressed by the porch and the slanting ramp that led to the yard. There was plenty of playground equipment, a cement wading pool, and even a patch of woods, within the six-foot chain-link fence.

She closed the door, turned to him. "Any questions?"

Tour over. He had a couple. "Cost per day versus by the week?"

She quoted him prices, including overnights and weekends. Kibble and snacks were included during longer stays. Grooming was also available.

"Affordable," he agreed. "Turbo's introduction to the other dogs?"

"Slowly. He'll be temporarily separated from the main group. We'll assign him two or three initial friends. Let them hang out for a day or two. Then bring in another dog, and another, until he's met each one."

"Add a friend a day. I like that."

"Anything else?"

"I'm good. Are you good with me?"

"I'll need to talk to Twyla first."

"Discuss or diss us?"

She dipped her head. *Diss.*

He was disappointed, but didn't know how to change her mind. Maybe Twyla would come to his defense.

Noise broke from the balcony. Running paws. The sound moved back and forth, room to room. There were no other dogs in the house. Joe needed to locate his rottie. "My boy," he said.

"I'm right behind you."

They climbed the staircase together. Stopped at the top—and stared. A tornado named Turbo had hit. Clothes and bedding were strewn across the landing. Pillows, sheets, a comforter. A black one-piece swimsuit, jeans, socks, shoes. An overturned dresser drawer.

Stevie's jaw dropped. "The bedroom doors were closed earlier." All four stood open now.

"Turbo *might* have"—no doubt *had*—"butted his head against the door, like a bull."

She checked out the doorknobs. Breathed easier. "Jarred, but not broken. Locks intact. Thank goodness."

Joe looked around, asked, "Who lives up here?"

"Lori and me. My aunt did, too, before she broke her leg. She's since moved to the guesthouse. Easier to get around." She bent and began to sort through the items. Dividing them into three piles.

"Where's Lori now?"

"Out."

Heavy silence, until he heard Turbo grunt. Not a good sound.

Stevie listened, frowned. "Coming from my room, two doors down."

He found his dog belly-flopped on the far side of a brass bed, tugging on the rounded corner of a brown, gold, and blue braided rug. Shit. A chunk was already missing by the time Joe reached him. Turbo spit it out. The rottie pushed himself up, darted around Joe, only to skid to a halt by a wicker laundry basket. He snagged something, took off again, leaving Joe staring at the torn rug. The wool appeared old, somewhat worn, the colors faded. Irreplaceable.

He nudged the loose piece with his booted toe, tried to fit it together. No go. Turbo had damaged the edges. Not a good impression. Maybe Stevie wouldn't notice. More likely she would. He blew out a breath. Silently swore. A vintage rug would be difficult to repair. Harder still to replace.

He should've chased down Turbo, but instead he took a moment to look around Stevie's bedroom. To satisfy his curiosity. Out-and-out simplicity. An armoire, an antique lamp, a cane rocker. His gaze narrowed and his grin spread when he caught sight of her blue garter on the bedside table. He circled the foot of her bed, picked it up, and twirled it on his finger. She hadn't thrown it away, as she had threatened. He could still picture it on her thigh, above her freckled knee. Frilly satin against soft skin. Nice.

"Drop my panties!" Stevie's voice was shrill, grabbing his attention. He placed the garter where he'd found it, and returned to the landing. The sight was not pretty. A tug-of-war was going on, as Stevie and Turbo pulled on a pair of red panties. The dog shook his head, and the bikini ripped. He immediately lost interest. Game over. He dropped the remains and bounded down the staircase.

Joe picked up the panties. The tear left them crotchless. To his liking—but not to Stevie's, he imagined. She snatched them from him. Stuffed them in the pocket of her shorts. Fire shot from her eyes. Her color was high. Her jaw worked. He waited for her to rant and rave, to rip him a new one. But whatever she might have said was interrupted by the *thump, thump* of Twyla's crutches.

The older woman now stood at the bottom of the stairs with Turbo by her side, all furry innocence. She called up to them, "I heard a commotion. Everything okay?"

Stevie expelled a breath. "Turbo invaded the bedrooms."

"Destructive?" Twyla inquired.

Joe descended the stairs, two at a time. Stevie was close behind. "Depends on your definition of 'destructive'," he defended his dog.

"That bad, huh?" from Twyla.

Joe played down the damage. "He discovered bedding and clothing. Dragged items onto the landing."

Twyla looked to Stevie. "Anything ruined?"

"A pair of my underwear."

Twyla shrugged it off. "Replaceable."

Joe spoke up. "I'll buy you—"

Stevie shook her head. "I don't want you getting into my panties."

Her words hung in the air. The connotation was overtly sexual. Stevie's whole body blushed, as red as the panties she'd just pocketed.

Joe fought back a grin. Inappropriate.

"My niece will make her own purchases," Twyla informed him. "Anything further?"

He came clean. "There's a small problem with the braided rug in Stevie's bedroom."

Stevie glared. "How *small* of a problem?"

"Turbo took a bite."

"It's a family heirloom," Twyla quietly said. "Dates back a hundred years."

Crap. Joe stood knee-deep in his dog's damages. He felt terrible. "I'll have it fixed," he assured Twyla. "I'll locate someone who restores rugs. Or I'll find a replacement through an antique dealer." Cost was irrelevant at this point. He needed to right Turbo's wrong.

"Incidents happen," Twyla said forgivingly. "We'll deal with it later." She changed the subject, spoke to Stevie. "You had a phone call moments ago. I took a message. A rather long one." She handed her niece a sheet of paper.

Stevie read the note. Her eyes rounded. Her voice held surprise, excitement. "The bridal event. I won a prize."

"Which one?" Joe asked. He'd stepped back on the boardwalk, watching her from a safe distance as she signed up for different drawings. Weddings gave him the willies.

Stevie answered, "A photo shoot with *I Do* magazine. The centerfold. I suggested several locales, and the editor chose Unleashed. She found it unique."

"Definitely different," Twyla agreed.

Stevie pursed her lips. "I was thinking it would promote the dog day care."

Her aunt smiled. "A lovely thought."

"The photographer will hold an open call for canines, and pick eight for the shoot," relayed Stevie. "Dogs that will add color, originality, and flow to the pictures."

Interesting, thought Joe. Turbo wouldn't stand a chance of being selected. He was too rough-and-tumble. Too chewy.

Stevie shifted uneasily. "There were hundreds of potential brides . . . at the event," she stammered. "I never imagined . . . I'd actually win."

"But you did, dear," Twyla said.

"There's a problem . . ." Stevie's voice trailed off. Her expression looked pained. Her face now pale.

"Something I can fix?" her aunt offered.

"Not unless you have a groom."

"Oh," from Twyla.

"Whoa," came from Joe.

A groom? It took two to marry. Something Stevie had dismissed. She'd gotten caught up in the festive wedding atmosphere, and she'd entered the drawings without even a significant other in mind. She'd accused *him* of being an opportunist, checking out babes on the boardwalk, while she filled up the contest boxes without even having a man in her life. Karma. A total payback. Bit her in the ass.

He grinned over her predicament. So broadly, so impolitely, that Twyla hit his boot with the rubber tip on her crutch. She was protective of her niece. He pulled it together. Put on a momentarily respectful face.

Stevie held her own. "I'll deal with it."

"I'm sure you will," Twyla assured her. "Moving on, where do we stand with Turbo?"

Joe stiffened. "My boy hasn't put his best paw forward."

Twyla rounded her shoulders, leaned heavily on her crutches. She eyed her niece. "Knee-jerk reactions aren't always fair. We all need second chances."

Joe breathed easier. "Seconds are good."

"What do you think, Stevie?" Twyla sought her decision.

"I'm not sure I can handle—"

The words hung in the air. Joe mentally filled in the blank. Him or Turbo, which did she fear the most?

Twyla's gaze shifted between them. Her expression was thoughtful. "A compromise, perhaps," she said. "Turbo needs doggy day care, and, to save face, Stevie requires a groom."

"A groom for an afternoon," said Stevie.

An alarm sounded in his head. Red flags unfurled. "What are you suggesting?" he asked Twyla.

"We'll accept Turbo's application—if you'll pose as Stevie's intended."

"No way," Stevie choked.

Joe felt the same, until Turbo nudged him with his nose. The rottie whimpered. Joe scratched the dog's ear. He'd arrived here with a purpose. One he would fulfill. He stepped up to the plate now. "Our posing together wouldn't be new, Stewie. We played a couple on the boardwalk. Our picture was taken together at Kuts for Kids. You take care of my boy, and I'll do you a solid— with one final stipulation."

"What more do you want?" she asked, wary.

He threw a curveball. "I need a place to stay. Rent me a room."

"That would be up to my aunt."

Twyla approved. "I'd planned to rent the extra bedroom. Eventually. I have no problem with you living upstairs." Pause. "One minor inconvenience. You'd have to share a bathroom with Stevie."

Joe nodded. "I'm fine with that, as long as Stevie doesn't hang her underwear over the shower curtain, and she knocks before she enters."

"You two can work it out," Twyla finalized. "I'm headed for a nap." She hobbled off. Left them.

Joe waited for Twyla to clear the back door, for the air to settle between them, before he asked, "Equal opportunity, sweetheart. Neighbors or not?"

Alone now, standing close, she met his gaze. They were two very different people. She was sarcastic, didn't like him. Much. He was drawn to her, for no logical reason. Lame.

Dissimilar, yet with matching desire, they breathed each other in. Woman. Man. He saw her uncertainty. Noticed her goose bumps. The clutching of her hands. She was a bundle of nerves. She touched the hickey on her neck. Bit down on her bottom lip. She warmed. He heated. Tension pulsed. Her sigh escaped. Low and throaty.

"I'll take that as a yes."

Four

Joe's teammates called him Zoo. He was aggressive, antagonistic, an animal at the stadium. Opinionated, too. No way were the Triple-A players taking over Rogue real estate in the locker room. Joe pulled the welcome mat, glaring at two Rebels until they retreated behind an imaginary line that separated the major and minor leaguers.

The Rogues' starting lineup filled the row against the south wall. As a veteran player with seniority, he was given two lockers so he could spread out and be more comfortable. No elbow-crowding from his teammates. The coveted lockers put him adjacent to the lounge and food cart, with additional easy access to the showers. He could settle on a La-Z-Boy, put up his feet after nine innings, and enjoy a snack or an entirely catered meal. Rogues' food. Not Rebels'.

He kept one eye on the side door. Dean Jensen had yet to arrive. The captain of the Rebels was late.

"Death stare, Zoo?" Jake Packer asked, amused. Pax claimed the neighboring locker. "Locker room is neutral ground, we're not on the field."

Joe cut his gaze to the back of the room. Watched as the minor league players talked, dressed, readied for practice. "I hate having them here."

Pax understood. "So do I. I've heard the players are

high-caliber this year. Any one of them could squeeze us right off the roster."

"So you keep telling me," Joe ground out.

Irritatingly rational, Pax added, "Rogues are a team unto themselves. The majority of minor league teams aren't owned by major league clubs; they merely have affiliation contracts with them. But the Rebels are owned by the Rogues. A huge investment. Our team owner and the front office track their progress as closely as they do our own."

His teammate's reminder and intentions were good. Joe just didn't take it well. Today the two teams would square off. Competition would be fierce from the onset. He would push himself, play as hard in spring training as he did during the regular season. He was fit, with strong arms, stronger legs. His focus honed. He ranked third of all left fielders in major league baseball.

Joe's competition, Dean Jensen, was an up-and-comer on the Rebels squad. He had potential. Was damn good, actually. As a prospect player, he was on-site to gain experience and face tougher competition. He had a lot going for him.

Joe locked his jaw. Fisted his hands. No one had ever given him anything. What he had was his and nobody else's. Left field belonged to him. The end.

Deep breath, and he cleared his head. Moved on, for the moment. He pitched his wallet and keys onto the top shelf of the empty locker that separated him and shortstop Brody Jones. Brody was a nice guy. A quiet, conscientious player. He got the job done. He'd injured his shoulder the previous season. Had undergone an operation. Extensive rotator-cuff surgery repaired the damage, but he'd yet to achieve full range of motion. He might start the season, but Joe doubted he'd finish. Retirement, sooner than later. He'd return to West Virginia with his wife and two kids.

Joe hiked his gray T-shirt over his head. Tossed it on the floor of his locker. He heel-toed his athletic shoes. No socks. Then unsnapped, unzipped his jeans. Shucked them. He stood in black boxer-briefs. Scratched his stomach, his hellhound tattoo.

Pax scanned the room. "Have you seen Will?" The starting pitcher. "I owe him fifty bucks. Bar game. We bet on the Blue Coconut jukebox, guessing what would be the next song played. Ten guesses. I lost, eight out of ten. The dude is fuckin' psychic."

Not psychic, but tall. Six-six and sharp-eyed. If they'd been standing anywhere near the Wurlitzer, Will could've seen the record drop. With little effort. Joe didn't blow his cover. It was Will's game.

"Will's probably in the bullpen," Joe returned. Pitchers and catchers began their workouts two weeks before the position players. Will was dedicated, perfection his goal.

Pax dropped onto the gray-enamel bench. Removed his socks and boat shoes. He'd recently purchased a sailboat. A forty-one-foot Morgan Classic decked out with two cabins astern. A third, larger cabin aft had a head and separate shower. Pax presently lived on the boat, which he kept anchored at Land's End, a cul-de-sac off Houseboat Row. "Where were you last night?" he asked Joe.

"At Unleashed."

Pax pulled off a worn and torn Rogues T-shirt. Frowned. "Not familiar with that bar."

"Not a bar. A dog day care."

"What the hell?"

Joe gave him the condensed version, from Turbo's destruction of the hotel room to his decision to move into the Victorian.

"Good move for your dog."

Good move for him, too, Joe thought, recalling the previous evening. He'd packed up his clothes and belongings at the Driftwood, and taken up residence in the second-floor bedroom next to Stevie. She'd been cool, but cordial, closing herself off in her own room. She'd skipped Twyla's lasagna supper. He'd eaten half the pan. Twyla had graciously allowed Turbo a few bites, too.

Afterward, the rottie went crazy in the backyard. Hiding in the doggy crawl tunnel. Climbing the wide, tiered deck platforms. Playing his heart out. Free.

Stevie's friend Lori had arrived just as he was helping Twyla clear the table, load the dishwasher. She stood in the doorway in a skimpy turquoise bikini top and cut-off shorts. Sunburned, smiling, and surprised to see him. Greetings all around, before she made a pot of coffee and requested the particulars. He was happy to oblige.

He'd filled her in as they sat around the kitchen table. She seemed extremely pleased. He swore Lori and Twyla exchanged a sly look when he raised his mug and sipped his coffee. An unspoken female exchange. He hated secrets, and hoped theirs didn't involve him.

Twyla yawned shortly thereafter. The day had worn her out. She called it an early night and left them to their second cups of coffee.

Joe eyed Lori. She had a nice body. Firm and athletic. "What's with the sunburn?" he asked. She would peel, could possibly blister.

"Testing out my new bikini."

"On men at the beach?"

"On one man only."

"And . . ."

"He took me in, and I took him out. He liked what he saw. First time ever. We went from childhood friends to possibly friends with benefits."

Her breasts swelled in the tiny top. High, front and center. Hell, he appreciated them. "You've known each other awhile, then?"

She sighed heavily. "Since middle school. He's never paid me any attention."

"Today?"

"A party at Sand Bar brought him around."

He knew the place. An enormous stilt chickee hut built offshore, on a solid, submerged ridge of sand and coral. Customers walked through thigh-high waves to reach the watering hole, then climbed a wooden ladder to get up on the raised platform. A palm-frond thatched roof covered a round center bar. Not much shade. No boats. No wake. Swimsuits. Bare feet. Relaxed atmosphere. Beer and wine.

Joe preferred coastal air-conditioning. Or at least a ceiling fan. "The two of you hung out?" he prodded.

"All day." She lowered her gaze to her arms and chest. Kicked out one leg. Winced. "I slathered on sunscreen, but I should've gotten out of the sun." She heaved a sigh. "I just couldn't leave him. It was my moment. My chance. I don't regret it for a second."

She might have a few regrets by tomorrow, when her entire body felt like it was on fire, and her clothes scraped her skin. "What about the guy? Sunburned, too?"

"He had a light tan to begin with, but he got a lot more color."

Color, as in *red*.

The two soon finished their coffee, then went their separate ways. Lori off to take a cold shower. Joe to toss a tennis ball to Turbo in the backyard. He wanted his boy tired out. To sleep through the night. Turbo had.

They'd awakened at the butt crack of dawn. Jogged two miles. He'd promised Stevie a calm Turbo. Although still somewhat antsy, the rottie had greeted her with a tail wag, not the knock down of the previous day. Joe hoped Turbo would behave himself.

He glanced up as Sam Matthews strolled into the locker room next. Wearing dark sunglasses and looking slightly disheveled, Sam wore the same clothes as he had the previous day. He clutched a large coffee in one hand, a bottled water in the other. "Hydrating," he managed.

Joe shifted his gaze between Sam and Pax. "Where'd *you* land last night?"

"Started at the Blue Coconut," said Sam. "Moved to the Lusty Oyster. By midnight, Hurricane's. It was recommended, but turned out to be a real dump. Flat beer and dirty glasses. Broken mirror over the bar. Most of the tables tilted. Slanted wooden floors."

"Drunk-tilted and slanted?" Joe asked. He figured his buddies were likely red-eyed and staggering by that late hour.

Pax held up his hand, palm out. "I was buzzed, but not bombed. Took a cab back to my boat before two."

"You?" Joe eyed Sam. "How'd you finish the night?"

Crooked grin from the man. "Biker chick got me back to the Driftwood. Her Harley hauled ass. I thanked her the next four hours for the ride."

"You were missed, Zoo," Sam told him, as he removed his street clothes, put on his uniform. "Major disappointment. More ladies asked about you than were into me." He went for his wallet, removed scraps of paper. "Phone numbers." He passed them off. "Call them."

Joe pitched them onto a shelf in his locker, saving them for later.

"Your party posse pouted all night," added Pax. "Girls threw their own pity parties. I tried, but couldn't cheer them up. It was you or no one."

Joe grinned. It was good to be missed. But a different priority had kept him out of the bars the night before. He and Turbo had a new place to live. Being bedroom neighbors with Stevie had its perks. That very morning, she'd escaped the adjoining bathroom a mere second before he'd entered, seeking a shower after his jog. He'd knocked lightly. Had the water been running, she never would have heard him. The element of surprise. Sneaky. He'd glimpsed her bathrobe, pale blue, silky and trailing, before she'd slammed the door in his face. Good morning to her.

The locker room door opened once again. Dean Jensen eased inside. The man was so sunburned, he shone like a beacon. He had dark red hair, and this morning it was hard to tell where his forehead ended and his hairline began. He walked stiffly, slowly, across the room. His Triple-A teammates stared as he made his way to his corner locker.

Comments and concern reached Joe. He listened. "Bro, what the hell?" came from the minor league catcher.

"Too much fun, too much sun." Dean was paying for it now.

The catcher shook his head. "Hope she was worth it," he said, assuming it was a woman.

A hint of a smile from Dean. "Eye-opening."

Eye-opening. Zoo's ears perked up. Sunburns were a part of Southwest Florida, but the man was a mirror image of Lori. He wondered if the two knew each other. Had they hooked up? Had her sexy bikini turned Dean on? A distinct possibility.

He got his answer within seconds, when the catcher asked, "Beach or bar?"

"Sand Bar."

Joe didn't like his response. Down the road, would Dean and Lori start dating? If so, Dean would be coming by Unleashed, assuming the woman was, indeed, Lori. Joe's stomach soured. There wasn't room for both rivals at the dog day care. One would have to go. That would be Dean.

The side door swung wide, slammed against the wall, drawing Joe's attention. Team captain Rylan Cates, third baseman Landon Kane, and right fielder Halo Todd strolled in. Their conversation drifted to Joe as they approached. Wives and off-season vacations were the hot topics. No wife for Joe. He and Turbo had spent the summer months in Richmond. He had nothing to contribute to the conversation. He gave each man a high five. Then kept to himself and dressed.

Baseball pants, belt, navy jersey. The Rogues would be wearing batting-practice uniforms for the duration of spring training. He dropped down on the bench and pulled on his logo crew socks. His cleats came next. Adidas Z. Z for *Zoo*. His personal brand insignia. He had a lucrative contract with the company. They kept him well-stocked.

He fitted a wristband. Superstitious, he nabbed his lucky baseball cap. The one worn only for spring training. Sunglasses in hand, he turned when Rylan called his name.

"Zoo, I heard you got bounced from the Driftwood."

Townie grapevine. Word was out. Joe didn't much care. "I was away for the day, and Turbo tried to chew his way out of the hotel room." He didn't share where he was now playing house. Later.

Halo rounded on him. "Was that Turbs at Unleashed?" he asked. Joe nodded. "I caught sight of your boy when I dropped off Quigley." His and his wife, Alyn's, black pug. Handicapped after an accident, Quigs had been confined to a canine wheelchair, but his nerve endings had healed over time. The pug now ran and fetched with the best of them.

"Was Turbo behaving himself?" Joe hated to ask, but needed to know.

"Define 'behaving himself.'"

Damn. That didn't sound good. "He was supposed to hang out with two dogs today, two more tomorrow, and so on, until he's fully acquainted."

Halo frowned. "Stevie was in the office, cornered by

a pet owner. The woman wanted her poodle groomed. Last-minute. Turbo was running the hallway. Not sure where he was supposed to be."

Stevie had promised a slow initiation. That Turbo had been left to his own introductions did not bode well. It was essential to know what was going on. *Webcam*. His iPhone had too small of a screen. He needed a computer. Fast. He glanced at his watch. Twenty minutes, give or take, before they took the field. He didn't want to be the last player out of the tunnel. Rogues needed to set a precedent.

He quickly headed to the Media and Communications Center, where reporters gathered for coach and player interviews. The team had four high-tech computers at their disposal. Joe logged on. Located the Internet web page. Typed in his password. Unleashed was live. Six squares divided the screen, covering different areas of the dog care.

He leaned in close, and immediately saw Turbo, darting between the screens. Running, chasing, panting, he was everywhere all at once. He nearly knocked over the three-legged miniature pinscher. Fortunately, Triple Threat kept his balance. Turbo slowed down beside an English bulldog. Female, from what Joe could tell. Turbo sniffed vigorously, nearly inhaling her. She snapped at him. Not good. Misfit. Misbehavior. Major problem.

Stevie soon came on-screen with a short leash in hand. She hooked it to Turbo's collar. Momentarily kept him by her side, restricting his freedom. Joe decided to call her. He kept his eye on the screen while he dialed.

Stevie slipped her cell phone from her shorts pocket. Eyed the incoming name and number. Visibly debated answering. Seven rings and a sigh. "Unleashed."

"I've got you on the webcam."

"Who is this?"

"Who do you think it is?"

"What do you want?"

"I'm waving."

"I'm not waving back."

So he noticed. Her expression was set. Narrowed gaze. Compressed lips. Her arm flexing as she held Turbo in check. The bulldog ambled by, and Turbo gave her his best smile. A smile Joe recognized—with one canine tooth showing—but it had no effect on the bulldog. Another *snap* his way. Stuck-up female.

"What's with the snotty bulldog?" he asked Stevie.

"Etta is not a fan of Turbo."

"Why the hell not?" His boy was likeable.

"She's not into roughhousing. Or humping."

"Turbo's neutered."

"Hasn't stopped him."

"What happened to his slow launch into the group?"

"Didn't happen. He ignored my 'sit and stay.' Took off on his own."

"Adventurous."

"Troublesome."

Turbo took that moment to stick his nose right into Stevie's crotch. He inhaled the crease right out of her shorts. Joe couldn't help smiling. Turbo was his boy.

"Stop smiling," she hissed, sidestepping.

"How'd you know?" He wasn't on webcam—she was.

"I know you."

He wanted to know her better.

Another pass by the bulldog. Etta side-glanced Turbo. The rottie strained against his leash. "She's flirting with my boy."

"Not flirting. She's making sure he's secured."

"Who's her owner? Maybe I could set up a private play-date between the two."

"Or not." Pause. "She belongs to Dean Jensen."

Shit. The Triple-A asshat. Of all the female dogs at the doggy day care, Turbo had to go after his adversary's pet.

Joe wanted them separated. It was irrational, perhaps, but that was his mind-set. It would not change.

"How well do you know Dean?" he asked.

"We're . . . acquainted." Slightly evasive.

"He and Lori, too?"

"She likes him."

Stevie affirmed what he'd already guessed. They were sunburn buddies. Stevie apparently knew Dean through Lori. Bad news. He returned to his dog. "Can you keep Turbo and Etta apart?"

"What happened to their playdate?"

"The standard poodle is cuter."

"Good-bye, *Joey*."

"Later, *Stewie*."

She hung up, and he signed off the computer.

"Zoo, you're second to the last man out," Pax called to him from the doorway. "Move it."

He wondered who lagged behind him. "I'm there."

A pass through the locker room, and he discovered Dean Jensen still getting dressed. He stood in profile to Joe. In his sliding shorts. White shorts. Red skin. Joe had never seen anyone so sunburned before. Stupid man. Hot for a woman, he'd lost track of time in the heat of the day. There'd be no sex in his immediate future. Despite his newly ignited interest in Lori.

Dean grunted, loudly, struggled to pull on his uniform pants. His breath caught. He closed his eyes, gritted his teeth when he drew on his jersey. Joe's own skin felt sore and stretched just from watching Dean's exertions. Even the man's feet were bright red. He'd soon be agonizing over his socks and athletic shoes.

No reason to stay. Outta there. Joe ducked around a locker, knocking the corner with his shoulder. "Carl?" he heard Dean call out. Pathetically. He'd mistaken Joe for the custodian.

To respond or not? There was real pain in Dean's voice. Joe could be a dick and disappear. He hated the guy and all he represented. Notwithstanding, there'd be entertainment value in seeing Dean on the field, sunburned and hustling. Cringing and hurting. Falling short. Not at his best.

Dean's misery drew Joe's smile. He reversed. "Not Carl. What the fuck do you want, Jensen?"

Dean was uncomfortable. Having Joe come to his aid was unbearable. He screwed up his face. His shoulders stiffened. He waved him off. "Nothing." *From you.* Unspoken.

"It's me or nobody."

"Son of a bitch."

Silence widened the gap between them, thick with animosity. Dean ran his hand through his hair. Cringed. Sunburned scalp. He gave up, gave in. "Cleats," he mumbled. "I can't wear my present size. Eleven. Too tight with socks. My feet are swollen, will bleed. I'll need a half size larger."

"I wear a twelve." Joe's tone said *take it or leave it.*

Mental debate from Dean. "I'll make them work."

Joe exhaled slowly and further offered, "Adidas supplied me with Superlite socks for spring training. Climacool ventilation. Not uniform-approved, but I wear them anyway, during practice. Cushioned and comfortable. They'll take some pressure off your feet."

Dean was skeptical. "You'd lend me both your socks and your shoes? Knowing I'm out for a spot on the team?"

Not just *any* spot, either, but *Joe's* position. "My sharing won't help you today, dude. You can barely raise your arms. You won't be doing a lot of running. I've got you hands-down. I'm still the star."

"Twinkle, twinkle, while you can." Dean smirked.

"My sunburn will fade, and I'll outshine your talent. I'm here to stay."

Ungrateful bastard, Joe thought, as he retrieved the footwear. He dropped a new pair of Adidas cleats and complimentary socks on the bench next to Dean. "You're late on the field, and you've made me late, too," he stated. "I'm totally blaming you."

Dean sucked air as he raised one foot, worked on a sock. "Expected."

Joe snapped his fingers, as if just remembering something important. "Initiation. Last minor league player out of the locker room shaves his head." Dean's shaving his sunburned scalp would hurt like hell.

Dean jerked. The sock he'd been pulling on popped off. "Bullshit. Wasn't in effect last year."

"New season. New rule."

"According to whom?"

"Rylan Cates." Ry carried more weight than Joe. Especially in a lie.

Joe snickered. Left his rival. He jogged the short tunnel. Sunshine broke around him when he stepped onto the main field. A blue, cloudless sky. Four practice fields stood empty. Awaiting player assignments. The bullpens were beyond the fence in right center field.

The head coach wound down his morning introductions and briefing, which Joe had missed. He'd heard the speech before: Staying in good health, and getting the team to be competitive right out of the gate were the primary goals. The players soon spread out, warmed up. Muscles stretched. Mind-sets strengthened.

Four groups eventually formed for batting practice. The hitting coach joined the starters. The projected rotation would be established within a week. No later than two. Joe presently batted sixth, the middle of the order. He was aiming for second or third by Opening Day. Which meant bumping Halo Todd or Landon Kane down the roster. Difficult, but doable. Joe was determined.

He kept his eye on the visitors' dugout, awaiting Dean Jensen's arrival. How long did it take a sunburned man to finish dressing? Nearly thirty additional minutes by his watch.

Joe purposely shouted at Dean when he did show. "Nice of you to join us, Jensen." Which drew everyone's attention. "Must be sweet to sleep in so late."

The coaches frowned. They cut him no slack. During scrimmage, they positioned Dean in the outfield, chasing down balls. To the best of his ability. He had limited range of motion. His guttural groans reached the dugout.

Joe had near-perfect placement at-bat. He intentionally airmailed Dean a fastball that sailed right over his head. On a good day, Dean would have run his ass off, snagged it. There was no run in him today. Barely a jog. He stepped out of his left athletic shoe—twice. The fit was too big for him. He made a poor showing. Too bad, so sad.

Triple-A next went on the offense. The Rogues, on defense. The Rogues' pitcher, Will Ridgeway, took the mound. First day out, and he took it easy, toyed with the batters, setting his own pace. He allowed hits. Left them complacent. The Rebels grew cocky. A significant smugness especially from Dean when he laid down a bunt. Their downfall loomed. Imminent.

An exhibition game was scheduled for Sunday afternoon. At the end of the first week. Promotion. The two teams would face off. Will would be ready for them. An ace force, he would dominate with his precision pitches. Firing strikes. Going for a shutout. The Rebels wouldn't know what had hit them.

Joe wasn't sure whether Dean's face was sweating or

if there were tears in his eyes by the end of practice. Six hours of scratchy material on sunburned skin had to have rubbed him raw. While he hadn't played up to par, he'd survived scrimmage. He now staggered into the locker room and fell onto the bench, his chin dropping to his chest. He appeared ready to pass out.

"Hydrate, dumb-ass." Joe grabbed a bottle of orange Gatorade from an ice cart directly inside the door. Drinks were available to the players after every practice. He tossed it to Dean. Dean barely caught it, he was so weak. Joe stood off to the side, waited, while Dean polished off half the bottle. He held up his head, and Joe moved on.

Pax trailed Joe to their lockers. "Fraternizing with the enemy?" he asked.

"People die from dehydration. We don't need a Triple-A corpse in our locker room."

"Here, I'd thought you'd gone soft."

"Hard-hearted as ever. Dude's on my shit list."

"I snuck a peek at two coaches' performance scorecards. Sunburn or not, Dean sucked," said Pax. "He'll be pressed to make our roster."

Joe wasn't a fool. Dean would heal. He gave the man two days to recover. He'd return stronger than ever, a left field threat.

Sam joined them, sweaty and stripping down. In need of a shower. "Plans for tonight? I'm up." He left his comment open-ended.

"Parrot Pete's?" suggested Pax.

Sam wrapped his naked ass in a towel. Slung a second towel over his shoulder. "Pete has two parrots now." They perched on swings in a long, narrow cage that hung over the bar.

"I hate them both," said Pax. "The parrots swear like sailors and spit sunflower seeds."

"Quarter beer happy hour makes up for the cursing," from Sam. "Your fault that Geraldo dropped seeds on you. He didn't like being called Gerry."

Pax grunted. "Like he knew the difference."

"Parrot spit said he did."

Pax was slow to agree. "Fine, but we sit at a table, not at the bar. An hour, max. Then we move on to the Blue Coconut." He glanced at Joe. "Joining us?"

Joe debated. He had two hours before Unleashed closed for the day and Turbo became his responsibility again. He hadn't signed up for evening care. He needed to hang with his boy. "Not sure, guys. Errands and Turbo take priority."

"You know where to find us," said Pax.

His teammates were easy to locate. Bars burst at the seams when the Rogues arrived. Crowds spilled onto the sidewalk. The players kept their fans happy with rounds of free drinks.

His thoughts turned to Stevie. He liked thinking about her. He owed her a new pair of panties. After a dozen phone calls, he'd also located a man who restored vintage carpets. Braided rugs weren't George Eagan's specialty, but he'd offered to take a look, late that afternoon. Joe would meet him at the dog day care at four.

He went on to shower, skipped the shave, and dressed. He left the locker room behind Rylan Cates. One foot out the door, and Dean Jensen called to Ry, giving him a thumbs-up. "Initiation. Shaved head tomorrow."

Rylan's brow creased in confusion.

Joe nudged the team captain out the door before Ry could address Dean's concern. "Fine by Rylan," Joe shouted over his shoulder.

He bumped into Ry two steps out. Rylan gave him *the eye*. "What's fine by me?"

"It's actually better for me than for you," Joe admitted. He relayed what had gone down earlier. He ended with, "I hate that guy."

"Yet you lent him shoes and socks and gave him Gatorade."

Joe's jaw worked. "How'd you know?"

"I'm here, there, and everywhere."

Joe believed him. Ry was uncanny. He kept his finger on the pulse of every player. He was aware of their daily and nightly activities—good, bad, or ugly. He reined in the Rogues before management fined them. Joe had always admired the man. Even though Rylan had spoiled his fun on occasion. What Joe considered a "good time," Ry usually termed "juvenile."

Joe shoved his hands in his jean pockets now, and awaited Rylan's censure. He expected the team captain to put a halt to Dean's bald head. Ry took his time, finally saying, "Two seasons ago, you followed the trend when my personal assistant and later wife Beth, gave me a haircut and accidentally chopped it too short."

Joe recalled the moment he'd seen Ry and Halo in the locker room with their asymmetrical cuts. The rest of the Rogues had fallen in step. Joe had gotten a Mohawk. Fans also filled the stadium with irregular haircuts and high spirits. A bonding preseason.

Ry rubbed his jaw, evaluated. "A shaved head will be painful for Dean."

"Yeah, I know." No sympathy from Joe.

"Not fair to Dean."

"We want to be fair."

"Don't be a dick, Zoo." Rylan's tone sharpened. "You are your own worst enemy. Stop competing with Dean and compete with yourself. Don't let him distract you."

"Dean's close to signing a major league contract."

"Close, but he hasn't arrived," Rylan reminded him. "No one's handed him an ink pen. Landing on the expanded roster is a long way from starting lineup."

Joe released a breath. "Thanks, Ry-man." He meant it.

Rylan ended with, "The front office in Richmond likes you, for whatever reason. I've heard Kason Rhodes is a fan." He left Joe standing in an empty parking spot.

Kason was a legend. He'd played left field prior to Joe. He'd left his reputation on the field. Hard-ass, fierce, a warrior. Once retired, he'd moved into administration. Had been appointed senior vice president of international scouting. He carried a lot of weight, showcasing new, ambitious players. Which meant he also had to have his eye on Dean Jensen.

Joe focused on the positive. He crossed the lot, climbed into his Jag. The sports car fit him tight, like a hug. He needed one. He drove to Saunders Shores, the northern sector of the Barefoot William boardwalk. The two neighborhoods showcased very different lifestyles.

Barefoot William was as honky-tonk as the Shores was high-profile. Waterfront mansions welcomed the rich and retired. Yachts the size of cruise ships lined the waterways. Private airstrips replaced commercial travel. *Forbes* listed Saunders Shores as the wealthiest resort community in the country.

Joe preferred the carnival rides, amusement arcade, and specialty shops in Barefoot William. Tourists and townies packed the boardwalk during the day. Neon lights flashed at night, and music poured from the many shops. People danced down the boardwalk, free and uninhibited. Many played black-light volleyball on the beach. Glow-in-the-dark Frisbees were thrown along the shoreline. Kisses stolen under the pier.

This afternoon Délicieux was his chosen destination. An upscale boutique for women's lingerie and undergarments. Joe knew the proprietress personally. Not as a lover, the way she would've liked, but as a friend. He parked off Center Street, which divided the two towns.

He left the cracked cement walkway of the Barefoot William boardwalk behind. Strolled the cocoa-brown bricks of the Shores. Here, there were no rickshaw pedicabs, in-line skaters, unicyclists, portrait painters, street singers, musicians, mimes, or vendors hawking hot dogs, nachos, or cotton candy. No one wore swimsuits or beach attire.

The patrons shopping the main city blocks were dignified and stylish. All but Joe. He'd tucked a gray T-shirt scripted with *Together We Can Fight Blue Balls* into white-seamed jeans. His attire was unsuitable for Saunders Shores, but when had he ever dressed appropriately? Never in this lifetime. He got a lot of female stares, and several suggestive smiles, even from the bejeweled and well-heeled. "A great cause," one woman whispered in passing.

The owner of the boutique met him at the frosted glass door. Celeste held it open for him. She greeted him with a red lipstick smile and a manicured fingernail touch to his arm. "So glad you called ahead of time," she said. "I've searched my designer collection and found a lovely selection for you."

He nodded. He wasn't at all sure what he was looking for. One replacement pair of underwear would suffice—he wasn't out to fill Stevie's panty drawer.

The women's shop immersed him in plush lavender carpet, pastel flowering plants in enormous ceramic planters, racks of lingerie, and mirrored walls. Celeste steered him toward a wide glass table against the far wall. Rows of neatly stacked undies offered diverse styles, colors, fabrics. Had he been shopping for any woman other than Stevie, he would've stuck his hand through a leg hole and spun it on his finger. Something held him back. Respect, maybe.

He'd yet to fool around with Stevie. He wanted to play it straight.

Celeste stood beside him at the table. "Close your eyes and envision your lady," she softly said. "Panties give a glimpse into the personality of a woman. They reflect how she's feeling that day. Sexy, playful, teasing."

Sarcastic, ornery, ungrateful was how he saw Stevie. She was not "his woman." Far from it. Turbo had ripped red silk. Perhaps something similar would please her. Or not. He rubbed the back of his neck, strangely ill at ease. Indecisive.

Celeste sensed his struggle. She wanted the sale, and so she gave further suggestions. She held up pairs of panties, and described each style. "Thongs are jaw-droppers, leave little to the imagination. G-strings cause a guy to sweat, show him exactly what he's getting. Bikinis are flirty, enticing. Boy shorts are seductive, playful. And never devalue the granny panty. Many men get aroused by full cotton coverage. Hidden fantasies."

"Bikini," he decided.

Celeste approved. "You can't go wrong. A safe choice."

Playing it safe was good with Stevie.

"Fabric?" she next questioned. "Silk, lace, nylon?"

"Silk." Cool and slick against female skin.

"Color, pastel, solid, paisley, flesh-toned or see-through?"

Joe went with, "Yellow."

"Yellow-gold, lemon chiffon, canary, yellow crayon, mellow yellow, sunshine?" she read the color-coded tabs on the panties.

A corner of his mouth curved. "Natural-blond."

Located at the bottom of the stack. "How many pairs should I gift-wrap?" she asked.

"One."

Disappointment creased her brow. "Anything else that might interest you?" she inquired.

He looked around, noticed the wedding section. "A bridal thong."

Her lips parted, surprise in her eyes. "I wasn't aware."

"Nothing to be aware of. I'm not getting married."

She didn't pry. Instead she shared a selection of the intimate apparel. Her favorites. Blush, cream, peach. Virginal to risqué. He made his choice. "Kiss the Bride." Designer crystals sparkled on the white low riders. Perfect for the bridal shoot on Saturday.

"Excellent." Celeste smiled. The high price tag pleased her. "A garter for the lady?"

Joe shook his head. "Got it covered." Previously purchased. Something blue.

He paid, and Celeste boxed the items separately. Floral gift wrap for the yellow panties. Satin bow, tied and nicely scented with a sprig of berry. The bridal thong was enfolded in silver foil, and secured with gauze ribbon.

The boutique owner linked her arm with his, walked him to the door. "Always a pleasure, Joe." He kissed her on the cheek. Then left.

He picked up his sports car, placing Stevie's gifts in the narrow luggage space behind the seats. He then drove to Unleashed. He anticipated seeing her. Even for just five minutes.

He rounded the corner, a block from the dog care. What he saw had him downshifting, cutting the wheel, angling toward the curb. Hitting the brake. Hard. His upper body jerked against the seat belt. Son of a bitch. Once parked, he unhooked his belt, jumped out. He placed himself at the end of the sidewalk. Waved his arms. Wildly. Turbo barreled toward him in a full-out charge.

Stevie huffed and puffed behind him. Clutching a leash,

holding her side, calling to the rottie. "Stop" did not faze his dog.

Joe put his thumb and forefinger to the corners of his mouth, whistled. Loudly. Catching Turbo's attention. The big boy skidded to a halt near Joe's feet. His sides heaved. He panted heavily, mouth foaming. Joe grabbed him by the collar. Held tight.

Stevie finally caught up. Her face was flushed, her legs so rubbery she could barely stand. Whether from fear or from exertion, he didn't know. He released his temper on a low growl. "You've never had an escapee?" he accused. "Turbo's on the run."

Five

Stevie stared at Joe. His expression had been trans-
formed. He looked hard. Annoyed. Fierce. Scary. She
barely recognized him. Gone was the genial man who'd
shown interest in her. He clutched Turbo's collar, taking
control of the runaway, his knuckles white.

She exhaled. The air leaving her body left her weak.
Her legs gave out, and she sat down on the sidewalk. Began to shake. "I–I'm sorry," she managed.

He came to stand before her. She handed him the leash.
He clipped it to Turbo's collar. Hooked the handle over
his wrist. It fit tight. His dog wasn't going anywhere. The
rottie lay on the grass, head on his paws.

Hunkering down, Joe rested his forehead against hers.
His breath was warm on her brow. His voice calmed. "I
apologize, too. I'm sure whatever happened wasn't your
fault, Stevie. Look at it from my perspective, seeing my
dog hauling ass down the sidewalk. He was so far ahead of
you, you'd never have caught him."

"I tried, but I'm no Olympic sprinter."

"No, you're not."

She punched him in the arm, with the little energy she
had left. He pulled a face, rubbed his bicep, and pretended
it hurt.

She tipped back slightly, noticed he'd relaxed. Relief

was in his eyes. Amusement cornered his mouth. "My heart was racing," he confessed. "As fast as when I'm running the bases at the ballpark or during sex."

Sex. "That fast, huh?" Her own pulse bumped at the thought.

"The sidewalk was about to end, and Turbo doesn't have the sense to stay out of the road. There's traffic."

"He was chasing a car."

"What car?"

"A black Nissan. It turned the corner, heading east. You arrived from the west."

"Why the pursuit?"

Stevie sighed, ill at ease. He would not be happy with her answer. "Let me preface this by saying that Turbo's continued interest in Etta was one-sided."

"The bulldog didn't give him the time of day?"

"Not one second."

"I'd rather have him play with the poodle, anyway."

"Princess Pom-Pom avoided him, too."

"Crap, I'd hoped they'd connect."

"Connect *how*?"

"Pal around, maybe. My boy needs companionship. You're not helping."

"I'm not a canine matchmaker."

"He spent the day alone."

"Hardly alone. There were seventeen dogs on-site today. Turbo had opportunities to play. The dachshund Felix followed him around, wanting to be his friend."

"A wiener and a muscle dog?"

"Felix is a little dog with a big presence."

"Don't expect them to bond. Turbo prefers females. He's a lot like me. We find girls we like, and go after them."

"A problem in the making," she stressed. "Dean Jensen picked up Etta early. Turbo pressed his nose to the glass pane on the side of the door and watched her leave. Dean loaded her, closed the door. Turbo went crazy, spinning in circles, whining, barking for her to return. Dean drove off. A pet owner arrived seconds later. Your dog dodged through the man's legs. Escaped out the door. He took off, tried to catch the car."

"Dean's car." It came out as a disgruntled growl. "You went after Turbo."

"I exercise regularly, but I'm not a runner."

"He outdistanced you by half a block."

"It won't happen again. Promise."

"I have a solution," he said seriously.

She was leery. "What?"

"Boot Jensen and his dog. No temptation for Turbo."

Wasn't going to happen. Ever. Dean was her cousin. Family came first. "Or Turbo could find a new dog day care."

"We're here to stay."

She'd been afraid of that. They were at an impasse. "We're getting married on Saturday. I need my groom on the staircase for the magazine shoot."

Joe went from relaxed to tense in a single second. The idea of marriage rattled him. Greatly. A muscle twitched at the corner of his eye. He tugged at the neckline of his *Blue Balls* T-shirt, swallowing. A death grip on Turbo's leash. A flex of his abdomen and thighs. *Nice clenching*, she admired.

"A designer involved with the photo session delivered three wedding gowns today. My choices for the center-fold."

He gave an acknowledging nod.

"Two tuxes arrived, as well. You'll need a fitting."

"No tux." Firm and final.

"*I Do* is a glossy international magazine. They have a reputation to keep up."

"So do I," he emphasized. "No formal wear."

She eyed him. "You're worn and torn. Unkempt."

"That's me."

He'd need to conform for an hour. "We have an agreement," she reminded him. "My wedding photo for your dog care and bedroom."

"Hard to forget." Short pause. "Why do you want to do the photo shoot so badly?"

She was honest. "Lori and I played dress-up as little girls. Fairy-tale fun. Bridal costumes and our mothers' high heels. We picked flowers from our gardens for our bouquets." Fond memories. "I have no desire to get married at the moment, maybe not ever, so the photo shoot is just a lovely chance to pretend again as an adult. A once-in-a-lifetime opportunity. And Unleashed is a unique local business. I wanted to involve Twyla. She's very dear to me." Their gazes locked. "Don't let me down, *Joey*."

"I'll be there, *Stewie*." He left it open-ended as to just how he'd show up, though. Uncooperative man. A conniving look crept into his gaze. His tone became cagey. "Trade-off," he initiated. Panties coming to mind. "I *might* try on a tux—if you slip on something for me."

Hesitant, she asked, "What might that be?"

"We'll discuss it later." When they both had time. "You're still on the clock."

She glanced at her watch. Almost four. Owners would soon be picking up their pets. Unleashed offered door-to-door service. There'd be a short list of dogs to be driven home. She hoped the VW bus would be able to make the rounds without another mishap. She drew in a breath. "Back to Unleashed." She pushed herself up. Dusted off her hands.

His own hand wrapped around her ankle. "Stand

still," he said when she would've sidestepped. He tied
her shoelace. "Don't want you tripping, walking Turbo
home."

Home. Permanence. All of them together under one
roof. Warmth filled her chest. Unexpected. Unexplained.
Uninvited.

He looked up then, his gaze hot, touching on her legs,
belly, and breasts. Her hips shifted. Fluttery stomach. Then
her nipples did the unthinkable—they pointed at him.

Wicked grin. Perceptive man. Joe hopped to his feet
with the grace of an athlete. Smooth. He lightly brushed
her damp bangs off her sweaty forehead. Then skimmed
a finger down her nose. He traced her lips. Upper and
lower. They parted. Hopelessly breathless. She was slow
to recover.

He raised the collar on her polo so he could look un-
derneath. His thumb massaged her hickey. "Fading," he
commented, before readjusting the neckline.

His bite would disappear. Yet the memory of his teeth
scraping her neck, his warm breath, lingered. She'd
dabbed on flesh-toned concealer that morning, but it had
long since worn off. She'd been careful to keep her collar
in place all day—until her run after Turbo. The chase had
left her disheveled. She tucked the ends of her shirt into
her shorts. Exhaled.

"Behave," Joe said to Turbo. He handed her the dog's
leash, then retreated to his car. The Jag was a two-seater.
She and Turbo wouldn't both fit in the car with Joe at
once, so the two of them walked back to Unleashed
while Joe drove behind them. She felt him eyeing her
butt.

"Heel," she commanded. The rottie cooperated. No
tugging or pulling. He slowed to her pace. She talked to
him, gentle-toned. "No more chasing down Etta." The

word *Etta* had Turbo's ears twitching. He recognized her name. He whined. "I know you like her. It's only your first day, and she could still come around to you. Give her time. No roughhousing. No humping. Play nice."

Turbo eyed her, as if taking in her advice. "Don't tell Joe that I'm on your side. He'd have a fit. Etta's a very sweet bulldog. Princess Pom-Pom—with the rhinestone tiara and painted toenails? Sorta stuck-up."

Turbo nudged her hand with his nose. Agreeing.

Joe met them back at the dog care. He parked his sports car in the side driveway, alongside the house and out of view, then met them on the veranda. He held the door for her as they entered. Twyla and an older man were standing just inside the entrance.

"There's someone here to see you, Joe," Twyla announced. "George Eagan, from Rug Doctor."

"My rug man," Joe was quick to say.

"My niece, Stevie," Twyla went on, including her.

George shook everyone's hand. He was a nice-looking, well-dressed older man, Stevie thought. Dark hair, a hint of silver at the temples. Classic black glasses. She noticed how his gaze shifted back to her aunt. His gray eyes brightened. Twyla had more color in her cheeks than she'd had for days. A soft, responsive blush to the man. Interesting. Her aunt had never married. Animals had been her life. And there was no ring on George's finger. Not even a white mark. Male companionship in her aunt's future would be nice.

Stevie unhooked Turbo's leash, set him free inside the house. He surprised everyone by lying down by the office door. She regarded her aunt. "We've had our adventure for the day."

Twyla nodded sympathetically. "So I heard. Berkley was worried sick when you took off after Turbo. She'd been handing out snacks. She came and got me, thinking I should be on-site, so here I am." She lightly touched Stevie's arm. "You're back now, dear. Happy ending."

As happy as it could be, after an escapee. Stevie was grateful that Berkley had enlisted her aunt. A responsible move on the young woman's part. She'd acted quickly. Out of chaos had come calm. Order had been restored.

"Where's the rug in need of repair?" George inquired.

"Upstairs," Joe told him. He turned to Stevie. "We'll need to enter your bedroom."

She nodded. She'd made her bed that morning. No clothes were strewn around. Joe led the way to the stairs. George followed. The older man paused at the bottom. He glanced over his shoulder, sought out Twyla, and asked, "Will you be here when I return?"

Her aunt's breath hitched, ever so softly. "I'll be in the kitchen, preparing supper. Do you like cheeseburgers, George?"

"Very much."

"Might I prepare one for you?"

"I'd like that."

Politeness had Twyla including Stevie and Joe. "Lori's away for the evening. How about you two?"

Stevie liked burgers, but not tonight. She sensed a hint of romance in the air, and she decided to let her aunt and the rug doctor explore their feelings for each other. She shook her head, said, "Thanks, but I'll pass. I'll make the VW run to take the dogs home. I've got plans for later."

"Plans with me," Joe inserted. "Dinner date."

Twyla raised an eyebrow. "Since when?"

"Since now," affirmed Joe. Surprising Stevie. He had apparently picked up on the vibe between her aunt and George, as well. He was freeing up the house for them to be alone. Generous on his part. Sensitive for such a hard-ass. But he didn't have to include her. She could find her own fun.

"There's an all-you-can-eat fish-fry special at Molly Malone's Diner tonight," he added. "Stevie likes snapper."

"She does?" Twyla was skeptical. "I've never seen her eat more fish than a tuna salad sandwich."

Stevie tolerated seafood, but it wasn't her favorite. Joe had put her in an awkward position. She was hungry, and would enjoy dinner out. She momentarily considered a disguise. Going incognito. Floppy hat, sunglasses, baggy clothes. Ducking her head. Walking several feet behind him. Joe would think she was crazy. And she would be, taking such a chance. Someone would surely recognize her.

Gossip was a favorite pastime on the boardwalk. Their dinner could appear to be a date to the casual observer. Word could easily reach DJ that she'd shared a meal with his nemesis at the popular boardwalk restaurant. Her cousin was already dealing with a severe sunburn. No need to raise any concern over her and Joe. Supper at Molly Malone's wouldn't happen. However tempting. She couldn't be seen with the Rogue.

"Fried snapper, French fries? I'm there," she tentatively agreed. Cancellation of the date would soon be forthcoming.

"If you're certain," from her aunt.

"Absolutely," Stevie reassured her.

Joe moved the night along. "Then I'll meet you at Molly Malone's in an hour," he suggested. "Workable?"

Stevie nodded halfheartedly. She crossed the hallway to check the sign-out list. Three dogs were in need of a ride. Two boxers, Truman and Capote, and a Pekingese, Ming. "I'll load the dogs into the VW and head out," she said.

"Turbo can stay here while you two have supper," Twyla offered. "Not a problem."

"I had a Rottweiler as a boy," George said, smiling at the memory. "Great dog. Protector, babysitter, and companion."

"We're good, then," Joe said, as he climbed the stairs ahead of George. The two men reached the landing. Joe pointed out Stevie's bedroom.

"George seems like a nice man," Stevie casually commented. "I hope he can fix the rug."

"Even if he can't, it's been a pleasure meeting him," Twyla said softly.

Stevie collected three leashes, hanging from a long peg near the front door. She whistled for the boxers and the Pekingese. The dogs immediately came to her. Once they were leashed, her aunt held the door for her. Twyla gave her shoulder a squeeze, smiled, and said, "Enjoy your supper."

Stevie grinned back. "Enjoy yours more."

Her aunt's cheeks pinkened in a flattering blush as Stevie and the dogs departed. She loaded the three in the VW bus, and they immediately lay down. Destination, south side of town. She keyed the ignition, and Otis turned over with a *chug* and tailpipe smoke. She crossed her fingers on the steering wheel, and hoped the vehicle would make the rounds one more time. She backed out of the driveway. Accelerated. The bus crept up to thirty miles per hour.

Cutting through town wasn't an option. Tourists preferred to cruise Gulfshore Boulevard, a palm-lined street that ran parallel to the beach. Lots of vacation action. Bumper-to-bumper traffic. Slowing and stopping for red lights might kill the engine. Permanently. Her alternative, Ten-Mile Sand Dune Drive that skirted Barefoot William. She took the back road.

Her stomach growled as the bus bounced over the dirt and gravel. Supper would come eventually. Just not with Joe.

Joe Zooker entered Molly Malone's Diner on the corner of Center Street and the boardwalk a few minutes ahead of schedule. He was looking forward to seeing Stevie. He was surprised by how much. Readiness tightened his gut. He'd never had first-date jitters before. They weren't fun.

The *Please Be Seated* sign freed him from waiting for a hostess. The atmosphere was casual and bustling as he made his way to an open corner booth. He sat on a black leather bench, his back to the wall, and rested his elbows on the white Formica table. Steepled his fingers beneath his chin. Breathed deeply.

The polka music from the carousel entered with the next group of customers. A family of six. Joe glanced out the wide front window that faced the pier and carnival rides. He caught the first turn of the merry-go-round. The Ferris wheel circled slowly, while the swing ride whipped out and over the water. Neon lights flickered, revitalizing the dusk. Crowds thickened on the boardwalk and pier. Weeknights felt like weekends at the beach.

Joe scratched his chin. It was a public place, he was alone, and a few people approached him. Fans wishing him well for the upcoming season, and several seeking his autograph. He made small talk and signed carryout menus and napkins, until waitress Sally Ann welcomed him with a glass of ice water, a paper place mat, and napkin-wrapped silverware. His fans dispersed, but the stares continued. Sally Ann relayed the nightly specials: meat loaf and a chili bread bowl.

No fish fry, he mused, smiling to himself. Fish had been the first thing to cross his mind when he'd proposed a meal to Stevie. They'd be away from Unleashed, which was all that mattered. He'd noticed the sparkle in George's eye when he'd looked at Twyla. And Twyla could barely catch her breath. Love at first sight, or longing for companionship? Happiness either way.

George had indicated that he could fix the braided rug. He'd need to roll it over, but he had the tools and know-how to get the job done. Satisfactorily. Twyla seemed pleased with his return downstairs. Joe believed they'd be seeing the man long after the repair was complete. The two had a tangible spark between them.

That catalyst had prompted Stevie's agreement to meet him at Molly's. She'd obviously wanted to give her aunt and the rug man time alone, too. Turbo wouldn't be a problem. The dog adored Twyla. He'd fall asleep at her feet.

Sally Ann approached him a second time, order pad in hand. He told her to give him a few, that he was waiting for someone. She brought him a complimentary plate of cheese nachos. He polished it off. Checked his watch. Almost seven. Stevie was late. That left him uneasy. He wondered if she was standing him up. Always a possibility. Just when he thought she might be into him, she backed away.

Frustration settled into the booth beside him. Hell, he'd even changed clothes for the woman, leaving his *Blue Balls* T-shirt and aging jeans on the floor of his bedroom. Took the time to select a lightweight cream pullover and khaki slacks. He looked decent, with no one to impress. Stevie wasn't all that impressionable. Still, he'd made the attempt.

He debated ordering. Thought about leaving. A long waiting line had formed at the door. Weaving around the corner. He was taking up valuable space. Sally Ann needed to turn over her tables. Tips were all-important.

He motioned to his waitress. "Appreciated the nachos," he told her. "My date's running late, and I'm not going to tie up your booth."

She winked at him. "Sit as long as you like. I'm in no hurry for you to leave. A Rogue in the restaurant brings in more business."

Despite her offer, he was ready to go. He didn't do alone well. He liked company. A nearby table of women glanced his way. A redhead patted the empty chair next to her. An invitation for him to join them. He smiled in their direction. But he didn't approach. He'd come to Molly Malone's to have dinner with Stevie. No one else.

Wallet out, he handed his waitress a twenty. Big tip for little service. Turning slightly, he nodded toward the five ladies still eyeing him. He drew out a fifty. Passed it to Sally Ann. "Their supper's on me." He wove around the tables to the door.

Where to next? he wondered while standing on the sidewalk. He needed to locate Stevie. Standing him up was one thing—he could live with that, despite his disappointment. But what if something had happened to her? That possibility bothered him most.

Concern walked with him to his sports car, restlessness on his heels. He removed several pieces of paper from beneath the windshield wipers. His Jaguar was well-known. He collected a fistful of women's names, phone numbers, and sexual proposals, then climbed into his vehicle and tossed them into the glove box. The space overflowed. He shoved hard to get the compartment closed. Next car wash, he'd clean it out.

The engine ignited with a guttural rumble. His sports car had never failed him. He'd had great make-out sessions on the front seats. He'd finessed around the stick shift. But he'd never gone all the way in the car. Tonight, no sex. He needed fresh air to clear his head. He had a need for speed. The Jag was fast.

Ten-Mile Sand Dune Drive came to mind. Desolate at this hour. Only townies traveled the road to avoid city traffic. Pedal to the metal, he could punch the accelerator, howl his freedom for a few miles. Nothing crazy, just a fleeting mental release.

He rolled down the windows, moved into traffic. He traveled the busy Gulfshore Boulevard for a short distance. People waved and called to him. A jogger ran beside his car. He felt like a one-man parade. The Joe Zooker float.

He cut down Gull Lane, turned onto Pelican Way, and connected with Ten-Mile. Headlight beams on high, he focused on the road ahead. Not a car, bike rider, or jogger in sight. No stray animals. His palms itched on the steering wheel. His legs flexed. He gunned the engine, fired through the gears. Zero to sixty in seconds.

His chest expanded. The Jaguar roared. Joe did, too. Wind smacked his face. His long hair blew wild. The pressure in his chest soon eased. He tapped the brakes, slowed. He felt better. Less irritated, despite the fact that Stevie had obviously ditched him. Should he find her safe, she would owe him an explanation. Perhaps even an apology.

He got clarification sooner than he expected. A half mile ahead, his headlights picked up the Unleashed VW bus, parked on the side of the road. It tilted, the emergency flashers dimming as the battery slowly died. A shadowed woman was bent over, elbows deep in the rear-mounted engine. She held a flashlight in one hand, what appeared to be tools in the other. She glanced up on his approach. *Stevie.* He wondered about her mechanical skills. She was stranded far off the beaten path.

He pulled in behind her. Watched through the windshield as she glanced over her shoulder. Their eyes met, and he saw a flicker of surprise, unease, then awkwardness. She stomped her feet, shifted her stance, returned to the engine. He admired the sexy roll of her hips. Sweet cheeks. Nice legs.

His relief was short-lived. Realization sharpened. The VW bus faced north, far afield from Pelican Way, the road leading to the diner. She'd been headed *away* from him. Shit. The truth hurt. She hadn't planned to meet him after all. A punch to his gut.

Decency had him opening his car door. Setting his jaw, he slid out. She needed his help. He had a head for mechanics. He walked toward her, pebbles scattering beneath his boots. She twisted, faced him, a flashlight in one hand, a wrench and a screwdriver in the other. Two of her knuckles were scraped. The steam from the engine rose like a sauna, dampening her bangs and brow. Grease-smudged cheek. Teeth marks marred her bottom lip, as if she'd bitten down hard in her frustration. Her polo was wrinkled and hung outside her shorts. Her expression was defensive.

Neither initially spoke. He let his actions do the talking. He took the tools from her. Rolling his shoulders, he fanned the steam, and leaned forward. "Any engine noises?" he asked.

"Little rattle. Wheezing."

"You should've pulled over."

"Otis is always making odd sounds."

Evaluation came quickly. The vehicle had drawn its last breath. He held up the dipstick. No oil. No sugarcoating. "Your engine seized."

Her lips parted. Panic filled her voice. "Lori added oil yesterday."

"You've got a leak. Didn't the oil light flash?"

"It's . . . broken."

"Bad for you."

"Can it be fixed?"

No good news forthcoming. "Irreversible damage, I'm assuming. Without oil, the seals and pistons scrape along the sides of the cylinder walls and cause permanent damage to the block. Your best option is a tow truck. Sell the bus for scrap."

She pressed her palm to her chest. "Otis has always been a part of Unleashed." She spoke of the bus as if it were family.

He went easy on her. "Otis wasn't safe. You're fortunate to have transported the dogs to their homes before it died."

Her shoulders sagged. "I hate to break the news to my aunt. Another van isn't in her operating budget. Even a secondhand one."

"Call Twyla," he insisted.

She removed her iPhone from her shorts pocket. Her hand shook as she opened her contacts, and pressed the number for Unleashed. Joe stood close enough that he could listen to her call. A brief rundown on the incident, indicating that she was fine and that Joe was with her, left her aunt breathing easier. Twyla was realistic. His assessment was accurate. They would tow Otis to the junkyard.

Joe took the phone from Stevie and spoke directly to her aunt. He offered to handle things on their end. Twyla was grateful. She asked about the fish fry before signing off. Joe came back with, "Our fish wasn't nearly as good as your cheeseburgers, I'm guessing."

He could hear the smile in Twyla's voice when she said, "Delicious dinner." They disconnected.

He was hungry as hell. Supper was his top priority once he'd called for a tow. The truck driver indicated a thirty-minute wait. Time enough for him to question Stevie and get some answers.

He leaned against the side of the VW bus, tools in hand, his ankles crossed. The night closed around them, dark with unanswered questions. He side-eyed Stevie. She spoke first, softly, sincerely. "Thank you."

He shrugged. "It's all in the timing. I had a date tonight, and she stood me up."

"Maybe she had a good reason." Pause. "Would a locked engine qualify?"

"Only if the vehicle was headed *toward* the diner, not away from it. You passed Pelican Way."

"That I did." Stevie licked her lips. He tracked the tip of her tongue. Pink, moist. Suckable. "Going out for a meal seemed like a great escape earlier. It allowed George and my aunt some private time."

"My private time came later. Sitting alone in a booth at Molly Malone's Diner."

"You are your own best company."

"What changed your mind?"

"It's personal."

"So personal you couldn't share it with your best friend?"

"You've changed your name to Lori?"

He tapped the screwdriver against the wrench. Admitted, "You're a first for me, Stewie."

"A first what, Joey?"

"The first woman to break a date with me."

"I'll let you take me home."

"I haven't offered."

"You will." She was sure of herself.

And she would be right. He took her hand and led her

to his sports car after the tow truck came and went. Her small hand disappeared within his own. He held tight. The truck driver had been nice, accommodating, presuming them to be a couple. An avid baseball fan, he'd only charged them half price, and he promised a decent value on the van, once crushed.

Settled in the Jag, they hooked seat belts. Joe fitted the tools under his seat. They stared forward. He glanced at his watch. Eight thirty. "Neither of us has eaten," he commented. "No fish fry, but I can feed you. Fast-food row on Commercial Boulevard. Lots of choices."

"A burger would be nice, same as George and my aunt."

"Served without romance."

Was that a flicker of disappointment in her eyes, or a reflection of the rising moonlight cast across the windshield? He wasn't sure. She'd kept him at arm's length. It was hard to believe she might have underlying feelings. Of any kind.

She gazed down at her hands, her clothes. Both were dirty and greasy. "Takeout might work best."

He nodded. He knew just the place. He'd let her clean up first. "There's a small bottle of hand sanitizer and a box of Kleenex in the glove compartment," he told her. Only to regret his offer seconds later. A release *click*, and fragments of papers popped out like confetti. Spilling across her lap, knees, and feet.

She picked up a couple of them, and pulled a face when she realized how many women had given him their names and numbers, wanting to hook up. "Such a popular guy." Her tone was dry as she reached deep into the compartment and found the sanitizer and tissues. And a pack of condoms. She shifted her hips. Uneasy. "Tell me you haven't had sex on my seat."

"Virgin Jag. Not broken in yet."

"Then why—"

"The condoms?" he asked. She nodded. "Stashed, in case I run out of the ones in my wallet."

"Does that happen very often?"

"Often enough." He left it at that.

He stretched his seat belt, tipped toward her. Went on to swipe the papers off her lap with a smooth slide of his hand. His thumb flicked over her zipper. He whisked papers from her thighs, right along with her. Their fingers touched, momentarily linked, until she shook him off.

"I can do it myself." She tried to slap his hand away.

He cupped her knee. Squeezed. Brushed down each calf. "Faster together."

"Your hand's moving slow."

"The better to feel you."

She kicked out her leg. "What about all the papers on the floor mat?" They piled up thickly.

"Leave them." He didn't want her handling them any further. "I'll toss them in the garbage back at Unleashed."

"No saving them? Not even one name?"

"I don't know these women."

"They obviously want to know you."

"Not the same. I like doing the choosing."

"You have a lot of choices." She sanitized her hands. Wiped her face with a Kleenex.

He met her gaze. "The one I chose for tonight didn't choose me."

She put the sanitizer and Kleenex back in the glove box. Said, "Maybe some other time."

"Limited time, Stewie. No honeymoon after the wedding shoot."

"No honeymoon planned."

"Baseball's my life," he replied seriously. "You won't be seeing much of me once the season starts."

Her expression fell, hinted at regret. Surprising him.

She turned aside, clasped her hands in her lap. Gazed out the open passenger window. Collected herself. "I'll see you at Unleashed."

"There, and you can always find me at the ballpark," he said. "Come watch me play."

"Maybe . . ."

Maybe not. "Do you even know what position I play?"

"Missionary? Girl on top?" Sweetly sarcastic.

He grinned. She had a sense of humor, at the most un-expected times. He would give her a preseason pass, on the off chance she'd catch a game. He had the sudden urge to show her where he worked. He keyed the Jag, and it roared its readiness. "Let's eat." He was starving.

"Where are you taking me?"

"Left field."

Six

Stevie settled deeply into the leather seat. She clutched her seat belt. No traffic. The intimidating vibration of the Jaguar raised goose bumps. She expected Joe to drive fast, crazy, on the deserted back road. He did not. With one hand on the steering wheel, one on the gearshift, he kept within the speed limit. Silence slowly massaged the evening, leaving them comfortable in each other's company.

Glancing his way, she took him in. Liked what she saw—a little too much. Strong profile. Windblown hair, slightly crooked nose, firm mouth. He could be a distraction, if she let him. He felt her gaze, raised an eyebrow, but didn't take his eyes off the road.

"Look, but don't touch, Stewie." It sounded like a dare.

She purposely poked his thigh.

"Higher."

The man was impossible. She turned away.

He took a left on Commercial Boulevard. Fast-food heaven. Big signs and bright lights. Increased traffic. All restaurants had drive-through windows. "Pizza, subs, Chinese, fried chicken, waffles?" he asked. "Burgers are good, too."

She stuck with her original thought. "Cheeseburger with the works. Extra onions." *No kissing.*

He patted his pants pocket. "Altoids."

He carried breath mints.

A half block farther, and he whipped left into Burger Brothers. The Jag crawled up to the big board with all the food choices. He came to a stop, and Stevie leaned in to his shoulder, scanning the items. Her eyes widened. She was impressed by the selections. "Salads, sliders, cheese fries, mozzarella sticks, onion rings, chili. One of each," she joked.

Joe twisted slightly, and his jaw pressed against her cheek. "That hungry, huh?"

"Toast for breakfast didn't stick with me."

He lightly kissed her forehead. "I'll fill you."

Fill me how? She shivered, straightened on the seat. Dipped her head. She hoped he couldn't see her face. Her neck flushed hot. Her cheeks even hotter. She squeezed her thighs together. He'd meant he'd fill her with food, but her thoughts went straight to sex. She could picture him naked. Atop her. Inside her. Deep penetration. Filling her. Fully.

Don't go there, she scolded her imagination. Shocked by her thoughts. They sat snug in the sports car. Fantasy friction. All body heat and awareness. Rubbing. His knuckles grazed her thigh each time he shifted. She fell against him with each sharp corner. Shoulder, arm, and hip contact. It was hard to separate what she wanted and what she couldn't have. No Joe.

The speaker box activated. A disembodied voice requested their order. Joe responded. He systematically went down the board, and chose a lot of food. Stevie's mouth watered. He added soft drinks and two chocolate cream–filled cupcakes.

They received their food at the window. Joe paid. Stevie held the sacks and boxes on her lap. The scents undid her. She snuck a mozzarella stick. Split it in half.

Shared with Joe. He flicked his tongue, caught her fingertip. Moist heat. Sensation shimmered. Her body responded—her breasts heavy, her hips shifting, her toes tingling.

Joe headed for the stadium. An enormous sign announced their rural destination. *Richmond Rogues Spring Training Facility.* A chain-link fence wrapped the grounds. Facility Operations had a strong security crew. Day and night. The guard at the gate greeted Joe. Frank indicated that three other ballplayers were on-site. Either in the workout room or batting cages.

"Have you ever been here before?" he asked her.

She shook her head. "I'm only in town because my aunt got hurt and needed help with Unleashed. I haven't seen much beyond the boardwalk and hospital. I like baseball, and I'd hoped to catch a game."

"Do you like ballplayers?"

"Your friends Pax and Sam seemed nice."

"I'm nicer."

"To each his own opinion."

Joe drove around the edge of the lot. Stevie peered out the window. The parking lot lights and the headlights of the car shone brightly on the winding sidewalk that wrapped around the stadium. She was in awe. Hundreds of footprints had been left in the cement for generations to come. All different sizes and shapes, from boots to flip-flops. One set was barefooted.

"Team members left their mark in Rogues Plaza near the front of the stadium," he told her. "Large cement squares showcase our cleated footprints, along with the players' names."

She wondered about the future. "Do new players get their own squares?"

He eyed her curiously. "I assume so," he said. "There are no additions to the team at the moment."

"Aren't minor league players in contention for some positions?"

His jaw tightened a fraction. "What's your interest?"

She chose her words carefully. "Dean Jensen and Lori are friends. She talks about him. Lots of concern."

"Worry about him less. Concentrate on me more."

"I'm with you now." For supper.

Joe parked on the west side of the facility. He climbed out, walked around the long bonnet of the Jaguar, and came to her. He opened her door, then took some of the food from her, but not all of it. The bags weren't heavy, yet both of her hands were full while he had one hand free. He used his free hand for touching.

His hand on her shoulder, he directed her around the back of the stands, and down a walkway, until they reached a low gate. He pushed it wide, then stroked his palm down her back until it rested on her butt cheek. He nudged her ahead of him. She wiggled her hip, and he squeezed her ass. She gave him a dark look over her shoulder. He smiled. His hand remained at her waist.

They walked onto the field. Moonlight glinted on the grass. Enchantment lingered over America's favorite pastime. The night air crackled with anticipation of the season ahead. Tangible with home runs and defensive fielding. Fans would become family, as boisterous cheers filled the now-quiet stadium.

Stevie clutched the food to her chest and turned around in a full circle. "So this is where you work." Impressive.

Joe scuffed his boot across the grass, then swept his arm extensively and spoke with pride, "Total adrenaline rush. I back up third, cover the left field foul line, warning track, and left-center. My office is mowed twice a week."

She bent, set down the bags. She moved her hand over the grass. "Very nice carpet." As short and bristly as a crew cut.

"I don't have a blanket or a tarp for our picnic. We can move to the dugout if you'd rather not sit on the ground," he offered.

"Grass is fine. Nice starlight. Nice stadium."

"Nice being with me."

"Combination of all three," she gave him.

"At least I'm included."

She dropped down, sat cross-legged. He settled, one leg straight, the other bent at the knee. They opened the brown bags and shared the food containers. Her first bite of cheeseburger was deliciously juicy. She sighed with pleasure.

"Orgasmic?" he asked, munching an onion ring.

"Better than sex."

"You haven't been with me."

"I'm fine with my burger."

"For now."

"Forever."

The corners of his mouth twitched, telling her otherwise. He had his own agenda. *Why me?* she continued to question. Spending time together was a mistake. A broken promise on her part. DJ would be hurt. Deception gave her heartburn.

She ate with purpose, concentrating on her food. Ignoring Joe. Until he commented, "You're wearing your meal, babe."

Messy? Her gaze widened. She grabbed a napkin. "Where?"

He reached toward her, lightly touched her face. "Cheek." Ketchup. He traced lower. "Chin." Tomato. Embarrassing. His finger tipped her collar, dipped down, flicked a bit of bun from her breast. She inhaled, her nipple rose, grazed his fingertip. She jerked back. Quickly wiped her face clean.

"Brake, woman," he said. "We're not going anywhere

until I've finished. I'm taking my time." He bit into his burger. Chewed deliberately slow.

She sighed. He was her ride. The food was good. She reached for a French fry, as did he. Same fry. Tallest, thickest. Saltiest. Their hands brushed once again.

"You take it."

"It's yours." He gave it to her.

"Halves?" She broke it in two.

"Half? You need a ruler. More like a fourth."

"Stop complaining, you're lucky I shared." She savored. "Best fry ever."

"I've had better."

"Where?"

"Here at the ballpark."

"You like concession-stand food?"

"I often sit alone in the stands once they've cleared after a game. Both here and in Richmond," he revealed. "I pay a vendor to bring me two hot dogs, fries, and a beer. I reflect on the nine innings. Visualize what I did right, what I could've done better. The cleaning crew sweeps around me."

She ate another French fry, thoughtful. "Here, I thought you'd be the first player at the bar."

"I always locate my teammates," he told her, after an onion ring. "Once I've showered, dressed, and gathered my party posse."

"Ah . . . your posse." Hot babes.

"Ladies who celebrate with me when we win. Console me when we lose."

"Support is good."

"I've always found them comforting."

"I'm sure you have," she said, tight-lipped.

He smiled. "The more the merrier."

"Aren't they distracting?" she had to ask. "How do you concentrate on baseball?"

"Baseball's always on my mind. Women cut in and out."

"No one's ever stayed?"

"I have a short attention span."

She was looking for lifetime love. "No female's touched your life for long."

"I've been touched."

"I don't mean sexually, Joey," she contended. "I'm talking feelings."

"Feelings are overrated."

"Underrated," she said. "Honest emotion opens hearts. Unifies lives. Clarifies the unclear."

"Clarity comes with a six-pack."

"Beer goggles?"

"Don't judge me."

"I'm not," said with conviction. "I'm sharing what I believe. You don't have to agree with me."

Long silence on his part. He finished off his second cheeseburger. The last of the onion rings. Then said, "I understand your sentiment, but it isn't me. I don't need a relationship to define me. I'd never pay you lip service just to keep the peace."

"No pacifying, huh?"

"I'd rather air it out. Argue with my woman until we're nose to nose, breathing heavy."

"I don't like confrontation."

"Disagreement leads to great makeup sex."

"Sex is your happy ending?"

"Climax steals the anger. Clears the air."

Intense. She'd never gotten that mad at a man. Raised her voice. Had a rapid heartbeat. Never experienced the release. Body shaking. Thoughts shattering. Losing herself in a guy.

She preferred calmer lovemaking. A compassionate oneness. Pillow talk and snuggling. A forever memory.

Joe drew her attention. He tapped the dessert box, asked, "Cupcake?"

She had a sweet tooth. She held out her hand. He set one on her palm. She tasted vanilla cream with the first bite. Thick. Decadent. Sugary. She took her pleasure, closing her eyes, polishing off the dessert with a low moan.

She was soon to learn that Joe was at his most dangerous when he was eating a cream-filled cupcake. Watching him eat was her undoing. He was a sinful tease. His own gaze hooded, he licked the chocolate frosting. Then bit the bottom cake. He swirled the center vanilla cream with his tongue. Tasted deeper. More intimate. Erotic. So oral, he turned her on. Stevie felt his mouth on her. Her panties dampened. She'd never been more embarrassed.

She swallowed hard. Shifted her hips on the grass. The blades tickled her bare thighs. She dug her hands into the ground. Uprooted chunks of grass.

"You're destroying my office," Joe mumbled, his mouth full.

Unable to sit still, she collected the empty boxes, stuffed them into one big bag. She pushed to her feet. Stood over him. He looked up her body. Hot, interested. She barely managed, "It's getting late."

He glanced at his watch. "Little after ten."

"I'm tired." Actually she was wired.

"No rolling around on the grass?"

"Not a chance." She'd nearly jumped his bones.

"Next time, then."

There'd be no next time.

Joe got to his feet, took her free hand. Engaged their fingers. Loosely. More friendly than romantic. He drew her beside him as they left the outfield. She dumped the trash in an outside receptacle. A breeze kicked up, carrying the significant *pop-pop* of a batter hitting baseballs.

Along with a series of painful grunts. Agonizing moans. Profanity.

Joe slowed, squinted through the chain-link fence. "Son of a bitch." He ground out the words. "Jensen's hitting balls."

She peered over his shoulder. Dean pounded baseballs in a batting cage. His sunburn was as bright as the overhead lights. His face contorted. Each swing pure torture.

"Determined bastard," from Joe. His expression was tight.

She had no words. Obviously, the men weren't friends. She stood in Joe's shadow, not wanting Dean to see her, should he glance their way. Dean did not. His concentration was on the ball machine, and what appeared to be well-timed pitches. He connected with every other one. Swore when he missed.

Joe's nostrils flared. "I hate the guy," he said flatly.

Joe's dislike of her cousin hit Stevie low. Her heart hurt. Supper sat heavy on her stomach. Her feet dragged.

Silence walked them to his Jag. His large body towered over her at the passenger door, swallowing her in his heat. "Sorry," he breathed against her forehead. "I have an aversion to Jensen. He wants what I have."

She was aware of their competition for left field. She refused to complete the family puzzle. To tell Joe that Dean was her cousin. There was no reason to. Not now, anyway.

He dipped his head, scuffed his boot. "Lori and Dean are hooking up. Can I ask you to stay away from him?"

Her cousin had asked the same of her and Joe. For her to keep her distance from the Rogue. She couldn't take sides. She lightly goaded, "I like him better than you."

"No, you don't." Cocksure. He didn't press her further.

They settled into the sports car. He curved her hand over the gearshift, then covered it with his own. Hand over hand, they shifted together. Cohesive. Smooth. Intimate. They soon arrived at the Victorian, and entered through a side door. They cut through the grooming room. The place was spotless. The cleaning team had come and gone. Hallway lights were dim. A brighter light peeked beneath the kitchen door. They checked it out.

Twyla and Lori sat at the small round table. Talking. Stevie noticed that both women had a glow about them. Her aunt's expression was soft, her eyes sparkling. Her friend was all smiles. Turbo lay in front of the refrigerator. Joe went to him first, gave his head a knuckle scrub. The dog wagged his tail.

Greetings next, all around. Joe eyed Lori's T-shirt with its washed-out Roanoke Rebels logo. A muscle flexed along his jawline. No comment from the man.

Stevie hugged her aunt around the shoulders. Took a chair beside her. "You look happy," she noted.

"Relaxed," the older woman replied. "There's chamomile tea, if you'd like a cup."

Stevie raised an eyebrow at Joe, who shook his head. They both passed on the tea. She was still full from supper.

Joe flipped a chair around, its back to the table, straddled it. "How was my boy?" he asked about Turbo.

"He took a liking to George. They bonded," said Twyla.

"Did *you* take a liking to George?" Joe teased her.

Twyla blushed as red as Lori's sunburn. "He's a nice man with a strong work ethic. He'll be here tomorrow to work on the rug."

"Do I need to chaperone?" from Joe.

Her aunt giggled. Stevie had never heard her do that before. Very sweet and unassuming. Almost girlish. She waved Joe off. "He'll be upstairs, and I'll be down."

"There's always the stairs."

"He's here to do a job," Twyla reminded him.

"And when the job's done?" asked Joe.

"Maybe Turbo can take another bite of braid," Twyla joked.

They all laughed.

"How was your evening?" Lori asked Stevie.

Stevie gave her the condensed version. "I drove the dogs home, Otis died, Joe saved the day, and we had supper."

"Poor Otis." Lori was sympathetic. "You . . . and Joe." She raised an eyebrow.

Stevie sent her a look only a close friend could interpret. *Not what you're thinking. Don't go there.* "Your night?" she volleyed back to Lori. She prayed Lori wouldn't mention Dean. Joe didn't need the aggravation.

Lori was evasive. Stevie was grateful. "I met up with friends," she said. "Showtime at the pier. Workers set up a large screen against the bait shop, and moviegoers brought their own beach chairs. Tourist season, and tonight's *Pete's Dragon* drew a big crowd. Families and couples. Kiosks sold sodas and snacks. Magical Disney animation. Good time."

"Did Dean like the show?" asked Joe. Nonchalant.

His question silenced them momentarily.

Twyla didn't pick up the undercurrent. She sipped her cooling tea. The girls had purposely kept her in the dark. Her aunt had enough on her mind. The conflict between the two men would worry her.

Turbo took that moment to rise, stretch. He crossed to Twyla, nudged her with his nose. Requiring her attention. "I'll take Turbo outside." She hobbled out on her crutches with the dog on her heels.

Lori collected herself. She folded her hands on the table. Faced off with Joe. The inevitable was spoken. "Dean didn't stay long. He had business to attend to."

"Batting-cage business," Joe said dryly.

Lori started. "How'd you know?"

"I'm psychic."

"No, really."

Stevie arbitrated. "We saw him at the stadium."

Lori was puzzled. "You were there because . . . ?"

"Picnic in left field," Joe said.

Lori skirted their meal, blew out a breath. Sought reassurance. "How was he doing?" she asked.

Stevie was cautious. "Doing his best."

"Your man looked like shit."

Heavy sigh. "He's not my man."

"He got sunburned for you." That said it all.

"Stupid on both our parts," Lori said regretfully. "He's sore, blistered, and jeopardizing his spring training."

"Damn straight." No sympathy from Joe.

"He'll recover." Lori was hopeful.

"Time's ticking," he pronounced. "Do or die."

Twyla and Turbo came in through the back door. The dog charged Joe. He braced for the impact. Still, the rottie hit him hard enough that the chair rocked. Joe planted his feet to keep his balance. "Full of yourself, I see." He scratched his dog's ears.

"He ran the whole time," Twyla said. "He wore me out watching him." She yawned. "I'm turning in."

Stevie stood and gave her a hug. "Sleep late tomorrow. I'll catch the early drop-offs."

"Thank you, dear." Twyla left them.

Lori followed shortly thereafter. "I'll be at the door by seven," she told Stevie. Hugs were exchanged. "I want to see Dean when he drops off Etta, before he heads to the park."

Etta drew Turbo's bark. He'd welcome her, too.

Joe's expression was far less inviting.

"Bedtime. I'm ready to call it a day, too," said Stevie.

"Alone, or do you want company?"

"Alone . . ." sounded weak. The man was hard to resist.

Rough and rugged. Experienced. Desired. She looked down at her grease- and grass-stained clothes. "Give me fifteen minutes in the shower, and it's yours."

"We could do thirty minutes together." He was persistent.

"We'd run out of hot water."

"Cold water, hot bodies."

"Give it up for tonight."

"Tomorrow night, then."

"Not going to happen, Joe." Longing would share her bed. Not him.

"Do I get a good-night hug?" he finagled.

He was pushing it. Standing now, arms open. She couldn't resist. She'd hugged her aunt, Lori, but their embraces couldn't compare to holding Joe. His bad boy enticed her good girl. Her body took to his, as if they were already lovers. She fit him tight. Perfectly. Secure. Her cheek pressed his chest. The steady beat of his heart lulled her. He massaged her back. Slow kneading. Satisfying. He released her too soon, withdrawing before she was ready to let him go. Her body missed his. She suddenly felt lonesome.

"Night," she managed.

"Enjoy the shower massage."

How did he know?

She hurried up the stairs.

Seven

Joe came down the staircase two steps at a time. He'd jogged with Turbo at first light. Two miles, in his ragged gray sweats. He hated throwing out worn workout clothes just when they were the most comfortable. The sky reflected a box of crayons. Long streaks of color. Returning to the dog day care, he stopped by his Jag on his way inside. He grabbed the two gift boxes holding the panties for Stevie, then he hid them in his bedroom closet to be presented when the time was right. Soon. He wanted her to wear the crystal bridal thong for the wedding shoot. Along with *their* garter.

He met up with her at the door on his way out, after a quick shower, shave, and change of clothes. She eyed his T-shirt, said, "A good way to solve arguments."

He smiled. A great shirt, navy and printed with the slogan *Let's Settle This Like Adults*, with hands shaping rock, paper, scissors. Tucked into frayed and holey jeans. Leather flip-flops.

He reached out, spiked the collar on her yellow polo. "My bite's almost gone." Barely a hint. He handed Turbo over to her. Short leash. "Take care of my boy," he told her.

The Rottweiler bumped her affectionately. "We'll be fine. Today will be better than yesterday."

"A good day is no runaway."

"You don't need to remind me."

"I'll track him on the webcam to be on the safe side."

"Concentrate on your baseball."

"Always time to sneak a peek."

A suited man wearing wingtips arrived with his whippet. She was a shy white female. He had the air of a professional. Joe pegged him as an attorney or a banker. Joe hated ties.

"Ron," Stevie greeted to the man. "Willow," to his dog.

Ron unclipped the leash, released his dog. She trotted down the hallway to the open door that led to the backyard. He glared at Turbo. "No knocking Willow off the dirt piles." His tone was firm. "You are not king of the mountain. Share." He departed.

Turbo is king, Joe wanted to say. Stevie's look told him to hold his tongue. All narrowed eyes and flattened lips. Turbo whined, anxiously. His attention was on the door, his head tilted, as he awaited the arrival of additional dogs. Joe hated to think his boy was seeking Etta, Dean Jensen's bulldog. He hoped he was wrong.

Two teenage girls came next, carrying a wicker basket with four golden retriever puppies between them. Roly-poly, happy puppies, trying to escape the basket. Turbo stretched, poked his nose into the carrier. The smallest blond puppy yelped, ducked down.

The shorter of the two girls spoke directly to Joe. "Your dog tried to pee on Bella yesterday."

He looked from Stevie to the Puppy Room, asked, "Aren't they closed off from the bigger dogs?"

"All of the large dogs were inside when the puppies had supervised yard time," she told him. "No one realized Turbo was hiding in the crawl tunnel, until he jumped out. He"—pause—"lifted his leg on Bella. She's not a hydrant."

Crap. "Did he get her?"

"A sprinkle," said Stevie. "The groomer gave her a bath."

"Ah, Turbo," was all Joe had. "Sorry, girls."

They accepted his apology with stiff nods.

A lady in a flight attendant uniform, along with her Afghan hound, found her way inside. The grayish, long- and silky-coated geriatric female moved slowly. The curl at the end of her tail drooped. Her muzzle was white. The flight attendant handed Stevie a paper sack, said, "Anastasia's medication for her arthritis. Once a day, with food. I'm scheduled on an international flight, and Stasia will need an overnight, please. I'll pick her up on Thursday."

"No problem, Sophia," Stevie readily agreed. "Anastasia's always welcome here. A very good girl."

The woman eyed Turbo. "We know who the bad boy is."

More criticism? It ticked Joe off. Fly Me was a snob. Apparently Turbo's true personality didn't shine on the webcam. It was one-sided. He was really playful, not a bully.

"Yesterday was the Rottweiler's first day," Stevie informed Sophia. "Lots of stimulation. He'll settle in, find his place in the group."

"Don't let him take over," said Sophia. "He's dominant. Aggressive."

"Anastasia can have the Quiet Room with the older dogs," Stevie reassured the woman. "We have four geriatrics today. The Rottweiler won't corner her to play. Promise."

Sophia nodded, relieved. "Stasia's fourteen. She was a

show dog for many years. She has enough trophies and ribbons to fill a room. She's earned her rest. We've been with Twyla for ten years now. I'd hate to change her day care." She gave her dog a hug, then sent Joe a dismissive look. Wishing Turbo gone.

Joe's nostrils flared. Snotty lady. He and Turbo weren't going anywhere. He saw Stevie look at his shirt, then to the flight attendant. She formed a fist. He read her mind. She challenged him to be nice. He clenched his own hand, and they discreetly shook out. Rock for her. Scissors for him. Rock crushed scissors—she won. Shit.

Sophia now walked to the door, and Joe beat her to it. "Let me get that for you." All manners and charm. "Safe travels," he called to her back. "See you soon."

Sophia gave him a reluctant smile.

Stevie, a thumbs-up.

Pet owners and their dogs trailed in. The entry hall grew crowded. Turbo did some solid sniffing as the dogs passed by him, but he didn't tug on his leash to follow. Questions were asked about afternoon delivery, which gave Stevie pause.

Joe angled toward her, whispered near her ear, "You'll have transportation," he guaranteed.

Her lips parted. "How?"

"I'll take care of it."

"You're *not* the boss." Her tone was firm. "Check with my aunt first."

"I'm capable of making a decision."

"Not when it comes to Unleashed."

"Done deal. Too late now." He left it at that.

Stevie didn't have time to question him further. Lori made her way downstairs moments later. She was fresh-faced and casually dressed in a flowing white blouse and baggy shorts. Clothes that barely touched her sunburned skin. "Dean?" she anxiously asked Stevie, afraid she might have missed him.

Stevie shook her head. "Not yet. Any minute, though."

"He texted, mentioned an 'initiation'"—she used finger quotes—"and that he'd shaved his head. Bald."

Joe could barely contain his laughter. "My cue to leave." He patted Turbo. "Be the best you can be." His dog's expression was pure innocence. He touched Stevie's arm. "Later."

Joe arrived at the stadium to find a newspaper article taped to the front of his locker. "Zoo, thought you might like a copy," Rylan Cates called to him. "Good publicity. Jill was pleased. It's also been posted on the Rogues' website."

Jillian Mac-Cates, executive liaison for community affairs, was all about positive promo. She connected with the locals and involved them in Rogue activities. Zoo glanced at the paper, seeing six photographs, followed by two columns dedicated to the superheroes and Kuts for Kids. Excellent coverage. Photographer Eden Cates-Kane had captured the moments. Beautifully.

He scanned the pictures, his gaze returning to the top-center photo. The one in which Super Zooker had kissed Stevie on the forehead, following her haircut. Her expression was soft, his attentive. Their attraction evident to anyone who really looked. He folded the article, placed it on a shelf in his locker.

Pax and Sam sauntered in moments later, their own newspapers in hand. They sat down on the bench. Eyed him speculatively. "Dude, what's up? You've been ditching us."

"Not purposely," he returned.

"CliffsNotes." Pax wanted a short accounting.

Joe wasn't ready to enlighten them yet about Stevie. "Turbo, Unleashed, complications. Working through them."

Pax covered his mouth, coughed in his hand. "Working through Stevie, too?" His voice was muffled.

Joe shot him a dark look.

"She gives new meaning to going to the dogs," from Pax.

"It's not what you're thinking," he denied.

"I think it's more than we know. Maybe even more than *you* know," said Sam. He shook out the paper. Flashed the Features section. Pointed to Stevie and Joe's photo. "Looking pretty sweet."

Pax grinned. "Like a couple. She appears vulnerable; you, protective."

Joe snorted. "You're seeing more than is there. You saw Eden take the photo. Stevie wasn't into me."

"That was then," said Pax. "How about now?"

"Get real. What do you think?"

"No fuckin' idea," admitted Pax. "You've gone all private on us. Too damn quiet, dude. You're neglecting your party posse."

His posse fell all over him. Loved on him. Stevie kept him at arm's length. "I'll make up for lost time on Friday, Happy Hour, the Blue Coconut."

Pax grinned. "We'll spread the word. Nude water polo at Rock Creek Cove afterward?" An inlet north of Houseboat Row, where he docked his sailboat. There was nightly skinny-dipping.

"I'm there," Joe agreed.

He would request an overnight for Turbo at the dog care. He was in need of a woman. Under, over, beside him. But he respected Twyla, and wouldn't bring a lover to Unleashed.

On the Rogues' schedule, Saturday was a free day. Joe

could sleep late. Recharge. Playing groom for an afternoon would suck his soul. He disliked weddings, even
make-believe ones. He was doing the shoot for Turbo. His
dog was getting a bad rap, and Joe needed to secure their
residence. Sunday was the exhibition game. He'd prove
his worth then and earn his salary.

The side locker room door swung wide. No one immediately entered. Then, after several seconds, Dean Jensen made an appearance. Joe stared, along with the other
players. The man looked odd with his sunburned face and
shaved white head. Quite a contrast. Eyes went wide. Jaws
dropped. No comments. His teammates looked as pained
as Dean himself.

"What the hell?" Halo Todd scrutinized Dean. "What's
with baldy?"

"Minor league initiation," Joe responded.

Halo's brow creased. "We don't have—"

"Yeah, we do," Joe cut him off, containing his grin.

"Damn, dude, you didn't," came from Landon Kane.

"I did."

Rylan Cates joined them. "Painful haircut."

Dean dropped his gym bag, approached Ry. Two minor
leaguers shadowed him. They had his back. He ran one
hand over his bald head, asked, "Good enough?"

Rylan side-eyed Joe. "You tell him."

"Barber missed a spot behind your left ear."

Dean touched the spot. Appeared confused.

"You are so damn gullible," from Joe.

Dean visibly tensed. "Not following."

Halo gave Joe up. "It was all Zoo. Look to the source
next time before you act. No team initiation."

"*My* initiation," said Joe.

Dean's face pinched. "Asshole."

"What-the-fuck-ever."

The catcher for the Rebels edged toward Joe, in Dean's

defense. His hands fisted. Pax and Sam backed up Joe. Rylan came between them. "No fighting. Not now, not here. Never in the locker room. It's only a shaved head."

"*My* head," argued Dean. He flipped off Joe. "You'll get yours." He retreated to his locker.

"A threat?" Joe asked Pax and Sam.

"Watch your back," from Pax.

"Rylan's in center—he'll referee," Sam said.

Uniforms soon replaced street clothes. Joe glared at Dean on his way out of the locker room. Dean scowled. The man was pissed. Joe didn't give a rat's ass.

After a thirty-minute warmup, Coach Jackson instructed the position players to double up in the outfield. Side by side. It was his own developmental drill. Which Joe disliked. Jackson made comparisons. Pitting Rogues against Rebels. Looking for attention and aggression. Speed. Responsiveness. Joe and Dean claimed close to the same space. Inches apart in left field. On defense.

The coach waved them apart. "Spread out."

Neither man moved. "Get off my shadow, dickhead," Joe ordered.

"Make me."

"Guys," Rylan shouted, just as Joe was ready to throw down his glove. "Separate." Ry and a Rebel shared center. Not amicably, but not adversarially, either.

In right field, Halo and a minor leaguer split turf. The Rebel played close in. Halo, back by the warning track.

Joe had no share in him. Dean was still sunburned and sweating bullets. The batting coach smacked balls throughout the outfield. Fly balls, line drives, grounders. The occasional foul. Joe allowed Dean a ground ball. He watched closely as Dean scooped it up. Pain strained his face. He sucked air. His throw to third was soft, off mark.

"Good one," Joe taunted. Time after time.

Joe ignored Dean as he jogged for a pop-up. Easy catch, if he hadn't been bumped from the back. Then tripped. Joe pitched forward. Dean's outstretched arm was the last thing he saw before landing facedown in the dirt. *What the fuck?*

Dean hung loose. If he hurt, he hid it well. He fired a ball home with major league precision. The batting coach gave him an affirmative nod. Joe was not pleased. His inner animal growled. He talked himself down.

The batting coach jacked dozens of balls to left. Testing the two men. Despite the fact that Dean called Joe off numerous hits, Joe went after them. Screw Dean. He overlapped his glove with Dean's and stole a fly ball. They both collided over grounders. Bumping, banging. An all-out battle.

Until Rylan hollered, "This isn't sandlot ball. Grow up, boys." A team captain reprimand.

Joe had played sandlot. Vacant lot behind a neighborhood grocery store. Basic rules, most ignored. No umpire. The play was dirty. Bats shaken in intimidation. Scuffles and fights broke out, often ending in a total slugfest.

He rolled his shoulders, pulled his act together. As did Dean. They gave each other space. Joe continued to play for himself. He claimed his position with each dive and difficult catch. Up until the defense was called to bat. Joe jogged with Rylan to the dugout. Dean lagged behind.

"What's with you?" Rylan asked him.

"Kicking the competition's ass. I didn't see you giving ground in center."

"Can't. I'm captain."

"I'm setting my own example."

"You're such a role model."

They both grinned.

The day progressed. Short break, and Joe headed for

the locker room. He needed to check on Turbo. The Media and Communications Center was empty. He booted up a computer, went to the Unleashed site, viewed the webcam. He went through all six frames before locating his dog, then shook his head. Not happy. He immediately dialed Stevie. She must have recognized his number, and she took her sweet time answering.

Her "hello" was curt.

His gaze was fixed on the camera footage. "Why is Turbo in the grooming room?" he pointedly asked. "I didn't request a bath."

The rottie sat beside a bathtub, his jaw on the rim. Bubbles on his nose. A second dog's head popped up, and Joe understood the "why" before Stevie could even explain. Etta was being shampooed. Great, just great.

The bulldog had snapped at Turbo the previous day. Growled, even. Not so today. They bumped noses in mutual affection. Joe ran his hand down his face. Could his day get any worse? Dipshit Dean in left field. Their dogs bonding.

Stevie appeared in the corner of his screen, iPhone in hand. *Pretty lady*, Joe thought, admiring her. Her sigh was heavy. "From your silence, I'm assuming you've seen Etta."

"Seen, and I'm ticked."

"Turbo's calm when he's with her. Not one problem this morning. They're staying together, like it or not."

"I don't like it."

"Get over it."

The groomer was attentive to Etta, adding more shampoo, scratching her ears, rubbing down the bulldog's shoulders. Turbo waited until the groomer's back was turned, then made his move. He jumped into the lower tub with Etta. Water waved over the side, splashing the groomer and Stevie. Full-frontal wetness.

"Tsunami." Joe chuckled. His gaze held on Stevie. "Wet T-shirt contest." Nicely defined breasts.

Stevie shut him down. Disconnected. She tossed her phone onto a side table. He watched as she grabbed handfuls of towels off a shelf, knelt down. Terry cloth soaked up the puddles. All the while Turbo and Etta were having a bubble bath together. Damn if his boy wasn't smiling. Content.

Stevie looked directly into the camera. She stuck out her tongue at him, showing her pique. A turn-on for him. She brushed her bangs off her forehead. Tugged her shirt away from her chest, then walked out of the room. No doubt to change clothes. He signed off of the computer.

He left the room, then spotted Dean seated on a locker room bench. Shoulders bent. Alone. He'd taken off his baseball cap, his bald head as white as a butt cheek. He conversed on a flip cell phone. Dude needed to upgrade. Joe leaned against the corner locker, purposely spying.

Dean's voice was subdued. "Yeah, joke's on me. Zoo's initiation, not the team's." Pause. "It happens, Lori. The man may be a dick, but he's a hell of a ballplayer. Can't deny him that. He has my respect. I'm pushing myself, trying to keep up. Screw my sunburn. It won't hold me back."

He listened, smiled over something Lori said. "We're getting there, hon, making up for lost time. We'll be good together, when we can finally touch without wincing. Soon." His watch beeped. "Break's over. Got to go. I'll never be last man on the field again. Call you later." He cut out.

Joe crossed his arms over his chest, rewound the conversation. Two thoughts stuck out in his mind. First, Dean respected him. No one had ever said that about him before. He was known as the loose cannon. Trigger temper.

Unpredictable. Daring. Some said he had a death wish. Second, Dean and Lori were soon to make love. No couple could do it with a major sunburn. Too painful. A day, maybe two, though, and they'd be getting busy.

Lori had scored Dean with her sexy bikini. He wondered what Stevie would wear to purposely attract a man. She had a tight little body. Skin, alone, worked for him. Bare and laid out beneath him.

Joe headed outside. The teams divided up, with three practice fields in play. The Rogue starters were on the main diamond, where the coaches put them through their paces. The strategy sessions and scrimmages lasted two hours. Joe's body was primed. Despite the strenuous, high-energy workout, he felt not a muscle twinge or soreness.

Practice ended, and the players moved back to the locker room. Joe observed Dean cutting across the far field to the batting cages. Dean was a perfectionist. No quit in the man. He'd hammer it out for another hour. Maybe longer. He admired Dean's stamina. For all of a second.

"I'm taking the Morgan for a sunset sail," Pax announced after the players were showered and dressed. "Casting off at five. Anyone interested? Couples, singles."

"I'm in," said Sam. "No date, but I'll bring a cooler of beer."

"Beth likes sailing." Rylan spoke of his wife. "We're in, as long as you dock by eight. No late-night partying. I'd rather be home with her."

"Old married man," Sam teased.

"Damn straight," said Ry. "Settling down was the best thing that ever happened to me."

"Alyn does it for me, too," agreed Halo. "We'll pick up hoagies. Chips."

"Eden has a children's birthday party to photograph and video-record. It's a pass for us," said Landon.

Pax eyed Joe. "You in?"

Joe hesitated. He had a priority errand that couldn't be left until tomorrow. He had no idea how long it would take. "I'll try to make it," he said. "If I'm not there by five, leave without me."

Pax raised an eyebrow, asked, "What's more important than sailing?"

"Buying a transport van."

"What are you carrying?" from Sam.

"Dogs."

Stevie stood by the front door of the dog day care, looking out the window. Joe had called Twyla a half hour earlier. A lengthy, private conversation ensued. Her aunt hung up, called to Stevie, happy tears in her eyes. She'd sniffed, barely able to speak. She'd requested her niece watch for Joe. He'd be arriving shortly. With a surprise.

Pet owners streamed in, picking up their dogs. Lori leashed and praised each one. Twyla believed a compliment ended the day on a high note.

Time passed, and soon, only Turbo; the Afghan hound, Anastasia; and the four dogs in need of home delivery remained. Two Scotties, a springer spaniel, and a basset hound. Turbo now lay in the office with his big head visible in the doorway. He appeared sad that Dean Jensen had already picked up Etta, leaving him alone. He grumbled.

Poor bald Dean—Stevie's heart went out to her cousin. He had a nicely shaped head, and, surprisingly, shaved worked for him. Lori liked his look. She ran her hands over his head, kissed him on the forehead. Called him "edgy." Hot like the Rock and Vin Diesel.

But Joe's initiation didn't set well with Stevie. She found no humor in a lie. Especially one that was meant to hurt someone else. A team initiation was one thing. Joe's personal campaign was another.

She knew Dean well enough to know he was upset. Yet he held his anger in. The newspaper photo of Joe and her at Kuts for Kids bothered him more than his baldness. The idea of the two of them together annoyed him greatly. He hated the fact that Joe resided at Unleashed. Neither he nor Stevie wanted to involve Twyla in the players' feud. Her aunt didn't need the aggravation. Her healing took priority.

Lori joined her at the window, asked, "Where's Joey?"

"He should be here any second."

"Check out the transport coming down the drive."

The driver parked the new white Dodge Sprinter near the door. Joe hopped out, and Stevie's jaw dropped. He entered, his presence filling the entrance hall. A key ring hung from his forefinger. "A donation to Unleashed," he said.

"Donation . . ." Stevie repeated.

"Twyla's aware of my gift."

"Gift . . ." Hard to comprehend.

"Otis bit the dust. Time for a dependable vehicle."

"*Woot-woot!*" Lori couldn't contain her excitement. "I'm taking it for a spin around the block." She snagged the keys, dashed out the door.

Astonishment held Stevie in place. She couldn't move. Could barely speak. Her gaze met his. "Why?" she finally managed.

"Because I can."

"You didn't have to."

"It was important that I did."

She had spent a restless night, tossing and turning, searching for a way to buy a new van. To take the pressure off her aunt. She'd awakened weary, with no immediate fix.

Joe had saved the day.

Twyla appeared, hobbled toward them. "I'm over-whelmed by your generosity," she said, emotion in her voice. She hugged him. Like family.

"There's rubber padding in the cargo area," he told them. "And more to come. Metal carriers are on order. They can be permanently installed, for safety's sake. The name *Unleashed* can be detailed on one or both sides."

Twyla was impressed. "You've thought of everything."

"And so quickly," said Stevie.

"I can be quick when something needs to be done," Joe affirmed. "I wanted to help. I'll pay the insurance for a year. The title to the Sprinter will arrive within two weeks."

Stevie released a breath. "You bought it outright?"

He made light of her question. "I had extra change in my pocket."

"A blessing for us." Twyla sighed.

Lori returned with the van. Once she'd parked, she came through the door, her steps light, bouncy. Bright eyes, big smile. She hugged Joe, too, despite her sunburn. "The Sprinter drives like a dream," she expressed, de-lighted. "Let's load up the dogs. I'll make the inaugural run."

"I'll ride with you," Stevie said. "My mechanic called, and the alternator's been replaced on my Miata. It's ready to be picked up."

"I also need a lift," stated Joe. "I drove the van here and left my Jaguar at the Dodge dealership. I'd hate to leave it there overnight."

"Pile in," said Lori. "One in the passenger seat, one in the back with the dogs."

"I'll keep Turbo until you return," Twyla offered.

The dogs were loaded in minutes. Stevie's checkmate stare with Joe didn't earn her the front seat. His gaze darkened dangerously. She shifted her hips toward the passenger door, and he inserted his knee between her legs. That stopped her cold. He buffed his thigh against hers. Jeans against skin. His knee rose higher, closing on her female V. He rubbed her. Her breath stalled in her lungs. She grew light-headed.

She clutched the front of his T-shirt for leverage. Suggested, "Rock, paper, scissors," to determine who rode shotgun.

They shook their fists. Stevie played paper, Joe scissors. Scissors cut paper; he'd won. She reached for the sliding back door, and his hand covered hers. "Take the front," he said, ushering her into the van. Being a gentleman. Which she hadn't expected. He then climbed in with the dogs. "Drop me off first," he called to Lori. "Dodge car lot is five miles south, off of State Road Twelve."

Lori talked nonstop, extolling the beauty of the van. They soon reached the dealership. Lori thanked Joe a hundred times over for his generosity. She twisted on her seat and kissed his cheek as he climbed out. "I like you, Joe Zooker," she said. "Despite the fact that you dislike my man."

"Find another man and we'll be fine."

"I've wanted Dean for much of my life. He's a keeper."

"No need to list his good qualities."

"We don't have enough time anyway."

He then exited the side door. He tapped on Stevie's rolled-up window. She cracked it. He then flattened his hand against the glass. She pressed her palm to his, an impromptu gesture. "Later?" he asked.

"I'll be around."

"Around Unleashed?"

"Around town. We have a new van. We'll be cruising."

"Definitely a vehicle to use to pick up guys." He left her.

Lori let the engine idle. Stevie watched him go. Not for the first time did she admire his backside. His overly long hair. The strength in his shoulders. The width of his back. Tight-as-sin butt. Muscular legs. Badass walk.

Car salesmen waved to him until he disappeared around the corner of the main building. Out of sight, but not out of mind. The man stuck with Stevie.

Lori pulled back onto the state road, heading for the first dog drop-off, a home within a few miles. "Pushing Joe away only brings him closer," she casually observed. "He's hot for you."

"Hot for the moment."

"I glimpsed the two of you in the passenger side–view mirror at Unleashed. He was pressed up against you, dry-humping."

"He always leaves an imprint." A male brand.

"I'd flirt with the man myself if not for Dean."

"I'm keeping my distance, because of my cousin."

"Dean's request that you stay away from Joe isn't fair. I've told him so. Let the two men battle it out at the stadium, and leave the women out of it."

Stevie was thoughtful. "Family loyalty. I'd never break my word to Dean."

Lori pursed her lips. "There's loyalty, and then there's loss," she pointed out. "Don't miss out on Joe. He's bedworthy. A once in a lifetime."

"Not sure I could handle him."

"Let him do the handling. I'm sure he's quite good." She stopped at a red light, glanced at Stevie. "The guys need to think about us and not their rivalry. When they next have free time, let's distract them. Win-win."

A win with Joe would be short-lived. She would be just one of many women, standing in line for his attention. His party posse took priority with him. "Are you seeing Dean tonight?" she asked her friend.

"We made a date when he picked up Etta. Dairy God-mother. Ice cream cones to keep us cool. Our sunburns will be gone by Friday night. That'll be *our* night." She grinned. "I've cleared time off with Twyla. She's fine with it. Rebels have Saturday free, same as the Rogues. I may not make your wedding, married lady."

Stevie rolled her eyes. "It's not a real ceremony. Merely a magazine shoot."

"Have you tried on the dresses?"

"I'd planned to do that tonight."

"The off-the-shoulder gown has my vote. Classic and romantic."

"It's my favorite, too—if it fits."

"Fits?" Lori laughed. The traffic light turned green, and she moved forward. "You are put together, girl. Flaw-less. Designers would kill to have you model their gowns."

Stevie took the compliment in stride. She'd never thought of her body as perfect. Far from it. Her cousin Dean had called her "*skinny*" most of her life.

Lori soon pulled into a crushed pale-pink seashell driveway fringed by red hibiscus bushes. The owner of the springer spaniel hurried out, happy to receive her dog.

The next destination was close by. Still, Lori pro-grammed the address into the GPS, for fun. "I love this van," she gushed. "Joe saved the day."

Stevie didn't see him as a knight in shining armor. More of a hardened mercenary. Rough and raw. A law unto himself despite his generosity.

Stevie got out of the van at Violet the basset's home. She slid open the side panel, unfolded a pet loader ramp, and hooked it to the door track. Violet of the floppy ears and short legs walked the ramp with ease. As if she'd been born to walk the runway. Her owner greeted them with high praise for the new Sprinter.

The twin Scotties remained. Their owners weren't home when Lori parked by the curb. There was no huffing and puffing with the new van. They'd arrived ten minutes ahead of schedule. The friends chatted.

Lori confided, "Dean's reserved a suite at Sandcastle for the weekend. No interruptions from his teammates. Room service, a balcony, Gulf view. *And*"—she stretched the word—"a raised king-size platform bed. The bathroom has a waterfall shower. Built-in water jets cover the ceiling. Like an outdoor paradise."

Sandcastle, a five-star hotel on Saunders Shores. World-class service. A honeymoon couple had boarded their Chinese crested several weeks ago. The purebred hairless came with a diamond collar and gourmet canine chef. The newlyweds requested transport for their dog to the hotel. Stevie had waited for them, just inside the main doors. Enormous chandelier. Terra-cotta tiles and Peruvian rugs. Original artwork. Wealth and luxury.

"Etta will be boarding," Stevie assumed.

Lori nodded. "Both Friday and Saturday. Dean cleared it with Twyla."

Etta's sleepover would make Turbo happy.

Long pause from Lori. Her lips pinched. "There's something you might want to know, or might not . . ." she began hesitantly. "Locker room talk from Dean. There's a Rogues all-night party at Rock Creek Cove on Friday. It's for the single players. Bonfire. Booze. Naked water polo."

Single players would include Joe. His posse. Baring it all.

Stevie's chest squeezed. She had difficulty breathing. Joe's actions shouldn't surprise her. Not one bit. She had no reason to feel hurt. To feel left out. But she did. Disappointed, too. He was done chasing her. She wondered if he'd leave her at the altar on Saturday. Depressing thought. The photo shoot meant a lot to her. She needed a backup plan.

"Thanks for letting me know," she managed.

"I'll be back at Unleashed Sunday morning, before the exhibition game. Want to go together? We can cheer on Dean," Lori said.

"I want," Stevie agreed. Her heart was not in the game.

The Scotties' owners honked behind them. Punctual. The husband unloaded the dogs. "Much safer," he said, admiring the van. "No exhaust trail when you leave."

Lori next drove Stevie to pick up her red Mazda Miata. With the new alternator, it ran like a charm. Stevie was glad to have her own transportation again. She no longer had to depend on Lori for a ride. She followed her friend back to Unleashed. No cruising the main beach drag.

Lori headed upstairs the moment she entered the house to change clothes for her date with Dean. Turbo wandered toward her, looking for Joe. "Want to play in the backyard?" she offered. "I have a few free minutes."

The rottie shot down the hallway. Stevie followed more slowly. It was early evening, and the air had cooled. The yard was clear of other dogs. Geriatric Anastasia was sleeping. Turbo had the agility equipment to himself. He climbed the piles of dirt and howled. He ran and ran, as if being chased. He brought Stevie a tennis ball. They played catch until her arm grew tired. Turbo dove into the crawl tunnel and never came out. Time to call it quits, she decided. She called to him, with no response. She could see his outline in the spy holes. Her calling "Treat!" didn't draw him out, either.

Difficult dog. "Don't make me come after you," she said, issuing a warning. What could she do but push him through the tunnel? With a long-suffering sigh, she crossed the yard. Hands on her hips, she challenged, "Out, *now*." No movement whatsoever.

She bent down, angled her shoulders into the tunnel. Leaned on her forearms. Glared at the Rottweiler. "Your ass is grass, buddy," she mumbled as she wiggled deeper inside.

Eight

Turbo's *ass was grass*? Joe arrived just in time to over-hear Stevie's irritation. He stood at the back door, looking out. Watching her wiggle her butt as she inched into the crawl tunnel. He barked his laughter. Unable to resist, he pulled his iPhone from his pants pocket and took her picture. A sweet-cheek memory.

He stepped outside, walked across the yard to her con-tinued mumbling. He could see the stub of Turbo's tail wagging through the spy holes. His boy was playing with her, but Stevie didn't find it amusing.

Joe snuck up behind her, braced his legs, and leaned down. Doggy-style came to mind, inappropriate but fit-ting, as he grabbed her by the hips, and hauled her out. With her back against him, her ass fit his groin. Nicely. His dick jacked.

A small scream died in her throat when she realized it was him. "You scared me," she accused.

"You could've gotten stuck."

"Hardly," she huffed. She swatted his arm. "Stop press-ing me."

The pressing felt good. He liked holding her. He sur-prised them both by kissing her neck, right below her ear, where his hickey had faded. The contact was arousing. She stiffened slightly, but didn't shove him away. He breathed her in.

"You sniffed my hair."

"I like your perfume." Faint citrus.

"Don't smell it all up."

He nuzzled her ear, flicked his tongue to her lobe. Then nipped, gave a gentle pull with his teeth. A sexual tease. He absorbed her shiver. He kissed her again, and her elbow caught his thigh. Dangerously high. Too near his boys.

He muttered, "You have bony elbows."

He eased back, uncomfortably hard, and shook out his leg. Making an adjustment. Stevie faced him now. She dipped her head to hide her awkwardness. Long hair would've concealed her blush. Short hair opened her face to his view. He tipped up her chin with his thumb. Her eyelids fluttered, not flirty, but nervous. She worried her bottom lip. Peaked nipples were visible beneath her polo. Her legs squeezed together. He'd bet she was wet.

He had provoked. She'd panicked. "Don't be embarrassed," he said. "Desire shows itself." He was still half-cocked.

"I don't want you."

"I say you do."

"Believe what you will."

"I'm a believer."

She blew by him, all heightened color and heaving breasts.

"Turbo," he called to his dog. The Rottweiler shot out of the tunnel as if he'd been fired from a cannon. He barreled toward Joe, body-slammed him. Joe barely kept his balance. He knuckled Turbo's ears. "I'm glad to see you, too." The rottie accepted his greeting, then hauled ass after Stevie.

"It's feeding time," she called over her shoulder. "I'm off your clock. Take care of your dog."

Joe tracked them to the kitchen and found Stevie reading a note from Twyla posted beneath a Saint Bernard magnet on the front of the refrigerator. He scanned it, too. *Braided rug is fully repaired. Entertaining George at the guesthouse.*

He grinned. "'Entertaining,' huh?"

"Cards," she explained, clearing his mind of sex. "My aunt plays gin."

"What do you play?" he asked. Opening a cupboard door to the left of the sink, he removed a dog dish and a bag of kibble. He gave Turbo dinner. Gone in thirty seconds. Joe poured out more, called it "dessert."

"Cards are fun," she told him, "but I also like Jenga, Yahtzee, backgammon, Scrabble."

She went to the pantry off the kitchen for a package of light butter flavor popcorn, then placed the bag in the microwave. She leaned against the countertop, asked, "Your board game of choice?"

Loaded question. "Adult XXX. Dirty Minds, Lust, Sexdrive."

"You're making this up?"

He shook his head. "I recently played Sexdrive." He and his party posse. "Challenges of sexual know-how, show-how, and tell-how. Players answer questions or perform 'body shop' tasks to show what they know about sex. The goal is to obtain your 'sex driver's license,' move to the 'inner course.'"

"Is there nudity?"

"With the advanced version."

She went so still, he wasn't certain she was breathing. He stuck his finger under her nose to be sure. She swatted his hand away. Neither spoke. *Pop-pop-pop* broke the silence.

The microwave beeped; the bag was ready. She opened it, tipped the contents into a large plastic bowl. "Invitation to your popcorn party?" he asked.

"I'm headed to the sitting room to watch TV."

"So was I."

She cut him a curious look. "Why aren't you out with your friends?"

"You are my friend."

"No, really."

"Pax took several single players and couples sailing. Sunset's a nice time to be on the water."

"Why didn't you go?"

"I was at the Dodge dealership, wrapping up paperwork on the Sprinter. I missed cast off."

"I'm sorry."

"There'll be other times."

"Twyla's very grateful for the van."

"She's a good woman. I don't give many gifts, but when I do, I like them to be meaningful."

"You have a place in her heart."

"What about yours?"

"I don't need mine broken."

He frowned. "I'd never purposely hurt you."

"I'd never take that chance."

Her response was telltale. She was protecting herself from him. That explained a lot. Why she was so stand-offish, sarcastic, despite their sexual burn. He sensed there was more to it. That she still hid something from him. A secret? Hopefully to be revealed. When she was ready.

"I need to check on the Afghan hound," Stevie said, as they left the kitchen.

Turbo took off ahead of them.

Stevie next.

Joe followed.

Dusk snuck into the house, leaving deep shadows in the hallway. She flipped on lights. Anastasia blinked awake in the Geriatric Room. Plenty of leftover noon kibble in her bowl. Soft chewy snacks on a tray. Fresh water. Stevie left the door cracked in case she wished to join them.

They took the stairs together. The staircase reminded him of the bridal shoot. "You prepared for Saturday?"

"Pretty much. You?"

"Ready or not, I'd do anything for Turbo."

She scrunched her nose. Unexpectedly cut him some slack. "Don't feel obligated, Joe. Your dog can stay—you, too, even if you back out of our deal."

She mixed him up. "Are you wanting to replace me?" That didn't set well. Women desired him. Yet Stevie remained distant.

She stopped on the landing, the popcorn bowl clutched to her chest, looking serious. "Your call. You dislike weddings. You've said so. I have four days until the shoot. Enough time to find a substitute groom if necessary."

He had an escape. Yet he didn't want to run. "I'm cool."

"No freaking out at the last minute."

"Under control."

She smiled her appreciation. Her first real smile of the night. Bright eyes. Color in her cheeks. Pretty curved lips. A natural beauty. "You nervous at all?" he asked her.

"I've yet to pick my dress. You've yet to try on your tux. Enough said."

"You could model the gowns for me tonight."

"Bad luck for the groom to see his bride in her wedding dress before the ceremony."

"Superstitious? It's make-believe, sweetheart."

"No fashion show."

"Planning to wear our garter?"

"Something blue? It's still under debate." Her expression softened. "Something old from my aunt, a lace handkerchief. Something borrowed from Lori, a pearl bracelet. I know it's all pretend, but I want it to be perfect."

"I have something new for you." The bridal thong.

Her expression showed apprehension, then curiosity. "What?"

"To be presented prior to the shoot."

"I'd rather know now," she insisted.

"I'm not telling." He left her in suspense.

They continued to the sitting room. A small space with a short fabric couch, ottoman, an overstuffed chair, TV mounted on the wall, narrow bookshelf, and a round game table. Turbo claimed the chair. Stevie sat on the sofa. Joe dropped down beside her, settled deep into the cushions. Purposely crowding her. She squeezed sideways, gained an inch. An inch he soon took back with a shift of his hip. The Afghan hound slowly found her way upstairs. She curled up on the floor at one end of the couch.

Joe dug into the popcorn. Salty, buttery. He went for a second handful, only to skim Stevie's thigh when she held the bowl away from him. "One piece at a time. Don't scoop with your palm."

He laughed at her, earning her frown. "One piece is girly."

"I want the popcorn to last."

He took a single piece, tilted back his head, tossed it in the air, and caught it in his mouth. "Hardly worth the chew."

"The remote." She felt around between the cushions. The back of her hand brushed his hip, butt, low on his back. "Sorry," she mumbled.

"I'm not. Keep searching."

Remote found, she turned on the TV. Channel surfed. "Preference?" she asked him.

"Sports."

"Second choice."

"*The Walking Dead.*"

"Reruns. Next."

He eyed the TV listings in the corner of the screen. "*Supernatural* starts in an hour." It was fantasy horror, and Joe's all-time favorite show. "Claiming it."

"I like Sam and Dean," she tentatively said.

The two brothers followed in their father's footsteps as supernatural hunters, fighting evil beings. Monsters, demons, and gods that roamed the earth. Joe rubbed his hands together. "I like Crowley." A demon and the current king of hell.

"No surprise there."

"I have a hellhound tat."

"Good for you."

"Want to see it?"

"Mmm-hmm, no."

"Got to, babe. Chaos is worth a look."

An intake of breath. "You named your tattoo?"

"After my own state of mind." Joe lifted the front of his T-shirt, hooked his thumb in the waistband of his jeans, and slid them down his abdomen, one inch, then two. A hint of his hip bone appeared. Just enough so she could glimpse the red eyes of the mythical beast at his groin.

She darted a glance. Stared overly long.

So long, he had to ask, "Want to pet him?"

She blinked. "Your best pickup line?"

"It works."

A soft release of breath. An inquiring whisper. "Why a hellhound?"

He told her. "I read *The Hound of the Baskervilles* as a kid. One of the few stories I finished."

"Detective Sherlock Holmes."

"I got caught up in the mystery," he admitted, straightening his jeans, but leaving his T-shirt untucked. "The legendary beast left an impression. Too bad the demonic dog turned out to be no more than a mix of bloodhound and mastiff, painted with phosphorus to give it a hellish appearance."

"I read the book, too. I saw the 1959 movie on late-night TV. The Gothic setting gave me the shivers." Her brow creased. "Dartmoor in England's west country, I believe."

"The 1939 film is scarier. Black-and-white feels more menacing than color. More horror elements, too. A lethal tarantula." He scooped a handful of popcorn. She didn't complain. Once he'd finished it, he went on to say, "The Rogues' players got inked two years ago. Team unity. The hellhound fit me. Strong. Fearless. Aggressive."

"Nothing carnal?"

"Don't need a tat for sex."

There was a break in the conversation, and they simultaneously reached for the popcorn. Touching fingertips. Palms. He ran his thumb over her wrist. Her pulse jumped. Arousal raised goose bumps on her forearm. He affected her. She got to him, too. Want surged hot and vital. He shifted on the sofa. Drew the hem of his shirt over his ridged zipper, attempting to hide what could still be seen.

Back to the TV. "We've got time before *Supernatural*. What do you want to watch?"

A corner of her mouth twitched in a subtle grin. "*It's All About Me*." She located the channel.

A bridal show? There went sixty minutes of his life he'd

never get back. Joe sat in silence, squinting at the screen. Not wanting to watch the program full-on. He didn't need to be brought up to speed on what was happening. The reality show was scarily explicit and would shock any groom as brides morphed into unidentifiable creatures under the stress of wedding arrangements and unrealistic expectations. Their worst sides were quickly revealed as they stepped on anybody who got in their way. Each of these brides selfishly believed it was her day, the groom insignificant. Damn.

He ate popcorn, but found it difficult to swallow, as one wife-to-be tried to select the perfect wedding gown. Trying on dress after dress. "Brunette's picked twelve effing gowns." He snorted. "She's driving the bridal consultant crazy. Me, too. The first one looked the best. What's her problem?" he asked Stevie.

She explained, "The bride wants to be sure there's no dress better than the one she chooses. A friend of mine once tried on forty-five."

"Women need to make their minds up quicker."

"She wants to be her most beautiful."

"How many dresses would you try on?" He seemed concerned, for no apparent reason.

"I have three available for the magazine photo shoot. It's still a tough decision. Each one is unique."

"Coin toss?"

"Could come down to that."

Joe's hands were sweaty by the time the bride finally selected a dress. She returned to the first, but only after running the sales associate in circles. The poor woman scurried from the dressing room to the revolving couture racks, hauling heavy layers of satin and lace. Long and short veils. He grew tired and irritable just watching her. Still he couldn't look away. A wedding train wreck.

The bride soon met with a professional wedding planner. Joe edged forward on the couch cushion and took in the reception consultation. "Bride wants a confetti cannon fired as the couple leaves the church?"

"She's decided to change out the colorful paper for white rose petals. That sounds romantic."

The planning continued: The formal reception would be held at a prominent hotel with a lavish sit-down gourmet dinner. Menus were discussed. Six courses. Joe curled his lip over the main item. "Pan-seared Chilean sea bass with coconut shellfish broth. Why not just steak and potatoes?"

"Too hearty," Stevie explained. "Sits heavy on the stomach. Guests would be yawning at the table, wanting a nap. The bride's going for elegance."

Elegance, his ass. Seating of the bridal party and decorations came next, giving him heartburn. He noted the enormous hanging centerpiece to be displayed over the head table. "Those floating white orchids seem to defy gravity. Impractical."

"Quite lovely, actually," from Stevie.

"White this and white that." He liked color.

"To symbolize innocence and purity."

"Are the brides on this show virgins?"

"Doesn't say in the program details."

"Couples need to know whether they are sexually compatible before exchanging vows. No man wants a surprise mannequin in his bed."

"'Mannequin,' huh?"

"A woman who just lies there."

The wedding coordinator guided the bride around the Crystal Ballroom. Five-tiered prism chandelier, thick Victorian columns, pale paneling, and wide-arched windows. Stevie sighed. "Check out the dance floor."

He did and gagged at the absurdity. It was a raised clear acrylic platform with bright yellow, pink, and purple flowers lit from beneath to create a garden in the middle of the ballroom. He had an alternate plan. "They could just set pots of flowers around the perimeter."

"Not the same effect. This bride's going for an illusion. Fantasy. Magic."

"The fairy tale ends with the ring on her finger. She looks the type to put more effort into the wedding than into the marriage itself."

"How can you tell?"

The back of his neck prickled. "Gut feeling. The chick is bitchy."

"The strain reveals the worst in her character."

"I think the show reveals her real self." The camera focused on her sending a nasty text to her mother. Arguing over the cost of her wedding. She'd already hit six figures. "Where's the groom?" he wanted to know.

"Most men leave the planning to the bride. They've selected the woman they wish to marry, they've proposed. They're done."

Joe grinned then. "Involve the guy, and fire-breathing, car-crushing robots might arrive at the reception. Xbox games on the tables. Camera drones overhead. Cool."

He ran his hand down his face when the discussion on-screen turned to having a private jet to take the married couple to an exclusive destination. He held up his hands. "Too much for me."

"Yet you watched the entire show," she teased.

"Sucked in. I've never seen anything like it before. Never plan to again." He fell back on the couch. Reached for a handful of popcorn. Scooped. "We've watched what you wanted. Now it's my turn."

Stevie clicked the remote, located *Supernatural*. His

show. He exhaled, and his body sagged against her. All tension left his expression. His shoulders. He stretched his arm along the back of the sofa. His hand brushed her shoulders. His fingertips, her upper arm. Lightly stroking.

"What are you doing?"

"Getting comfortable."

"You're making me uncomfortable. You're too close."

"I need to be close."

"Why?" She elbowed him.

"To kiss you. Practice for the photo shoot."

"There's no kiss scheduled."

"Last frame. Always a kiss."

Her breath caught. She jarred the bowl of popcorn on her lap. Half the snack rolled over the rim. Joe helped clean her up. She went fast. He, slow. His fingers collected popcorn from between her legs. Lingered over the pieces at her V.

She shoved his hand away. "All done."

"Not done, babe, just getting started."

"Watch your show."

A corner of his mouth curved. "Catch you at the commercial."

He'd warned her of his intention. Prepared her for his kiss. The idea was daunting, nerve-racking. Yet it left her expectant. Conceivably it would be no more than a kiss on her forehead. Possibly, parted lips and tongue.

Her breathing deepened. Her belly butterflied. If she was smart, she'd hop off the sofa, take the Afghan hound downstairs, outside, and settle her in for the night. Wash out the popcorn bowl in the kitchen sink. Then head back upstairs for a bubble bath. Early to bed.

Rational thought vanished when it came to Joe, however. The lines between right and wrong faded. One kiss would break her promise to her cousin Dean. She was a woman of her word.

All the same, the longer she remained, the more susceptible she became to the Rogue. To his kiss. They sat so close, air couldn't squeeze between them. Joe dwarfed her. A tilt of his shoulders, and she nestled against his chest. His very wide chest. Solid and muscled. His mouth interested her. Full lower lip, narrower upper one. He was an experienced kisser. Should she leave or stay?

She stayed. Apprehensive. Aroused. Afraid.

Joe flagged his hand before her eyes. "You okay?"

Her "Fine . . ." sounded weak.

He bumped his knee against hers. "You've been lost in thought. Staring at the television screen, but not watching the show."

"I'm watching."

"What was the last commercial for?"

She'd missed the ad. "Cereal." Wild guess.

"Super Poligrip. Not on my breakfast table."

Denture adhesive cream. She blushed. *Supernatural* returned. Her commercial window for a kiss disappeared. Had he played her? Wound her tight, let her spin? She'd waited, wanting him, and he hadn't made a pass. She felt let down.

She huffed. He heard her. "There're more commercials to come." Humor was in his voice.

"I don't care."

"Yeah, you do." He was so self-assured. "You expected me to kiss you within the first ten minutes. Give it time, babe. Anticipation. Sexual psych."

The postponement rode her last nerve as she sat through the next set of commercials. Her chest squeezed. Her stomach cramped. Ford trucks drove her back to the demon hunters Dean and Sam, brothers on the run. Chasing the king of hell, Crowley. She got lost in the action of the show. Her gaze was on the TV and not on Joe.

He took her unaware, waiting for no product promotions. Devious man. He smoothed his mouth over hers in the softest kiss ever. Gentle, pleasurable, skilled. It was short-lived, yet it had the greatest impact. Her scalp tingled. Her tummy fluttered. Her toes curled.

The man could kiss. Her lips parted slightly. The tip of his tongue touched inside her lower lip. He tasted her. But he never gave her time to respond. To fully kiss him back. He detached. Practice over. She sighed against his mouth. Which he heard.

"No sound effects at the photo shoot, Stewie."

"No visual aids, Joey." He was stiff.

He laughed at himself. "I'm better than PowerPoint."

He tucked her into his side. This man who cruised through life without commitment. She felt amazingly safe and protected. Reality reminded her that he had a party posse. Hot, sexy babes who were all about him. Women who would play naked water polo on Friday nights. Not her sport.

A potato chip commercial, and Joe kissed her forehead.

A kiss on her nose during a pet food ad.

Supernatural ended. Once again, Crowley had evaded Dean and Sam.

Joe never took her mouth again. Disappointing.

Instead of kissing, he wanted to talk. "I'm your groom for the afternoon on Saturday. Is the magazine only taking pictures, or will an article be attached?"

"No article was mentioned. Not yet, anyway."

"Your sixty-second bio, just in case."

"Born in Roanoke, Virginia."

"Richmond, for me."

"Stop taking my seconds."

A sarcastic, "Sorry."

"My mom is a triplet; Twyla is one of her sisters. I'm an only child. With lots of cousins."

He interrupted once again. "You mentioned a male cousin who always had your back."

Dean. "Our families are close." Enough said.

"Education?" he asked.

"A degree in professional bridal consultation."

Pained expression. "Yanking me, right?"

"You almost believed me," she teased.

"College of William and Mary. Williamsburg. Psychology. I'm in your head."

No smile from the man. His body tensed. He removed his arm from across her shoulders, distanced himself. "You're analyzing me?" The possibility seemed to bother him a lot.

"Not officially. I've yet to set up practice," she said honestly. "I see what I see. On the surface, the obvious. You're complicated. Mental bumps and bruises. Darkness and shadows."

His gaze narrowed. "Blame my childhood."

"We all grow up," she dared. "Elect our adulthood."

He leaned forward, rested his elbows on his thighs. Said, "I like who I am."

"Do you?"

"I can live with myself. Back off, Stevie." Firm and final.

"If you ever want to talk-"

"I don't." He pushed off the couch. Stood over her. Suddenly withdrawn as he recited his own rundown. "University of Virginia, Charlottesville. Sports medicine. Preventive care to rehabilitation. Fallback career if baseball fails. Broken home, which you've already guessed. I haven't seen or spoken to my parents in years. One younger brother. A hellion. Can't hold a job. Jason walks the fine line between justice and jail."

He jammed his hand through his hair. His jaw was set. "I work my ass off at baseball. Play hard outside the park. I have a few select friends. Hangers-on come and go. I know who's using me and who's got my back." Pause. "March birthday. I like to travel. I sleep in the nude. I'd have sex twenty-four/seven if time allowed. That's it. We know each other well enough now. I don't do close."

Her heart squeezed. Hurt. "I never thought you did," she whispered.

"I'll need an overnight for Turbo on Friday," he went on to request.

No explanation. She already knew why. Naked water polo. He and his posse. "I'll put his name on the weekend list."

A short nod, and he whistled for his dog. They left the room together. Solitude sat heavy on her chest. She hadn't meant to provoke him. Their sixty-second bios had ended the evening poorly. A hostile silence lingered in the room. Television no longer appealed to her.

Joe's reputation accounted him a hard-ass. Destructive. He didn't always play fair. Regardless, she'd witnessed his good side. He'd saved her from boardwalk security. Requested a wig for young Ashley. Bought a transport van for Unleashed.

Throughout their time together, she'd been caustic. He hadn't cared. He'd tenaciously pursued her; kept the beat going between them. They'd practice-kissed, in preparation for the photo shoot. She'd liked it. He had a sexy mouth.

Her mention of psychology had flipped his switch. He'd shut down. Lost trust in her. She'd had no ulterior motive.

His past was relevant, yet evaluating the man served no purpose. He needed to work through his own issues. He obviously had a few.

She would leave him alone. Let him return in his own good time. Hopefully he would be true to his word, and wouldn't stand her up on Saturday. Fingers crossed.

Nine

W hat happened with the Rogues, stayed with the Rogues.
What happened at Rock Creek Cove never happened.
Friday night, and Joe lowered himself onto a beach
chair on the banks of Rock Creek, a hidden inlet noto-
rious for skinny-dipping, naked neon Frisbee, and nude
water polo. Night crowded him. Tightened his breathing. Tiki pole lights flared, their orange and red flames
mirrored in the water. Inhibitions were left on the shore.
Eagerness and expectancy sent naked bodies into the cool
depths. Women shrieked, bounced, as the chill crept up
their thighs. Nipples puckered. The ballplayers claimed
"shrinkage." Laughter and teasing filled the air. A good
time—for all but him.

Joe took off his tennis shoes and socks, and let the rip-
pling waves and wet sand suck his toes. Water swelled
about his ankles, dampening the frayed hem on his jeans.
A missed throw by Jake Packer into the opponents' goal
smashed the shoreline. Splashing him. The ball floated
back into play, accompanied by giggles and profanity.

"Who is she, Zoo?" was asked of him. Impatiently.

One of the girls in his party posse passed him a beer.
Alyssa was hottest of his twelve groupies. Wavy dark hair,
exotic amber eyes, and a suggestive body. Men projected
their fantasies onto her. She sat beside him on a beach

blanket, her long legs curled beneath her. Her ample breasts and rounded ass nearly escaped her bikini. Tempting. Accessible. She was just waiting for him to unhook her top. To release the string ties at her hips. To get into the game. He had yet to make his move.

She rested her hand on his thigh, her fingertips straying toward his zipper. He took her hand, stilled her strokes. Asked, "Who's who, 'Lyssa?"

"The woman who's got you thinking about her when there's naked water polo being played in front of you."

He took a pull on his longneck Red Dog. "I'm watching." Half truth. He'd seen enough to know the score. "Three to one. Pax's team is ahead. Sam's side would be doing better if the guys kept their eyes on the ball instead of on Cady's breasts."

Incredible double Ds. A total turn-on for his buddies. Joe was certain that Sam Matthews was sweating bullets in the cold water. His teammate was interested in the brunette, but he hadn't acted on his attraction. Out of respect for Joe. Cady was part of his posse. Party girls he had personally selected. Babes who stuck by him. His teammates might come on to his girls, but they never took them home.

Wild Cady had recently written a children's book. She'd shyly shown it to him. An inner glimpse of her softer side. She had a big heart. A love for kids. She deserved a decent guy. She glanced at Sam as often as he looked at her. Their gazes locked, and they lost the next point. The ball dropped between them. Sam retrieved it. Homed again on Cady, indifferent to the outcome of the game.

Alyssa nudged Joe. "Why aren't you naked?"

"Why aren't you?"

She drew his hand to her mouth, deep-throated his middle finger. Swirled the tip. "I'm waiting for you."

It would be a long wait. His ass wasn't leaving the chair until he cleared his head and came to a decision. One that involved Stevie. She staggered him. Stuck on his mind. The fact that he liked her, sarcasm and all, shook him. She gave him a hard time. And a hard-on.

He was a man of raw sex appeal. He raised women's heartbeats. Stevie quickened his pulse. Gentle was new to him. Their practice photo-shoot kiss had nearly undone him. Soft and slow. She had wanted their kiss to continue. He'd heard it in her sigh. A significant longing. He'd put on the brakes. They had chemistry. A subsequent kiss with tongue and touching would've led to sex. Assuredly. He'd been a week without a woman and had been horny as hell, sporting a boner and blue balls. Not to his liking.

He wondered where Stevie would fit into his life. She was unique. Unbelievably gorgeous. Kind. Smart, too. A psychologist. That revelation had been mind-blowing, and, if he was honest with himself, impressive. Her career shouldn't have mattered to him, but it did. He had a history with school guidance counselors and referral therapists that brought back difficult times and dark memories. Professionals had judged, criticized, and picked him apart, pointing out his faults and mistakes. Assuming reasons as to why he acted out. They never had a positive word for him. He'd grown combative, punching his way through his teens.

His life gradually improved with age. Sex brought him release. Calmed him. Women came and went. No woman stayed in his bed or in his mind too long. Up until Stevie. She conceivably knew him better than he knew himself. Whether that was a good or a bad thing, he'd yet to resolve.

Joe leaned back in the chair, stared up at the sky. There were a few stars. No moon. He finished off his beer.

Alyssa offered him a second, but he shook his head. She raised an eyebrow questioningly. He cupped her chin with his palm, stroked his thumb over her lips. She nipped his wrist. Her gaze softened, expectant. She was ready to strip down and play water polo. He wasn't there yet. He had a question for her. "Who am I to you?" he asked.

She blinked. "A trick question?"

"No correct answer. Just be honest."

"You're my favorite Rogue."

"Mine, too," from Cady. Out of the water, she walked toward them, all shivering flesh and chattering teeth. She leaned over Joe, kissed him full on the mouth. Her nipples nearly poked out his eye. Alyssa tossed her a beach towel, which she wrapped around her full figure. The ends gapped at her breasts. Split between her thighs. "I like my party guy," she added.

Roz of the red hair and low, sexy voice, the tallest of his posse, joined them. She slipped on a short terry-cloth cover-up that looked like a bathrobe and barely concealed her butt. She grinned. "You're sex to me, dude. Pure sin."

"Mmm-hmm," the ladies hummed. Agreeing.

"We all love Chaos," Roz said of his tattoo.

"You're bar night to me," brown-eyed, athletic-bodied Bo told him. Beach towel–wrapped, she wiggled her ass onto his lap. Settled square on his groin. No stirring. His dick sat still.

The remainder of his posse soon circled him. He looked deeply into the eyes of each of the twelve. All sexually hot, and altogether confused. They'd never seen him this serious before. Anxiety and concern had them shuffling their bare feet, clasping their hands, and gnawing their bottom lips. Tossing their dampened hair. Tightening their towels.

"What if I wasn't a ballplayer?" he went on to ask. Curious. Needing to know.

"But you are," said Alyssa.

"What if I didn't drink? Didn't close down bars?" Seeking insight.

"Red Dog would lose their best customer," Cady said. "You bring business to the Lusty Oyster and the Blue Coconut."

"What if I was a lousy lover?"

"Impossible." A small smile from Roz. "You were born for sex."

"We're grateful," from Bo.

Their responses weren't what he'd hoped. There was no depth. Regardless, a smile curved his lips. He'd created his posse to party. Shallow as it seemed now. He'd elected them for their looks, their sexual impulses and freedom. Intellect had never been a factor. Their time together was all about him. They lived up to his expectations. Feeding his ego. No jealousy. He could take any one of these women to bed tonight. Two, even. They offered passion. Pleasure. Satisfaction guaranteed.

He held the thought. Turned it over in his mind, like a coin flip. Heads: posse sex. Tails: principled Stevie. He felt an uncharacteristic loyalty toward her. Which freaked him out a little. Stevie was a psychologist. He wanted more than a mind fuck. He wanted her body. To make love. All night long.

His inability to commit to the ladies sent all but Alyssa back into the water for a second round of water polo. Sam, Pax, and his other teammates welcomed them with whoops and cheers. The guys had physically adjusted to the crystal coolness. Chests puffed. Cocks stood proud.

'Lyssa rolled off her hips and onto her knees. She leaned her elbows on his thighs. Licked her lips. Met his gaze. "Don't you want me?"

"You're my go-to, babe." So often. *If* he was wanting a woman.

"I'm available now." She spread her hands over his groin. Unbuttoned his jeans. She stroked his tat, then finger-walked his happy trail. His dick twitched. His balls pulled tight. A purely physical reaction. Painful as hell.

No more. He covered her hand. Gritted out, "Can't, 'Lys."

Unrelenting, believing he just needed further convincing, she snuck her free hand inside his *Living Hard* T-shirt. She palmed across his ribs to his nipple. There, thumbed and teased.

She turned him on.

He turned her down.

He caught her wrist. Shook his head. "Not going to happen." He set her from him. Went on to button up his jeans. To straighten his shirt. To stand, towering over her.

He offered his hand, and she took it. He pulled her to her feet. They faced each other. He had nothing more to say, but his silence seemed to speak to her. Her gaze rounded. Her lips parted. "Oh, dude. *Really?* You've met someone special. Hard to believe."

For him, too.

"Are you breaking up with us?"

"Short weekend break only."

"I'm betting longer."

Groom for an afternoon wasn't a lifetime commitment. A couple hours max.

He'd be back. No man got caught up in make-believe.

Ten a.m. Saturday morning. Joe was still sleeping. Noise and voices now rose from the first floor, echoing upstairs. He groaned. What the hell? No man deserved to be wakened from a sex dream. Especially one in which he was just about to undress Stevie. She'd stood before him, eyes dark with desire. A blush of longing on her cheeks. Her lips plump, swollen from his kisses. He'd left her breathless. She'd left him bone-hard.

Sunshine sliced through his bedroom window, warming his face and prying his eyelids open. He blinked the room into focus. He'd returned to the Victorian on the morning side of midnight, after leaving his party posse at Rock Creek Cove. He had a key, and slipped quietly into the house, tiptoed up to his room. Not wanting to rouse Stevie, Turbo, and Etta. Dean Jensen had requested a weekend sleepover for his bulldog. To Turbo's delight. The two were now inseparable.

Rumor in the locker room registered Dean and Lori at Sandcastle. Their sunburns had faded. Dean had left the practice field for marathon sex at the hotel. There was an exhibition game on Sunday, and sex could drain a man if he wasn't careful. Dean would hit the field already played out. Advantage Joe.

He presently lay flat on his back, naked, alone. A scrunched-up pillow under his neck. The wrinkled top sheet wrapped his ankles. He scratched his belly. Balls. Jacked to a sitting position. Ran his tongue over his teeth. Dry mouth. Tooth brushing, a must. Which meant knocking on the bathroom door in case Stevie was inside, hopefully in a state of undress.

He drew on a pair of black boxer jocks—as decent as he was going to get. It was gifting time. He tucked her presents under his arm. Yellow panties and wedding thong. He knocked with purpose. Heard her gasp, and swore she jumped.

"Coming in," he warned as he turned the knob.

"Stay out," she mumbled.

"Already inside." He found her at the sink, toothbrush

in hand, toothpaste on her upper lip. He liked the view. She wasn't naked, but her short gown dipped low over her breasts and flashed her ass. Cute bare feet. Nice.

Her gaze flicked over his face, chest, held on his Under Armour. A brand he endorsed. He bulged. Significantly. Unabashedly.

She held up her hand, palm out. "My time, not yours."

"Bad breath. Share the sink."

"Don't breathe on me."

He balanced the gift boxes on the corner of the countertop. Crowded her. She nearly spit on his hand. On purpose.

He stretched around her, located his Sonicare electric toothbrush in the medicine cabinet. Added Crest. "Grumpy, babe? I thought you were a morning person."

"I like mornings," she said. "However, two in the bathroom is one too many."

She rinsed her mouth, hung up her toothbrush, and twisted away from the sink. She grabbed her bathrobe off a hook, clutched it to her chest. "I should've locked the door," she muttered as she struggled into her robe. Jamming her arms through the sleeves. She tied the sash. Unevenly. She'd yet to request that he put on pants. He remained in his boxer jocks.

"But you didn't." Obviously.

"I didn't think you were home."

"I got home earlier than planned," he told her. "I didn't want to wake you when I came in, so I didn't shower." The pipes rumbled. The vintage plumbing needed an overhaul.

"Weren't you squeaky-clean after water polo?"

Word had spread. She was aware of last night's activities. If he'd chosen to participate. "Salt water, babe."

"You're itchy?"

"I never got wet."

His response obviously confused her. She crossed her arms over her chest, splitting the hem over her legs. Sexy thigh gap. "I'd have thought you—" She hesitated.

"What?"

"Would've been—"

"The first wearing only a smile."

"You, or someone from your posse." He heard the underlying hurt in her voice. Surprising, but there. She cared.

"Jealous, Stewie?" he guessed.

"Get over yourself, Joey."

"I'd rather get over you."

She pulled a face.

He winked at her in the mirror.

He switched on his toothbrush; it buzzed. He eyed her reflection as he cleaned his teeth. Rinsed. He replaced the Sonicare in the cabinet. Next gargled with Scope. He shifted his stance and saw her gaze slip from the back of his head, across his shoulders, down his back, then holding on his ass. She softly sighed, and her shoulders sagged. She liked what she saw, he was certain. A body bonus for him.

He eased around, looked her in the eyes. Honesty filled his words. "Naked water polo can get wild, and a helluva lot of fun. I could've stripped, screwed. Had a sleepover." She flinched. "But a groom doesn't cheat on his bride the night before his wedding shoot."

"So you didn't—" There was an expectant pause.

He shook his head. "Kept it in my pants."

"Difficult for you?"

"A first for me."

Her lips parted, her expression soft, appreciative, before reality reminded her, "We have no commitments."

"Not a single one," he agreed. "Marriage isn't my thing. This photo spread is as real as it gets for me."

"Me . . . too."

That he didn't believe for a second. "I can see you married with a couple of kids."

"Wish I had your vision."

He could imagine her as a wife. A mother. Chasing after kids and Turbo. *Turbo?* His dog. The thought tightened his chest. He massaged his hand over his heart. Loosened the pressure there.

She looked away from him, her gaze lighting on the presents on the countertop. Time for gift-giving. He handed her the floral-wrapped box with the satin bow and berry potpourri.

Her breath caught. "What's this?"

"A replacement."

"For what?"

"The Turbo mishap."

"You bought me panties?" Her tone was disbelieving.

"One pair for everyday; another for formal wear."

No ripping off the paper. She took her time, savoring the presentation. Her fingers trembled as she carefully freed the bow and the dried berries. Then removed the flowered paper, smoothing out the creases before setting it aside. She lifted the box top, spread the tissue, and stared at the panties. Stared without a word.

"I guessed your size," he admitted. "The color's all you." Natural blond.

She blushed. Her response was embarrassed, but yet polite. "Thank you."

"Try them on, see if they fit."

"I'm not modeling them for you."

He passed her his second gift. "Bridal."

She set the opened box on a small pink marble vanity table. "*How* bridal?" she asked.

"To be worn with our blue garter."

★　★　★

Their garter. Stevie's stomach filled with butterflies when she noticed the discreet gold oval sticker peeking beneath the gauze ribbon. Délicieux. Intimate apparel. Joe's eyes undressed her without taking her clothes off. Apprehension swelled her chest. She fingered the folded ends of the silver foil, afraid to open the box.

"What's inside doesn't bite," he teased her.

Joe, however, did. She self-consciously touched her fingers to her neck, recalled his hickey. The memory stuck with her, as fresh now as when he'd nipped her. Nerves had her tearing a corner of the foil. The paper was ruined. Emotion overwhelmed her. Tears filled her eyes. She felt ridiculous.

He reached out to her. "Let me help you."

"I can do it," she insisted.

"I can do it better." He rid the box of the foil.

She lifted the lid. Crystals sparkled on white satin. "A bridal thong." Her whispered words were barely audible. She'd never seen anything so beautiful. So innocent. So sexy. She read the designer label out loud: *"Kiss the Bride."*

And Joe did. He angled in, around the box, set on kissing her. The stubble on his jaw scraped her cheek. He stared deeply into her eyes and his blue eyes darkened. Dilated.

Gentle and hesitant was a turn-on.

The unexpected, raw emotion on his face switched her inside out.

No tentative touch of his lips this time. He fully mated with her mouth. Parting her lips, touching her tongue, stealing her breath. He knew what he was doing. He consumed her senses. She was being kissed by the best. They tasted each other. Fusing toothpastes. His mint. Hers cinnamon.

More. She rose on tiptoe, leaned closer. Her shoulders pressed his chest. Her satin and softness submitted to his muscle and strength. The primitive beat of his heart aroused her own pulse. Quickening sensations. Tingling. Temptation. Willingness. Rays of desire. Taken into him, without his touching her.

The fantasy of a wedding settled deep in her soul. Too deep. There was nothing real about this day. Joe had initially agreed to the photo shoot in exchange for dog care and a place to live. A trade that benefited them both. Still, she embraced their pretend kisses with her entire being. Enjoying the man.

He tilted his head, grinned down on her. "I like your mouth."

She touched her mouth with her fingertips. "You took advantage," she accused.

"Your lips said differently."

"How so?"

"They parted for me."

That they had. There was no denying it. "Our kiss comes at the end of the shoot. If then."

"Then and there on the stairs."

She'd been warned. He eased back, allowing them air. She inhaled deeply. He expelled slowly. The gift box and dangling bridal thong were now crushed between them. Cardboard corners jabbed them both, marking his naked abdomen and indenting her hip where the robe parted.

He lifted the thong with one finger, held it up to the light. The crystals sparked prisms as bright and colorful as rainbow confetti. It was a fairy-tale garment. Very romantic.

His gaze lowered to her hips. Held. "Thong should fit."

"It will." He was a man of many women, and had easily guessed her size. She wondered how many others had received gifts of lingerie from Joe Zooker. Perhaps a camisole or a teddy. Flowered nipple petals.

He tipped up her chin with a finger, said, "You have

a very expressive face." He read her mind. "I've bought ladies rounds of drinks at the bar, picked up dinner tabs, and purchased passes on booze cruises. I've shopped for lingerie, I'm not going to lie. But you're my first bridal thong." He handed it to her.

She believed him. Her concern was ridiculous. She had no ties to the man. Other than the fact that he was the groom in her wedding shoot. For one afternoon.

"What time does the shoot start?" he asked her.

"Officially at one." It was eleven now. "The creative director, photographer, and staff will arrive early."

"Turbo and I are headed out. Jogging. Where is he?"

"In the backyard with Etta. Take her, too. The bull-dog's here all weekend. The two are inseparable."

"Turbo and I have our own pace. We race. Hope she can keep up."

"Your dog will walk beside her if she can't."

He ran one hand down his face. "Puppy love."

"Could be worse."

"How so?"

"He could still be incorrigible. Rough and rowdy. He's manageable now. She's calmed him."

"Broken his spirit."

"He surrendered on his own."

"Hard to imagine."

"Watch them together. See for yourself. Take their leashes. Hers is pink."

"Pink." He rolled his eyes. Scratched his belly. It was flat, muscled. "I'll shower after our run. Don't panic. We'll be back in plenty of time. What's happening with you?"

"I'm tied up here. A makeup artist from the magazine will arrive any minute."

"I like you natural."

"The camera won't. I need a little color."

His grin came slow, sinful. "I'll stand behind you on the

staircase. Press against you. Whisper something naughty in your ear. So wicked you'll blush. Bright eyes, pink cheeks."

"Behave yourself, Joe."

"I've promised best behavior."

Joe's best behavior was still controlled chaos. "A bridal shop assistant follows makeup to help me into my gown."

"I could've done that for you."

"The back of the gown has forty tiny pearl buttons."

"I have fingers."

"The assistant is bringing a buttonhook. Works faster."

"Never doubt the speed of my fingers."

No doubt. No debate. He played ball. Sharp reflexes. Flexible fingers. Which would wander beyond the buttons. She couldn't take that chance. He was six feet, four inches of foreplay. His kiss seduced. The gift of the panties was a sensual promise. He still stood so close he boxed her between his body and the door. Yellow bikini and bridal thong in hand, she half-turned, softly said, "Thank you, Joe. I needed you today."

"What if I need you tonight?"

Sex snuck between them. Swelled. A hot flirtation. Common sense spoke for her. "We can't follow a pretend wedding with an actual honeymoon."

"It's our sexual reality."

"I thought your life was 'all about baseball.'"

"It is, starting with the exhibition game tomorrow. Tonight, it's all about us."

A night with this man would be a commitment for her, a one-night stand for him. Memorable, but not practical. She left the bathroom with sex heavy on her mind.

"The bride has gone to the dogs," quipped Liza, the creative director of the *I Do* magazine wedding shoot. Photographer Paige, a lighting technician, and Aronson, the dog handler, nodded their agreement. "The movie-wide staircase provides the perfect backdrop. Very *Gone with the Wind*. The bride is positioned perfectly. We just need some minor rearranging of the dogs." Pause. "No groom."

Of which Stevie was aware. Joe had yet to return. Ninety minutes was a long run. Unless he'd run away from her, and kept on going.

"He'll show," she promised Liza.

A tight smile from the director. "Soon, dear. We're on a tight schedule. Two hours. Sadly we can't use a male model, as this spread has been billed as an engaged couple's shoot. I'd hate to cancel and have to draw another winner."

Stevie would hate to have that happen, too. She presently stood halfway up the stairs. Her off-the-shoulder lace and satin gown fit tight across her breasts, pinched her waist, and shimmered over her hips. Beneath, the thong creased her butt. Crystal floss. The blue garter hugged her thigh. She peered beneath the gauze of her rhinestone circlet veil. Her long train was fanned out behind her, nearly reaching the second-story landing. She shifted on her five-inch glass fairy-tale heels. Narrow width. Squashed pinkie toes. She'd given up comfort for glamour.

Eight dogs surrounded her. Some higher, some lower on the flight of steps. All sizes. All breeds. All motionless. Almost surreal. Additional owners and their pets were gathered in the entry hall, forming two lines. Obedient canines were ready to hit their spot and pose.

Stevie listened as Liza stood away from her crew to take in the scene. The director hung back, hands on designer jeans–clad hips, and sighed as if she was heavily burdened. Her gaze narrowed. Her brow creased. Her lips pinched. Absolute silence. Stevie herself held her breath, until Liza snapped her fingers, and the dog trainer appeared by her side. Leashes circled his wrist. "The white standard poodle fades into the wedding gown," she noted. "Move Princess Pom-Pom two steps higher." Aronson was quick to act.

Stevie thought the poodle might outshine her, as Pom-Pom was wearing a pink rhinestone tiara and necklace. The dog's toenails were painted metallic silver. Shiny.

"What do you think, Paige?" Liza asked the photographer.

Paige crossed to the camera that was mounted on a tripod in the middle of the hallway. The lighting technician hovered close. She bent, studied the layout, taking significant time to check the shot. She eventually straightened, rubbed her lower back, and said, "I'd like to change out the Newfoundland and the mastiff on the landing, holding the corners of the train. They slobber, pant, and are too 'weighty'"—she used finger quotes—"making the photo top-heavy."

Aronson took the stairs and leashed the big boys. They lumbered down and were handed to their disappointed owners.

"Sleek dogs up top, Aro," Liza instructed the handler. "Two trained not to tug or tear lace."

"The Blue Ridge greyhounds," Aronson called out. "Heel," he commanded as he bounded up the stairs. His "sit and stay" staged the dogs. Descending, he suggested, "We'll have them pick up the train at the last second."

"A runaway," Paige called out.

Aronson went after a restless Jack Russell. The dog bounced up the steps. A minor interruption. Quickly suppressed.

Stevie felt like a mannequin. The dogs were like statues.

The director glanced at her watch. Tapped her foot. Her tone was sharp as she said, "Your groom—"

"Has arrived," Joe loudly announced from the front

door. Sweaty, winded, wild-eyed, he kicked it wide. Turbo shot through. Joe came in more slowly. He held Etta in his arms, her leash wrapped around his arm. He set down the fifty-pound bulldog, adjusted his T-shirt and gym shorts. Caught his breath, then took in the scene. Stevie wanted nothing more than to walk down and meet him. To hug him. The bridal assistant hovered on the balcony above. Jana had fidgeted and formed the gown into perfect angles. She'd ordered Stevie not to move an inch. Stiffness invaded her every muscle. Shallow breathing squeezed her lungs.

"Sorry we're late," Joe apologized at large. "I left on a run two hours ago. Back roads. We started at a good pace, reached our turnaround point, but then Etta gave out. She lay down. Stayed down. I couldn't coax her up. Neither could my dog, Turbo. No iPhone to call for a ride. I had to carry her back. I got here as soon as I could. Would have been sooner, if she hadn't gotten wiggly."

The creative director crossed over to him. She gave him the once-over, her look long and lingering. Recognition was in her eyes. She politely introduced herself, "Joe Zooker, I'm Liza. You were worth the wait. We'll give you some time to clean up."

"Quick shower, shave—"

"Leave the scruff," Liza insisted. "The look of the spread is coming clear to me. This shoot will play up the contrast between you and Stevie. Your bride's as beautiful and as soft as her satin gown. You're . . . earthy. Rugged. Muscled." She looked to her photographer. "No tux on this man. He can wear his own clothes. Sports coat, T-shirt, and jeans. Boots."

"I like," Paige approved. "The magazine has a wide circulation and it's known for its creative bridal shoots. Last month's beach-themed spread got tons of attention. The bridal party was staged on the coast against an approaching thunderstorm. Wind, and an unexpected waterspout, literally blew everyone away."

Joe headed upstairs. Turbo charged beside him. Etta dragged herself up, too. He stopped on the stair next to Stevie. Lifted her veil, despite Jana's indrawn breath. Her total disapproval was obvious.

"You made it," Stevie whispered. Boneless in her relief.

He winked at her. Then lightly kissed her lips. Jana cleared her throat. Censure. Which Joe ignored. He cut his gaze to Etta. "Turbo's girl quit on us. Next time we'll go a shorter distance."

"'Next time'?" she had to ask.

"Turbo wanted nothing to do with me," he admitted. "He ran beside Etta, until she stopped. Then he kept jumping on me when I picked her up, afraid I was taking her away from him."

"Separation anxiety."

He grinned then. "I felt anxious being away from you."

From the corner of her eye, she noticed Liza pacing the hallway. The lady was impatient. "Get going, get ready. I'm tired of standing. Save me from locked knees."

A second quick kiss. "I'm saving you for later," he said, and was gone.

Leaving her anxious. He shook her to her core. Her hands trembled. She clasped them before her. Her mind was reluctant; her heart ready. She'd thought only of him during her makeup session and fitting. Resolving that sex with Joe would be the perfect ending to an amazing day. As long as she could let him go afterward without questions or pain.

Her aunt Twyla entered through the back door. She leaned her crutches against the wall and eased down on a dog bone–shaped bench. She waved at Stevie. Stevie gave her a short nod, not wanting to muss her veil.

Joe returned, hair tied back, looking undeniably sexy in a navy sports jacket, white T-shirt beneath, scripted with *I Do You*. Liza was quick to suggest he pull the button side of his coat over the word *You*. He obliged. *I Do* fit the magazine's theme. He was himself in ladder-ripped jeans and worn boots.

Jada held up her makeup kit. "Powder, blush on the man?"

Joe curled his lip. Resistant.

Liza shook her head. "His hard face, broken nose, craggy cheeks appeal. He's a guy's groom, and a girl's perfect wedding night."

Joe started down the staircase. "Where do you want me?"

"The steps are wide. Snug in behind Stevie," Liza requested. "Let's show oneness on your wedding day."

Joe got in place. He defined closeness. His groin aligned with her bottom. Nearer still, he parted her legs with his knee, without disturbing the flow of her gown. The contact was sexual and erotic. His knee fit her thigh gap. Stevie shivered, nearly fell off the step. He splayed his wide hand over her hip, steadying her. She laced her fingers with his. More contrast: his calluses; her lotion-soft skin.

Turbo and Etta appeared suddenly, bounding down the stairs. Turbo sniffed nearly every dog, rousing them. The canine statues came alive, arching their backs and stretching.

"Stop!" Aronson yelled at Turbo. "You've disrupted the gallery." Leash in hand, he went for the rottie.

Joe eyed the handler sharply. "Don't touch my dog," he warned, deadly soft and dangerous.

The trainer drew back. "He's messed up the shoot."

"Turbo's being a dog," said Joe. "This whole scene sucks. Animal lovers have their pets at weddings. Dogs are as important as any other guests. They shouldn't be posed. Obedience shouldn't be a prerequisite. It's not natural. They should be barking, tails wagging, as happy as the couple is."

Aronson was horrified.

The lighting technician blinked.

The photographer looked piqued.

The creative director was stunned silent.

Stevie smiled to herself. Joe called it as he saw it. Fine by her. She felt stiff, like a plastic cake topper. She'd want to be relaxed and in love on her own wedding day. She squeezed his hand, approving his comments. Encouraged, his fingers strayed along her hip, discreetly feeling for the outline of her thong. Easily found. She sensed his smile at the back of her neck. Felt his breathing deepen.

"Garter?" for her ears only.

"Left thigh."

Low, animalistic growl.

Heightened color on her cheeks.

Liza soon motioned to Paige. Their heads went together. Discussion ensued. Until Liza tapped her fingertips on her lips and stared into space. Envisioning.

Her decision came on an exhaled breath. One that appeared difficult to admit. "Cancel the dramatic layout," she said to Paige. She looked up at Joe and said, "We'll title the new layout 'Woof, Woof Wedding.' Not quite what I'd envisioned, but eye-catching." Pause. "We'll see how it plays out."

Kudos to the director, Stevie thought. The idea hadn't been hers, but it was a great one. Joe had imagination. He'd put the whole shoot in perspective. He brought real life to an imaginary scene.

"No restrictions," she told the dog trainer.

"Free." Aronson moved among the dogs, putting them at ease. They wiggled, barked, then dropped and flopped where they were the most comfortable. There was no order. No pretense. A dappled dachshund rolled over, paws up, near the bride's glass slippers. Fell asleep with soft snores.

Aronson's jaw clenched when Turbo parked himself next to Joe. Etta sat, too. "They're not contracted for the shoot," he complained. "We're only using dogs from my obedience school."

"Turbo's with me. Etta's with him," Joe stated.

"I'll need releases on both dogs," said Liza. She sent the lighting technician up the stairs with the paperwork. Joe signed, his signature unreadable. "Magazine offers a flat fifty dollars. Checks payable to the owners."

"*I Do* can be added to your dog's résumé, should he continue doing shoots," added the technician. "Dog food companies, pet toys, and miscellaneous products are always holding auditions. Aronson's looking for a new furry face to represent his obedience school."

Turbo barked.

The trainer choked on the thought.

The photographer eyed each dog with a practiced eye. She commented to Liza, "Let's add the Shar-Pei puppy. Wrinkles would be a nice contrast to the smooth drape of the gown. The red Irish setter is distinctive. The black Scottish terrier. Interesting face. The hair is lightly trimmed and brushed forward."

The creative director smiled, pleased. "You'll be shooting in color, black-and-white, and later adding Photoshop sepia tones for an antique look. The magazine editor can decide which works best."

Aronson unleashed the chosen dogs, and they scampered up the steps, choosing their spots and settling.

"Finalizing," from Liza. She pointed to Jana in makeup. "Give Stevie her bouquet." Yellow roses and baby's breath. "The couple's just gotten married—we need wedding bands." Two gold rings were provided. Loose on Stevie's finger, tight on Joe's. "Toss white rose petals on the stair-case." The floral scent was fresh and pure. Turbo bit a petal. Spit it out.

Paige got behind her camera. Gentle lighting set the mood, making the scene romantic, yet natural. "Talk, joke, smile, kiss, fool around," she told them. "A feature editor will call in a day or two and set up an interview. She'll cover the fashion and human-interest angles."

Joe breathed near her ear. "I like interviews."

"You like talking about yourself."

"I'm interesting."

"To you."

They smiled easily for the first formal photographs. A few were taken straight-faced. Up until he poked her in the ribs. Startled, she gasped, giggled.

She playfully pinched his thigh. Felt his muscle flex.

He lifted one side of her veil. Kissed her on the neck.

She angled her head back against his shoulder. Closed her eyes, lost.

He next brought her hand to his lips, nuzzled her palm. His facial scruff tickled. More smiles.

She teased him, too. Squeezing his hidden knee between her thighs. Heat and moaning from the man. He raised his knee, almost to her thong. She shifted, and her hip brushed his groin. He groaned low in his throat.

Liza gave them a thumbs-up. "Love the chemistry. *More.*"

Joe eased to her side, turned her to face him. He raised her veil in heart-racing foreplay. He cupped one cheek, went in for a kiss. So tender, she softened to him. Her knees went weak. His arm circled her waist, secured her to him. They grafted themselves to each other, as close as humanly possible. Her lace and satin gown embraced his sports coat and jeans. Her glass slippers kissed the steel toes of his scuffed boots.

"You getting this?" Liza asked the photographer. Her words reached the couple. Super-excited.

"Oh . . . yeah," replied Paige. "They are hot."

Joe teased the camera. He broke their kiss, then slid his hand over her hip, along her thigh. She eyed him questioningly. His purpose soon became clear. He carefully grasped her gown with two fingers, drew it up her calf, beyond her knee. High on her thigh. Flashed her blue garter.

Stevie blushed.

Joe was all sinful satisfaction.

The creative director clapped.

The lighting director cheered.

The photographer put her hand over her heart. Sighed.

Turbo howled. Joe, too. Not surprising. He threw back his head, his own howl raw, carnal male. Barking ensued. Even prissy Princess Pom-Pom yipped. Dogs began wagging, moving about, and becoming playful.

"A few more shots," called out Liza.

Joe had his own agenda. He skillfully removed her circlet veil and placed it on Etta's head, hooking it behind the bulldog's ears. Turbo immediately sniffed the gauze. Etta cocked her head. Stevie swore she smiled.

Unexpected, yet as romantic as a fairy tale, Joe scooped her in his arms, held her high on his chest. His gaze held hers. "We're done here, babe."

Fine by her. She wrapped her arms about his shoulders, buried her face in his neck. Breathed in the man. Earthy arousal. She trembled. Lost a glass slipper on the stairs.

"Catch it!" the director shouted.

"Got it," from the photographer.

Joe took the steps easily. He paused on the landing, turned toward the camera with a wicked victory smile. He walked along the balcony toward her bedroom. The door was cracked, and he kicked it open.

The bridal assistant hurried toward them. "I'm here to assist Stevie out of the gown," she said anxiously.

"I've got it covered," from Joe.

"Sir, there are dozens of pearl buttons. Difficult to undo."

"Bill me for the gown," said Joe, as he carried Stevie over the threshold. "I'll undress her my way."

Ten

Stevie's heart beat so fast she could barely catch her breath. "Your way?" She recalled his comment on the boardwalk, during the bridal fashion show. *No man wasted time undressing his bride on their wedding night. He'd rip and pop the pearls.* "You're not really going to tear the back of my gown, are you?" she asked once Joe shoved the door closed with his boot. Then locked it behind them.

He held her tightly against his chest. She clutched her bridal bouquet with one hand. Clenched his shoulder with the other. Her breast pressed his forearm, soft and full. The arc of her left hip molded his groin. His desire was evident. His chin brushed her cheek. "I want you bad, babe. No row of pearl buttons will stand in my way."

Stevie shivered. No man had ever wanted her badly enough to strip off her clothes that way. The word *thrilling* came to mind. Joe would pop the tiny buttons, scrap the fabric, and fulfill her fantasy. If given her consent. The gown was exquisite. Ruining it would be outlandish. Disrespectful to the designer. She couldn't live with herself. Even if he had made the purchase.

"Take it slow," she appealed softly. She wanted their moments to last. To make the ultimate memory.

"I'm in no hurry," he assured her. "I can stretch us out."

A very long honeymoon.

Pretend vanished beneath the reality of sex.

He released her then, set her down gently. A trail of lace and satin sliding over the heavier fabric of his sports jacket and torn jeans. She stood on the brown, gold, and blue braided rug, tipping slightly from the loss of one glass slipper.

Her bedroom walls boxed them together. Intimately. The space was modest. The armoire door stood ajar, revealing her clothes on hangers. She'd moved in with only one suitcase. Her plans had been to support her aunt's recovery, lasting no more than six weeks. Sunshine slatted through the indoor-style Victorian shutters. A wall sconce shed light on a round marble-topped table near the cane rocker. A silver tray offered gourmet cupcakes and an iced bottle of Chateau De Fleur, a nonalcoholic champagne, to the couple. Two crystal flutes stood ready.

She crossed to the table, put down her bouquet, slipped off her pearl bracelet. It had been borrowed from Lori. Joe came up behind her. "From Twyla," he read over her shoulder. "*Celebrate your magazine shoot. I'll keep a watchful eye on Turbo and Etta.*" He kissed her behind the ear. "Sweet celebration."

"She knows I love cupcakes," Stevie confessed. "My mother baked them for all occasions, happy or sad. Cupcakes made me feel good."

"I'm better than a cupcake."

"These are rich and decadent."

"I have fewer calories."

He made her smile. She turned, faced him. Met his gaze. Seconds were magnified as each memorized the impact of the moment. Neither spoke. Neither looked away.

It was startling. Unnerving. And totally unforgettable.

Time slowed. He slipped his hands into her hair, held her still. Her scalp tingled. He looked deep into her eyes, seeking her soul. His expression suddenly turned serious.

She sensed something was on his mind, bothering him. He needed to get it off his chest. His voice was rough, unsure, when he asked, "How do you see me, Stevie? As a woman, not as a shrink."

His question surprised her. Sex took second place to her answer. It seemed so important to him. She weighed each word. Spoke from her heart. "I like you, Joe. More than you might expect. You pursued me when I pushed you away. We're together now. I wouldn't sleep with a man I didn't care about."

She touched her fingertips to his cheek. Affectionately. "You've come into your own in baseball, but you have yet to find yourself. You party, enjoy women. I separate what you do from who you truly are. A person is often defined by a few moments of existence, but that's not the totality of it. We all have room to grow, to claim our best. You're strong, driven, and generous. Decent. Your future will forgive your past. You'll pass the test of life."

Her words sank in. For the first time, he felt he was enough. He took her hand, kissed her palm. "I've blamed my parents for my childhood, which was complicated, misguided, confusing. My dad cheated on my mom. She had her own affairs. They were seldom around. When my old man was home, my mother wasn't. No clean clothes. No meal on the table. He would get mad, turn mean. Punch the walls and me. My brother and I fell through the cracks of our family. We have our own bond. Based on survival." Long pause. "My parents turned me off of relationships."

His admission touched her, saddened her a little. "Relationships are always risky." She was honest. "Not everyone's meant to marry."

"This from a woman with a wedding band on her finger."

"My ring's loose. Yours is pinching."

He glanced at his hand. The gold band indented his skin. "A little tight." But he didn't remove it. "You like me, and I like you. Want to fool around?"

She looked at the brass bed. It was made up with white cotton sheets and pillowcases. A down comforter for cooler nights. Three thirty ticked on the bedside clock. "It's the middle of the afternoon." She sounded silly. Virginal. She'd had lovers. But they were few compared to Joe. She wasn't "party posse" hot. Daylight shone on her insecurities. Her imperfections. Brightened her self-doubt.

"Sex doesn't tell time, sweetheart. We're now."

She drew a breath. "Now . . ."

"Want me?"

"Want you."

She sensed the shift of his energy, how it tangibly heightened. All doubt dissolved. Her heart pounded, and anticipation took hold. She didn't care how many women had come before her; she was his, for their honeymoon.

Their lips met. A light-as-air kiss. Gentle for a rough man. Tilting his head left, then right, he took her mouth from both angles, in a caress that was intimate and prolonged. Thorough. A kiss born of warmth and promised pleasure. The penetration of his tongue was slow, then fast. Raking the roof of her mouth. Thrusting deeper. A hint of urgency. Amped-up hunger. The kiss went on and on. Until they separated, to slow things down. To catch their breath.

Her mouth felt swollen, bruised. Her cheek, whisker-burned. Her smile was tentative. His grin X-rated. Her entire body blushed. His dark gaze stripped off her wedding gown and pulled down her panties. She'd never felt so naked while still being dressed. She was certain he could bring her to orgasm with just a look.

She slipped off her glass high heel. Stood barefoot. He turned her away from him. A man with big, callused hands and deft fingers, he had her unbuttoned faster than the bridal assistant had button-hooked her into the gown. He spread the material. Air tickled her bare back. He kissed along one shoulder, a nip, a flick of his tongue. Teasing. Arousing. He traced a finger down her spine, exploring, from the base of her neck to the dimples just above the waistband on her thong. Skin-hot deliciousness.

He brought her back to face him. He traced the heart-shaped neckline on her bodice. His thumbs dipped beneath the lace. A delicate built-in shelf bra supported her breasts. A lowering of satin, and he freed her. Her nipples puckered. He drew the gown to her belly. Released it. The dress drifted over her hips like a dream, down her legs, pooled at her feet. She stood exposed and vulnerable. In only her garter and thong. She'd folded, tucked, her aunt's vintage linen handkerchief beneath her garter. Something old. She plucked it, placed it on the table.

Joe stared so long, she thought to cover herself. He grasped her hands before she could do so. "Let me look at you." His voice was deep, raw. "Damn, you're gorgeous. You do it for me, woman."

Relief warmed her belly. Her anxieties vanished.

He squeezed her fingers. "My turn. Bare me."

She wanted to seduce him, to turn him on, as he had with her. She rose on tiptoe, claimed him. Still it took two tries to work the sports jacket over his wide shoulders. Even then the coat caught on one elbow. Dangled, before it dropped.

She bit down on her bottom lip. Worried. Apologized, "I'm not very good at this." She was certain his usual lovers could strip his clothes off with one swipe.

He stroked her cheek, calming her. "It's our first time together. You're doing just fine. Exhale."

She breathed a little easier. Steadier now, she worked on his T-shirt. She splayed her hands beneath the hem and pushed up. Eyeing his navel, the delineation of his ribs. He was even more muscular than she'd expected. Totally ripped. Curly brown hair dusted his well-developed chest. His skin was tan, taut. Her fingernails skimmed his pecs, lightly scoring hardened male nipples. He lost the shirt with her tug over his head. He shook out his hair. She loved the longer length. Total rogue.

He kicked off his boots. Got out of his socks. She concentrated on his jeans. No belt. She covered the ridge that ran the length of his zipper. His sex strained against her palm. Unsnapping, unzipping, she rid him of his Levi's. Boxer briefs came next. His hellhound tattoo appeared. Controlled Chaos.

Joe stood tall, all sculpted shoulders and killer abs. His legs stretched long. His feet large. He sported a major erection. A man in his prime. His body should be illegal. She admired him fully.

He bent, located his wallet in the back pocket of his jeans. Removed condoms, which he tossed on the bedside table. Good aim. The silver foil gleamed against the dark wood. Taking her in his arms, he walked her backward to the bed. She melted into him. His body betrayed telltale desire. The back of her knees touched the brass frame, and he laid her down on the mattress. He came after her, rolled atop her, then rocked back on his knees. He took her hip bones between his broad hands and pulled her toward him. A slow slide of her bottom on cool cotton sheets toward a red-hot man. The tips of his fingers slid down, tripping lightly across the crystal band of her thong. Easing his thumbs beneath the elastic, he stripped it down. The caress of silk, as soft as her sigh.

He eyed her thigh. "Garter stays."

She silently consented.

He kissed his way up her body. A man in need of a sexual fix only she could provide. He went for the most sensitive areas first. Licking his way up her inner thigh. Kissing her where she was most vulnerable. Her thighs flexed. A moan escaped. Then came the touching. So much touching. His hand moved within the shadows of her thighs. Stroking. He found her wet.

His fingers slid over and inside her. Desire consumed. Her hips rocked, and her stomach fluttered. Joe pressed his mouth to those flutters, kissing her belly. Tonguing her navel. Scraping his teeth over one hip. Her hips came off the mattress. She arched her back. Her body was sensitized. She longed. Craved. Climbed.

He palmed her breasts. Took her nipple in his mouth, rolled it with his tongue. His body heat nestled into her cleavage. He nipped the pulse point at the base of her throat. Nuzzled her neck and ear. His scruff was sandpaper sexy.

Foreplay was as arousing as a climax. She wanted to fit into his skin. Wanted the oneness only lovers experienced. He reached for a condom. Tore the foil, protected them. His legs pushed her own farther apart. He braced on his elbows, looked down on her. She loved the hard, heavy feel of him. Concern creased his brow. His mouth compressed. "You ready for me?" he asked.

"Been ready since you said, 'Hot, sweetheart,' regarding my garter on the boardwalk."

"You remember my words?" Amazement filled his voice.

"Along with your smile and your attitude."

"You were such a smart-ass, Stewie."

"I needed to keep you at arm's length, Joey."

He centered his groin at her sweet spot. Penetrated her slowly. A slide all the way to his hilt. "No arm's length now."

His body seemed larger than life. She bonded to his maleness. A commingling of warmth. A compression of flesh. They fit perfectly, an intimate pairing of hard planes and soft curves. Pleasure pulsed from her breasts to her belly and between her thighs—pure, raw, and endless. She was lost in him.

He moved—deep, circular motions that changed the angles of each thrust. The friction of their bodies grew desperate. Greedy. He demanded her response. Her nails dug into his back, scored his skin. Her thighs tightened on his hips. Her entire body throbbed.

Tension strained his every muscle. Sex on the edge. The mad *thump* of her heart matched his own. The muscles in his chest contracted. Tension spiraled in her belly. She could feel his body lock, jerk, at the exact moment she spun out. They climaxed together. Lights brightened, then burst behind her eyelids. She surrendered to a thousand pulsing nerves.

Time stalled, and a slow meltdown followed. He relaxed atop her. She welcomed his weight. They lacked the energy to roll apart and reveled in the ardent tangle of arms and legs, the remnants of pleasure. She hugged him with what little strength she had left. He remained hard within her. A solid length.

He eventually pulled out, kicked off the bed, and discarded his condom. He sheathed himself again. He was back on her in a heartbeat. "I want you again."

"I want a cupcake."

"Over me?" His expression looked pained.

"Persuade me to wait."

"I'll convince you."

He swayed her. Introducing her to his inner wild man, uncontrolled and aggressive. Tenderness gave way to lust. They rolled about, returned to the middle of the bed. Tucking into each other. Their hips bumped. Ground. He accidentally kneed her inner thigh, which was sure to bruise. Her elbow jabbed his abdomen. Brick-hard.

Mouths joined, and their tongues mated as fiercely as their bodies. She lost her breath and her inhibitions. She fell in with his fast and fearless foreplay. Hot kisses and hotter hands. His breath beat against her neck, moist as he nipped her chin, licked the base of her throat.

She bit his lip, and his dick bumped her belly. Overheated, her pulse ramped up, and her hips rocked. His fingers fanned out over her pelvic bone. He sought her readiness. He found her wet, slick, and open to him.

He streamlined inside her. His muscles flexed. His thighs pumped. He generated an incendiary passion that spiked her orgasm. A bolt of white heat ricocheted off him and into her. She was suddenly there. So swift and encompassing, she shattered a second time. Indescribable spasms. Intense satisfaction. He thrust a final time, growled, came hard. Chaos howled.

Spent and exhausted, he left her to rid himself of the condom. She rolled onto her side. In the afterglow, his large body framed her own. They spooned. He held her for a long, long time.

The cupcakes called to her. She finally stretched. Her body was languid. Her legs weak. She carefully eased off the bed. Slipped on her thong, despite his eye roll because he'd just seen and touched her everywhere.

She left him sprawled naked on her sheets with two pillows propped behind his head. A contrast of tan skin, ripcord muscle, and wicked grin against pure white cotton.

She reached the table, offered, "Cupcake?"

"I'll have a bite of yours."

She'd seen him eat. His bites were huge. "I want a whole one."

"No sharing?"

"Not when it comes to my favorite dessert."

"Choose one, and bring me your least favorite."

She looked them over. Six total. Flavors were designated

by wrapper. Chocolate, vanilla, lemon, confetti, peanut butter, and red velvet cake, each with a matching frosting and decorated with sparkling sugars and silver stars.

She glanced at him. "I like them all."

"I never took you for greedy."

"You've never been around me and cupcakes."

"Don't make me come over to the table."

"That's the only way you'll get one."

He jumped off the bed. Stalked her. Nude, semi-erect, and hungry-eyed. He evaluated the cupcakes, gave each his full attention. Deciding on the lemon, he touched his finger to the whipped peak of lemon-chiffon frosting, then spread it across her lips. She flicked her tongue. Sampled the sweetness. Right before he kissed her. Delicious frosting. Tasty man.

Sexually creative, they savored the cupcakes. In ways she didn't mind sharing. She fell a little in love with him when he gave her the last red velvet cupcake hours later. Her midnight snack.

Sunday, and Joe was the first player out of the locker room, uniformed and seated in the Rogues' dugout. He sat at the far end of the bench, beside the Gatorade cooler. The stadium pulsed with excitement and the anticipation of the exhibition game. The heart of the park beat baseball. He took in the white brilliance of the baseline and bases, and the newly designed on-deck circle. The seats were rapidly filling with Rogues fans, along with those cheering on the Rebels.

He leaned back, closed his eyes behind his bronzed-lens aviators, and fantasized about the sweetness of Stevie's mouth. He imagined tasting her. The woman and her cupcakes. Confetti was her favorite flavor. She'd flicked her tongue over the frosting, softly moaned, and nearly had an orgasm just from the taste. He'd gotten hard watching her.

He should've been drained after their night of sex. Instead she energized him. A first. Initially nervous, she'd slowly lost her fear. Of sex with him. Of him as a man. Once calmed, she'd gained a confidence that matched his own. Even gotten a little cocky. Which made him laugh. Their fantasies fused. They'd fed off each other, the cupcakes a sugar rush. Sexual fuel.

They'd gotten little sleep, both collapsing near dawn. He'd awakened two hours later, flat on his back, with her by his side, snuggled close. A natural fit. Her thigh and hip curved against his groin. His dick throbbed, and he swore his hellhound panted at her nakedness. Her cheek rested on his chest. When she parted her lips, her breath warmed his nipple. She'd gotten under his skin.

She made him feel and need. Two emotions he'd survived without until her. Indecision gutted him. What had he lost? What could he reclaim? What had he gained? Being single had always worked for him. He excelled at easy familiarity. Come and go. A relationship bound both participants. Commitment required staying power. For now, he walked away. Wanting time to think.

He'd lightly kissed her forehead, then rolled out of bed, careful not to disturb her. He'd memorized her body before covering her with a sheet. Sexy, delicate Stevie with her mussed-up hair, closed eyes, puffy lips, and reddened chin from whisker burn. His eyes fell on her garter. He'd tried to be careful with this woman half his size. She had beautiful skin. Sleek and supple. He'd made love with his entire body, and inadvertently bruised her. He hated that it had happened. A heated squeeze to her ribs had left behind his thumbprint. His four-fingertip grip marred her ass. She carried him with her now. Fortunately, no bruise was as visible as his previous hickey. These new bruises were known only to them.

He'd stared overly long at her wedding dress, hung on

a padded hanger on the door of the armoire. Stevie had looked amazing in the gown. She'd been the picture of bridal beauty. Someone had delivered her lost glass slipper after the photo shoot, leaving it outside her door. He'd scooped it up when he'd gone to the kitchen for bottles of water, after they'd consumed the Chateau De Fleur. He'd placed the heels together below the hem of her dress on his return. Completing the fairy tale.

He'd slipped out, showered, dressed, and then returned. He left Stevie a premium box pass for up to four people, seats within the first five rows behind the Rogues' dugout. She'd be right on top of the action. Enjoying every pitch and at-bat, as if she were part of the game herself.

He figured she'd invite Lori and her aunt. Perhaps even Twyla's beau, George. The two kept regular company now. His own role as groom for the afternoon—and the night—had come to an end. He debated removing his wedding band and leaving it on the bedside table. His gut clutched. Parting with it somehow felt like separating himself from Stevie. The idea of detaching from her left him cold, despite his uncertainty as to their future. Instead he switched it from his ring finger to his little one, where it was far less tight. Flexible.

He next went to locate his dog. He found Turbo and Etta in the kitchen with Twyla. She'd fed them breakfast, gone on to portion a plate of scrambled eggs. Turbo's manners surprised Joe. His boy was usually a food hog. But he now sat, took turns, and allowed the bulldog her fair share. Twyla didn't question Joe's night with Stevie. Instead she informed him that the two dogs would be together for most of the day, until Dean Jensen picked up Etta after the exhibition game.

Game time neared. MLB Richmond Rogues versus Triple-A Rebels.

Cleated footsteps now approached, and Joe cracked his

eyelids. Jake Packer dropped down beside him on the bench and immediately asked, "You fuckin' asleep, Zoo?"

Sam Matthews shook his head. "A nap? From the man who pulls all-nighters. What the hell?"

Pitcher Will Ridgeway grinned. "More important question, *who* tired him out?"

Pax's eyes narrowed. "You left Rock Creek early Friday night," he recalled. "We watched you go. Your posse stayed behind. All pouty and pissed. Sam hooked up with Cady, and—"

Sam tensed, sucked air. Looking guilty.

Joe rolled his shoulders, straightened. "And, what?" More interested than irritated. He'd left the women for Stevie. Sam and Cady had every right to make their own fun. Make love with their choice of partners. He'd often hoped Sam and Cady would connect.

"I bought Cady dinner, and she took me back to her place." Sam waited for Zoo's hammer to fall.

"Cool." Enough said.

Pax braved, "Roz spent the night on my sailboat."

Roz of the red hair; the low, sexy voice; and the kiss-me lips. She and Pax had a lot in common. Appreciation of the Gulf, fishing, and water sports. She had a speedboat and a cigarette racer. She would've fallen in love with Pax's vintage Morgan. Maybe even with the man himself. Given time.

Joe slapped Pax on the back. "It is what it is."

"You're sure?" Pax wanted full approval.

"It appears my posse is breaking up with me," Joe said honestly. He'd hinted, initiated the split, and the women had taken it to heart. "I want the ladies to be happy—with whomever they choose."

"Alyssa won't let you go without a fight," said Sam. "She's made her bed and wants you in it."

"I'm sleeping elsewhere."

His teammates grinned. Pax had the balls to say, "Unleashed."

"I'm renting a room." Which both men already knew.

"Stevie's your neighbor," said Sam.

Right next door, in the next bedroom. Where he'd spent the night. Brass bed, twisted sheets, tangled limbs. Hot bodies and satisfaction.

Joe went silent on his friends. Jaw locked, gaze slitted. His time with Stevie was too new. Privacy mattered. No need to put her name out there, if nothing came of their relationship.

The remainder of the players hit the main field for pre-game warm-ups. An hour of static stretches and short sprints, throwing and catching drills, and batting practice swings. Triple-A got ready on an adjoining training field.

Joe kept his eye on Dean Jensen. The guy looked strong. Seemingly his weekend of marathon sex hadn't weakened or slowed him down. The Rebels team captain was jogging, jumping, setting an example. Shit.

Joe homed in on his own drills. Rylan Cates joined him for catch-and-throw. "No need to babysit me, Ry," he said.

"Get over yourself, Zoo. You're one of eight. I watch all the guys."

Joe wasn't fooled. Rylan watched him closer than most. Ry knew he was hyped. That he had a trigger temper. Ry threw a wild-ass ball, on purpose, forcing Joe to stretch and dive. "What the fuck?" He got to his feet with one grass-stained knee. Before the damn game even started.

"Taking the edge off," said Rylan. "Today is exhibition. It doesn't affect our standings. Have fun, no crash and burn. Entertain the public. No individual conflicts."

"I'm not conflicted."

"You were born with clenched fists."

"You say that like it's a bad thing."

"Stay fixed on what's important."

"So you keep saying."

"And I'll continue, until you listen."

Joe smirked. "You're such a mom."

"Triple-A cuts happen next week. Most will go back to Roanoke."

"I'll pack Jensen's bag, put him on the bus." Joe powered a ball to Rylan; it smacked his glove. Ry shook out his hand.

"Switch up," Rylan called to the players. "Infield, at-bat." The outfielders shagged balls until it was their turn to step up to the plate. Once the starting lineup wrapped up their pregame practice, they returned to the dugout. Their muscles were now warm, loose. Focus honed.

Ry glanced into the stands on his way down the steps. He leaned against the short railing, said to Joe, "Your party posse just arrived to cheer you on."

The women were recognizable. Individually they were each sexy, but in a group, they knocked hotness out of the park. Each was skimpily dressed. Belly shirts, tube tops, short shorts. Displays of skin. Men all around them stared. Admired. Lusted. Joe watched as the women took seats in the field boxes. He'd purchased their seating. Before Stevie. Wanting them in attendance. They shouted and cheered, always supportive whether he struck out or slammed a home run. He'd see how he fared today.

"The girls are branching out," he told Ry. "They're not here for just me anymore. There'll be lots of applause for Pax and Sam, too."

"You're okay with that?"

"I set it in motion."

"The new you?"

"The old me. I'm not looking to be part of a couple. The girls deserve commitment."

"Alyssa's eyeing you for a walk down the aisle."

"Not happening." He'd been Stevie's groom for an afternoon. Her lover overnight. That was as close to a wedding as he ever cared to get. Or so he thought.

His heart jacked when he saw Stevie, coming down the center cement stairs behind home plate with her friend Lori. He was glad to see her. For all of a second. Lori came down first, wearing a Roanoke Rebels T-shirt and khaki slacks. But the sight of Stevie stopped him short. Same tee, worn with jeans. *What the hell?* He'd thought her to be a Rogues fan. *His* fan. His teammates boarded their dogs at Unleashed. He lived there. They'd had sex. He would expect Lori to support the asshole Jensen. But, Stevie? Hell no. He didn't understand. Where was her loyalty? Apparently not with him.

She had nearly reached the safety netting that separated the stands and the field when he caught her eye. She looked at him—through him—allowing no more than a tight smile. She was quick to glance away. As if he mattered little to her.

He watched the friends cut down a side aisle, winding toward the visitors' dugout, soon locating seats several rows behind the Triple-A team. Leadoff hitter Jensen stood on the on-deck circle, swinging two bats. Weighing his options. He nodded, and Lori smiled. Stevie gave a small wave.

"Who you looking at?" Halo Todd nudged past him.

"No one."

"Death stare says someone."

Joe ran a hand down his face. Baseball was his life. He was good at it. He'd wanted to share the game with her. To know that she was in the stands close by. To show off a little. To nail a home run. She'd denied him.

Had he been selfish? Not in his mind.

Illogical? He wasn't always rational or reasonable.

Crazy? Most thought him insane.

But despite everything, he'd thought they had an understanding. Of sorts. Apparently not. She now sided with the enemy.

He cut his gaze, refused to look at Stevie a second time. He had no idea what game she was playing—and at his ballpark. She and Lori were tight. Yet if Stevie wanted to be near him, the girls could've split up. She *knew* how he felt about Jensen. He hated the guy. But she now sat across the stadium, rooting on the Rebels. Low fuckin' blow.

Whatever he'd felt for her suddenly splintered. He was stabbed by shards of disappointment. He'd never been hurt by a woman. Until now. He collected his feelings. He'd gone soft to her overnight. Now he hardened his heart. Cursed his stupidity.

At one fifteen, the players were introduced. Starting with the Rebels. Applause was vigorous from the fans of Triple-A. Joe noted that Lori and Stevie clapped, cheered, and hugged each other when Dean was introduced. Joe swallowed hard.

The starting lineup for the Rogues got a standing ovation. The Cates family and townies rallied around Rylan. He was the most popular player. Halo Todd and Landon Kane received enormous welcomes, as well. Joe's name was called, and to his surprise, his posse stomped the bleachers, and others followed, creating a rumble. The women continued to support him. He couldn't help but smile. He glimpsed Stevie from the corner of his eye. Her hands were steepled beneath her chin, as if in prayer. He looked away. There was no point in speculating what her expression meant.

The remainder of the players' names were called. The national anthem was sung. The Rogues grabbed their gloves and took the field. *Game on.*

Will Ridgeway took the mound for the Rogues. Dean Jensen was the leadoff for the Rebels. Nearly all the action during a game was centered on the pitcher for the defensive team. Will delivered speed and precision. Jensen went down on three strikes. The next two batters followed suit. The first half of the inning was over in record time.

Rebels to the outfield. Joe and Jensen passed near third base. Jensen glared. Joe growled. They were definitely adversaries.

The Rogues picked up an early run. Halo connected with a fastball, and landed a line drive between first and second. Landon popped a fly ball. Caught. One out. Rylan powered what should've been a home run over the centerfield wall. The Rebels outfielder gave speedy chase, high-jumped, and snatched his chance. Two away. Halo stole second.

Shortstop Brody Jones batted fourth. He smacked a curveball into left field. Jensen charged the ball, but couldn't reach it in time. Which allowed Halo to round third and head home. Safe. Score!

Brody stretched off second, waiting on Pax to bring him in. Consistent, patient, Pax focused. Choosing his pitch. He got under the ball, it went high, fell short, right into the second baseman's glove. Third out. Rogues again took the field. One-zero.

Top of the second became a one-two-three inning. Will Ridgeway got all three hitters out, allowing no walks, errors, or hits. First preseason game, and Will was showing no mercy. Rogues fans went crazy.

It was the bottom of the inning—Joe's turn at bat. He switched his baseball cap for a batting helmet. Located his Louisville Slugger. Moved to the on-deck circle. The low chant of his name gained momentum. He was known as the "wild party" Rogue, and the bar crowd was in attendance. The chanting swelled with his practice swings, echoing as far as the parking lot. He appreciated their enthusiasm. The fans paid his salary. He owed them a hit.

He approached home plate. He slapped the head of the bat against his heel. Dug in. Took his stance. He batted left. Jaw clenched, his shoulders hunched, he blocked out the noise of the crowd and concentrated solely on the first pitch.

It was down and outside. He checked his swing on ball one.

An inside fastball shot by him, called as a strike.

He punched the next ball foul. It flew straight over the Rebels' dugout, landing close to where Stevie was seated. She ducked low, head down, afraid of being hit. A young boy wearing a baseball glove leaned over her and snagged himself a souvenir. He held it up to applause.

Stevie straightened. Wide-eyed. Pale. Joe hadn't been out to hit her. But he'd inadvertently gained her attention. He took advantage of her watching him. One ball. Two strikes. His entire body tensed, released, on a slider. Hit off the end of the bat, the line drive followed the left field chalk, stayed in play.

Jensen charged, scooped the ball. He had a powerful arm on him. He relayed the ball to first. Joe hauled ass. He was the second-fastest base runner on the team. His foot hit the bag at the exact moment the ball smacked the first baseman's glove. Too close to call. They both looked to the umpire. Awaited the call. That single second aged him.

"*Safe!*" was shouted.

Hot damn. Sam Matthews batted next. He seldom smashed it to the wall, but he was good for a single. His single took Joe to second. Sam on first. Joe took a long lead off the base, and when catcher Hank Jacoby knocked the ball over the shortstop's head, Joe took off for third. Jacoby landed on first. Sam on second. Bases loaded.

His fans were behind him. His name, a mantra. He stupidly glanced over at Stevie, and found her looking his way. He was on third, and Jensen out in left field. She could've been eyeing either one of them. Most likely the Rebel.

Pitcher Will Ridgeway took his bat. The two pitchers faced off. Noah Scanlon for the Rebels had a surefire fastball. He took Will to full count, three strikes and two balls. Will swung on a changeup, jammed it between first and second base.

The third base coach sent Joe home. The Rebels' right fielder had speed. He claimed the ball and fired it to the catcher, who blocked the plate. Joe slid low, feetfirst, a heartbeat ahead of the catch.

Earsplitting cheers from his party posse drew his gaze. The girls were excited, happy, giving each other high fives, hugs, dancing in the aisle. Supportive. He headed to the dugout. Each base still held a runner.

Top of the order, and Halo Todd gave him a thumbs-up from the on-deck circle. Joe received slaps on the back from his teammates. He dropped down on the bench between Pax and Landon Kane.

Landon whistled. "Damn, dude, you're cutting those bases close."

Safe by seconds. Lady Luck had kissed him on the lips. Slipped him a little tongue. He wished it had been Stevie.

Halo soon edged home plate. The Rebels pitcher made adjustments and came at the batters full-force. Halo struck out. Landon next popped up. Ball caught. Sam was cut off and tagged while trying to steal home. Three down.

Inning over. Rogues ahead, two-zero.

Top of the third, the Rebels flexed muscle. They gained two runs. One off an error by shortstop Brody Jones. The second came with Dean Jensen's home run. Over the right field wall. Halo launched himself in a rocket man attempt. Long and gone. Tied score. The next three batters went out on strikes. Joe and Jensen passed in the outfield. Glared at each other.

Pax entered the dugout behind him. "Let's get our lead back. No way can we lose to these guys."

"They've kicked it up. Playing decent," noted Rylan.

"We're better, and we need to put them in their place," from Sam.

"What place might that be?" asked Ry.

"Second to us," said Joe.

Agreement echoed down the bench. Triple-A was going down.

The tension intensified with each inning. Both teams pushed hard. The Rogues ran up the score. Eight to three. It was the top of the ninth, the Rebels' last bat, when the atmosphere in the park suddenly shifted. Anticipation electrified the air. Excitement shimmered. The vibe intensified. Fans stood, some on tiptoe, craning their necks. All staring toward the visitors' dugout.

Time stretched. Empty air. No batter on deck. The umpire allowed the interruption. No one understood the delay of the game. It only lengthened.

Rylan in center field, called, motioned, to Halo in right, Joe in left, to move in. Shortening their distances off the diamond to get a better look at what was going on. They stood a few yards beyond the infield dirt.

"Play ball!" the umpire finally directed. He positioned himself off the plate.

A cameraman, a TV reporter, and a batter simultaneously exited the dugout. The news crew took a spot near the stands off of first base. The batter came forward, his helmet low on his head, shadowing his face. He crossed to the on-deck circle, took three practice swings of his bat, then walked the walk to home plate. Assured swagger.

Joe squinted, taking him in. He was tall, large. His

confidence tangible. Far more certain than any previous Rebel. "Who the hell?" he muttered.

Joe caught Rylan's grin. "No, can't be. I don't believe it."

"Believe what?" Halo shouted their way.

"Take a good look at the hitter," said Ry. "Remind you of anyone?"

They watched as catcher Hank Jacoby tipped up his wire face mask, started, then took a step back, giving the player significant room to dig in. Pitcher Will Ridgeway shifted on the mound, looking oddly indecisive for a man who'd once pitched a perfect game. Only twenty-three pitchers held the honor in Major League history. A victory that lasted a minimum of nine innings and in which no opposing player reached a base. Twenty-seven up. Twenty-seven down. An incredible feat.

Halo raised his voice. "Dude's not wearing the Rebels uniform."

Rylan's grin broadened. "That uniform is a decade old."

Joe counted back. "The decade when Risk Kincaid captained the Rogues to the World Series and they won." The team had changed ownership shortly thereafter. Several of the Rogues had invested in the team, wanting to keep the squad in Richmond. Risk became the managing general partner/cochairman of the ball club. He was highly regarded, and known to be both fair and decisive. A man with vision.

The past had come to play in the present. Joe focused on home plate. The batter rested the Louisville Slugger against his thigh. Tightened the Velcro on his gloves. Adjusted his batting helmet. His face was momentarily visible. And recognizable. *Richard "Risk" Kincaid*. Rogues fans went ballistic. Explosive cheers and wild clapping rocked the stadium.

"Holy fuck," came from Joe. "The man himself."

"What the hell's going on?" shouted Halo.

"No idea," from Rylan. "Get in position."

They jogged deep into the outfield, awaited his pitch. Will Ridgeway threw one wild fastball, calmed, took possession. Kincaid went two balls, two strikes, before he delivered a hit, solid and streamlined, into right field. It dropped, bounced, and Halo was on it. Too late. Kincaid stood on first.

Joe walked a small circle. Staying loose. This was a game like no other. He'd been in high school during Kincaid's era. He'd watched and learned. Imitated the man.

Minutes later, the next batter appeared. Joe would've known him anywhere. *Kason Rhodes.* Broad-shouldered, thick-chested. His face spoke graphically of hardness. He didn't smile often, but when he did, it was sincere. Joe had stepped into his shoes when he'd retired. Rhodes had joined the front office as senior vice president of international scouting. He had an eye for athletic talent. He'd put the present team together.

The crowd welcomed him. A surge of clapping, stomping, shouting his name. He stood at home plate, game face on. In the zone. Determined. The pitcher laid a fastball over the middle of the plate. "*Strike!*" the umpire called. Rhodes reset, widened his stance.

Joe had a good initial read on the next pitch. A curveball, and Rhodes crushed it. A hook toward left field. Joe's real estate. He reacted, let his eyes guide his body. Crossover steps, then a full-out run, back to the warning track. He hit a spot where the ground was slightly uneven. He had to slow down to keep his balance, felt a heartbeat of fear that he wouldn't make the catch. Adrenaline pushed him. He caught it at the outlying cement pole that marked the ball in play. But he'd moved too far left and missed the

Safefoam, the stadium wall padding. His shoulder struck the post, jarring his neck and scraping his face. Right cheek and chin. He tasted blood on his lip.

He shook it off, and threw to third. Too late. Rhodes was out, but Risk Kincaid scored. Eight to four. The Rebels fans were on their feet. They couldn't sit still, screaming, jumping, proud.

A switch in the Rebels' batting order brought Dean Jensen on-deck. He was team captain and a Triple-A star. Joe couldn't see Stevie among the crowd, but he sensed that she was cheering him on. That sucked. Jensen followed the Rogues legends with a solid hit to center. He held on first. Two further Rebels landed singles, and the bases were loaded.

Low-flying planes could've heard the cheers rising from the stadium. Deafening. Not only for the minor leaguers, but also for the next player on-deck. The most identifiable Rogue of all time took his practice swings. *Cody "Psycho" McMillan.* Once arrogant, wild, and intimidating, he'd breathed baseball as no other player had. A feared contact batter and base stealer. A force to be reckoned with. Even now.

Direct, opinionated, take-charge, he'd claimed the title of senior vice president and general manager. He was responsible for the day-to-day operations of the club. The organization ran like a well-oiled machine.

Psycho stood at home plate now and surveyed the field. Owned the moment. He had every right. He had a financial stake in the team. He kept his finger on every player's pulse.

Joe admired the older Rogues from a distance. The earlier generation hadn't even seemed to age. They were in their late thirties now, and the legends still remained fit. Joe would often pass executives and officers in the athletic room at the Richmond stadium, working out. Players sweating with the front office bigwigs formed a bond. It was all about staying strong mentally and physically, whether on the field or behind a desk.

Psycho proved he still had it. An eye for the right pitch. The strength to kill the ball. He was ready for Will.

Will pitched with accuracy and velocity, taking Psycho to two balls, two strikes. The fans erupted. A fusion of cheers for the Rebels, for the present Rogues, and for the older returning players. Joe had never been bothered by the noise. But today the sound seemed to ricochet around the stadium, carrying out to the beach.

Will's next backdoor slider went in the dirt, a pitch that bounced before reaching the catcher. Psycho didn't move a muscle. He kept his stance at full count. Joe was antsy. His whole body alive. Waiting for the hit. It came with a grand slam. Undeniable power and placement. Over the centerfield wall.

Rylan Cates made a valiant attempt to save the runs. The ball sailed high into the second row of the outfield bleachers. Ry could jump; he just couldn't clear the wall. Four additional runs scored. Tied, eight-eight.

Commotion, chaos, a near-riot in the stands. Excitement sparked like fireworks. Fans congratulated each other, as if they'd hit the grand slam themselves. Psycho accepted the ovation with a cocky grin and a strut back to the dugout. Lasting applause brought him out for a second bow.

Joe looked at Rylan, then Halo. Their expressions said it all. They admired Psycho's ability, but they refused a loss. Will struck out the next two Rebels.

Bottom of the ninth, and the Rogues were anxious to bat. To raise the score by at least one run, for the win.

"Your face, dude." Pax eyed Joe.

"You're bleeding," from Sam.

"Kissed by the pole." His cheek felt raw. Sore. He

touched his face. A hint of blood smeared his fingers. No big deal.

"Let's do this," Rylan cheered.

"I want this one," said Joe. "Exhibition or not. Front office tied the score for the Rebels. We need to kick back."

The players nodded, grinned, and bumped fists. All were in agreement, wired to win.

Triple-A alone took the field. Risk, Kason, and Psycho stood and watched the game from the dugout railing, talking and evaluating every aspect of the play.

Batting order: Brody, Pax, and Joe. They needed to produce.

Brody started the rally. Doubled.

Pax struck out, leaving Brody stranded on second.

Joe walked from the on-deck circle to home plate. The fans were once again on their feet. He cut his gaze over to left field, saw Jensen bouncing, shifting, and anticipating.

Joe held true, found his pitch. A fastball, sliced to left field. He knew the moment he connected that it would fall short of the wall. Jensen was on it, capturing the ball before Joe crossed first base. Shit.

All was not lost. Brody rounded third and was headed home. His run won the game. Nine to eight. Joe jogged back to the dugout. Jensen passed him on the infield dirt, a huge smile on his face. Joe attributed his enthusiasm to having made the final catch, despite the Rebels' loss.

He dared to look over at Stevie. She and Lori were at the railing above the visitors' dugout. Stevie was grinning as broadly as Jensen. Visibly proud of him and his success. Joe's stomach sank. Son of a bitch.

The dugouts emptied, and both teams lined up and shook hands. Joe and Jensen exchanged short nods only. Had Joe shaken his hand, he would have squeezed to break Jensen's fingers.

The Rogues legends had supported the Rebels. Talent

was developed and grown in the minors, and the Rebels had several players who'd be wearing a major league uniform this season or next. Second string.

Risk, Kason, and Psycho spoke to the media, divulging hot Triple-A prospects and promoting the upcoming season. The remainder of the players waved to the crowd, then proceeded to the locker room. Showers and street clothes were in order. Joe eyed his face in the mirror. Cement rash on his cheek and chin. Split lip. He appeared rougher than usual. Couldn't be helped. The team physician located him on his way out, handing him a prescription tube of antiseptic salve to fight off any infection.

It was late afternoon when he finally emerged from the locker room, and the sun played with the clouds, dodging in and out. There was a light breeze. Both teams gathered in the parking lot, a convention of players. Talking with their bosses, relishing their surprise appearances. The three legends had fueled the fans' enthusiasm for a game never to be forgotten. The Rogues' popularity swelled stronger than ever. Joe was damn glad to be a part of his team.

Families and fans with full-access passes drifted among the ballplayers. Joe rested a hip against his Jaguar and waited for the stadium to clear. He needed some time to himself in the upper deck. A man alone with his thoughts. His order for a hot dog, French fries, and a beer was placed with a vendor. He'd replay the game in his head. There'd been a lot to take in.

He'd turned to leave when Kason Rhodes shouted to him. "Got a minute, Zoo?" he asked. An invitation to join him. Three parking spots separated them. Not enough space with Dean Jensen, Lori, and Stevie in the group. Not a circle Joe wished to join.

His chest tightened. He hesitated, taking a moment to consider his options. He had none. Rhodes had taken a chance on him years ago, back when Joe was wild and unmanageable. Disorderly and disruptive. In some way, his talent outplayed his idiocy off the field. Kason had signed him to the majors. Joe owed the man. Big-time. He sucked it up, crossed over to him. To *them*.

Kason welcomed him with introductions. "You know Dean," he said. "He caught your fly ball."

Dean topped Joe's shit list.

"His girlfriend, Lori."

Lori tentatively smiled. Joe liked her, despite her terrible taste in men. One corner of his mouth curved.

"And his cousin Stevie."

Time was suspended. He'd landed in the Twilight Zone. *"Cousin?"* No way! He choked on the word. Backstabbed, and he'd never seen it coming. His nemesis and his lover were related, their secret now exposed.

Anger and hurt slammed through his chest. He ran with mad. A joke on him? So it appeared. He didn't take well to being played. Stevie had known all along how he felt about Dean. Yet she'd hidden the fact that they were related. Had Dean put her up to it? Had he asked Stevie to distract him? She had done a bang-up job of it. Woman to man.

The wedding shoot flashed through his mind.

Pretend or not, he'd been deceived.

He'd married into their family.

Double hell.

Eleven

"What are you doing with my wiener?"

"I brought your hot dog, fries, and beer," said Stevie.

"Lou passed my food to you?" Joe's expression was cool, closed.

"I went back inside the stadium, looking for you. I saw the vendor, carrying a brown bag, and figured it was yours. I remembered you telling me the night we had the picnic in left field that you liked alone time after a game. Time to think."

"Alone, just me. Yet you're here."

She'd climbed up to the grandstand seats. Wanting, needing, to talk to him. To explain. However feeble her justification might be. He'd rebuffed her. Which she'd expected. Even understood. Still, she held her ground, here with the man and his nasty scraped face. She sought to reach out, to comfort him, but she knew he'd reject her.

Instead she handed him the bag. Their fingers brushed. Her entire hand tingled. "I don't plan to stay."

"Go anytime. You're breathing heavily. Going down the steps is easier than coming up."

If her breathing was a little rough, it was due to her concern for him. Her heartbeat raced. Her palms were sweaty. He'd issued no invitation to stay. He sat stiffly in a faded

T-shirt with the logo *Takes Gutz*, jeans with a rip near his groin, and black Adidas athletic shoes. His hair was long and damp from his shower. Heavy five o'clock shadow. She caught a glint from his gold band. He still wore the pretend wedding ring, now on his little finger. That gave her heart hope. Yet there was no eye contact. He focused on the field, waiting for her to leave. She stayed.

"Talk to me, Joe. Please." Her words were barely audible.

He remained as silent as the empty stadium. He didn't encourage or deny her. His indifference scared her. No more than a step separated them, but it seemed insurmountable. A sense of loss squeezed her chest. "I'm so very sorry," she managed.

He side-eyed her. "Sorry for what?" No slack.

He wasn't making this easy. "For not telling you that Dean is my cousin."

"Slipped your mind, huh?"

"I'd planned to tell you." Truth. "No time to explain."

His gaze darkened, his expression disbelieving. He was ticked. "No *time*? It would've taken seconds. Three short words: 'Dean's my cousin.' You knew how I felt about him. I've vented. You didn't come clean."

"My mistake. You deserved to know."

"Truth and trust are important to me."

"Dean was never meant to be a secret, a skeleton in my closet," she softly said. "He's family—we're close. He's kind, generous, one of the good guys."

Joe rolled his eyes. Made a rude sound.

"Dean's also competitive, same as you. He'd asked Lori and me not to associate with any Rogues during spring training. Long before we came to Barefoot William. It was important to him. Family loyalty. No consorting with the enemy. No conflict of interest. An easy promise. I gave him my word and I kept it . . . until you."

He raised an eyebrow. "Until me?"

"You made me like you." Possibly she loved him. "After Kason Rhodes left us in the parking lot, I told Dean I'd been seeing you—"

"Sleeping with me."

He was a naked memory on her bed. Never to be forgotten. "Dean was disappointed, but not mad. Lori will smooth things over. She gives him perspective."

"What's *my* perspective, Stevie?" His tone was caustically curious.

"That competition makes for better players. You and Dean are more alike than you realize. He reflects your strength and intensity, and he has the same drive to play ball. He wants what you have, Joe. Can you blame him?" No response. "I hope Dean succeeds. Not by replacing you in left field, but by landing somewhere in the majors. He is my cousin, after all."

"So Kason revealed."

Her heart sank. She was losing him. She had one last hope. "You can stay mad, hold a grudge, and I wouldn't blame you. Not in the least. You're justified. You can sit up here alone and enjoy your food or"—she drew the word out, daring him—"meet me at Unleashed for makeup sex." She'd never had makeup sex before. Now seemed the perfect time. With this man.

"So the shrink's telling me that sex can make it all better."

"That's my analysis. At least it's a start." She sighed. "If I could do it all over again, I would've told you about Dean between your kissing cupcake frosting off my lips and your taking off my panties."

She swore one corner of his mouth curved up. Ever so slightly.

She left him then. Didn't look back.

It was what it was. Unleashed or not.

★ ★ ★

How had Joe beaten her home? He hadn't passed her on the main streets. Perhaps he'd taken the back roads. He'd parked his Jaguar next to the Unleashed van. She stopped behind the Sprinter, climbed from her Mazda Miata. When she entered the building through the side door and walked to the hallway, she found Joe and Turbo seated on the staircase.

"Turbo looks sad," she noted. Joe, unreadable.

"My boy lost his girl," he told her. "Dean apparently picked up Etta right after the exhibition game. Turbo's lonely."

"Treats might help. He likes turkey jerky. My aunt recently bought a fresh bag."

"Whatever it takes to get him back to his old self. Etta's changed him."

"Love can do that."

"Love takes it out of a guy."

"Not when the woman gives love back."

He descended the steps, and they proceeded to the kitchen. A note from her aunt on the table indicated that she and George had gone out for a drive. Turbo had the run of the house. Stevie canvassed the cupboards, located the treats in one, high on a top shelf. A bit difficult to reach. She stretched on tiptoe. Almost there . . .

Joe came up behind her. Not beside her. A full-body press. She closed her eyes, absorbed his heat and strength. Felt his erection at the small of her back. He was fully armed. She held her breath when he snagged the bag, then rubbed against her, slow to back off.

Turbo heard the rustle of snacks and charged them. He sniffed the bag, nearly inhaled it. Joe gave him two pieces. One he scarfed with barely a chew. With the second, he took his time. Joe sealed and returned the bag to the shelf. Turbo lay down, one eye on the cupboard.

"More later, big guy," Joe told his dog.

The rottie wagged his tail.

Joe turned to Stevie, arms crossed over his chest, his stance wide. Hard-faced, hard-bodied, hard-on. His "So . . . ?" had a dark undertone.

"Make up with me."

He made her wait. Seconds of silence stretched to a minute. "Forgive and forget?"

"Our situation could be worse," she dared. "Dean could be *your* cousin."

The corners of his eyes tightened. His mouth flattened against his teeth. "Not funny, Stewie."

"I'm laughing, Joey."

"You're asking for it, babe."

"Give it to me," she risked.

He took one giant step toward her, and she took off running. Down the hallway, up the stairs, to her bedroom. The doorknob stuck, and she twisted it hard. Too late. She heard his footsteps, heavy, stalking, behind her. On her. All over her. A man demanding more than her apology.

The landing closed around them. He pulled her back against him. There was nothing slow or sensual in his move. He had his way with her. Not rough, but deliberate. Tauntingly sexual. Makeup, make out, he made her. A rush to orgasm. *Her orgasm.*

He grasped the round neck of her T-shirt and stretched it wide, kissing her nape, biting her shoulder. He felt her up, then down. He snuck under the hem, fanned her ribs with his fingers, and seduced her breasts. Lengthy caressing and a pinch to her nipples. Heat flicked, arrowed low, when his fingers stole beneath the waistband on her skinny jeans. No unsnapping, no unzipping. She sucked in her stomach. His hand scored her mound, parting her sex. Her arousal dampened his fingertips. He slid two fingers inside her. Drew them out, then delved deeper. His thumb rubbed her most sensitive spot. She responded, all hot need and urgency. Passion pounded in her bones, in her heart, and deep between her thighs.

She went up on her toes. Strained. Back down. Moaned. Short of breath. She rocked her hips. Built to climax. Spiraled, shuddered. Then collapsed against him. Undone. Her head fell back. Her spine was liquid. Her knees weak.

"Accept my apology?" escaped her lips, soft and breathy.

He turned her toward him. He held her hips tightly. His nostrils flared. His gaze was wicked dark. "You're not sorry enough. I'm still pretty mad, sweetheart."

He reached around her and opened her bedroom door with a slight flick of his wrist. He backed her inside, towering over her, but not overpowering. The door creaked closed. They stood on the braided rug. The air between them was electric. Raw excitement. Whatever anger he'd felt earlier had left his body hot. A fusion of heat and arousal. His erection was prominent. He wanted her, despite the secret she'd been keeping.

Dean was momentarily forgotten. Her full attention was on Joe. He raked his hands into her hair, and her scalp tingled. She looked up into his warrior's face, scraped and bruised. Sore lip. Being battered didn't stop him. He kissed her aggressively. Thoroughly. Biting her own bottom lip, the tip of her tongue. Then sucking it into his mouth. Deep. Her heart softened to this hard man. She cared for him.

"Lift your arms," he roughly said.

She raised them high. Her spine stretched. Her breasts lifted. He focused on her chest as he pushed her Rebels T-shirt over her breasts, her head. He tossed it to the floor. Her pale yellow bra was scalloped and lacy. Her nipples were visible through it. He fingered the front clasp. It popped open. Her breasts spilled into his palms. They rose and fell with her breathing. Erratic. Her nipples pointed. He squeezed and kneaded, his touch callused, hard, but not hurtful. Her bra went the way of her shirt.

She slipped off her leather thong sandals, amber-embellished. He took down her jeans. She sidestepped the denim. His gaze moved down her body. Narrowed on her V-zone. She wore his gift, the natural-blond panties. Sheer and revealing. Her pubic hair was a shade darker than the silk. He stroked a finger from her navel to the juncture of her thighs, then pressed the silk against her sex, rubbed her dampness. Her legs stiffened. Her knees locked. He held her on the edge. But didn't let her come.

She was wound so tight, her heart bumped, her stomach was a sexual knot. She stood nearly naked while he was fully clothed. She rectified the situation. She scored her fingernails under his T-shirt, over his six-pack, his pecs, then back down his sides. His muscles rippled, tensed. A streamlined push up his torso, and she pitched *Takes Gutz*. His expression was as tight as his body.

Confident, momentarily in control, she bent, pulled off his sneakers and socks, traced his toes, then got him out of his jeans. His boxer briefs came next. Still on her knees, she kissed up his thighs, and his dick rose, long and large. Looking for attention. No kiss, only a tease of warm breath along its length. She flicked her tongue to each hip bone, gave Chaos a kiss. She imagined the hellhound's howl. Her fingers stretched, sketched his abdomen. Solid. Tanned flesh. Breathing muscle.

Joe widened his stance. Exhaled sharply. He grasped her shoulders and drew her to her feet. "Condom," was a husky sound.

"Bedside drawer." A few left over from their previous night together. Their pretend honeymoon.

They stared at each other. The look on his face was a
subtle meld of anger and need. Need won out. Her body
ached, craved him. His erection was ready for her. She
made her move, bold and transparent, leading him to
the bed, and not by the hand. There she stripped off her
panties. Went flush against him. Clutching his shoulders,
she climbed him. Her legs wrapped his waist. Her thighs
squeezed. Sex to sex. Him hard. Her wet. He cupped her
butt.

Dusk crept through the window, casting shadows. On
Joe. On her. Obscuring the scraped side of his face, and
shading her cleavage. A rock of her hips signaled him to
the bed. He went down on the mattress, took her with
him. He hitched himself up against the headboard until
he was sitting. She straddled him. His erection nestled between her thighs.

Leaning forward, she brushed his dick, as her breath
bathed his neck, his cheek, his mouth. Their tongues soon
tangled, mated. Erotically. He palmed her breasts, circled
one nipple, and thumbed the tip, bringing exquisite pleasure. His hand flared across her belly, wide, coarse. Her
stomach fluttered.

A quick recovery of a condom, a ripped wrapper, and
she sheathed him. She rocked forward, then back, teasing his erect penis, yet refusing to take him in fully. He
curved his hands over her hips, squeezed her. His need
was raw, rushing, and intense.

She went on to frustrate him further. She stroked his
sex, holding him between her palms, suggestively rubbing her hands together. Friction and heat; slow, then fast.
Until air exploded in his lungs, jagged and sharp, his chest
heaved, and he took control. Slipping inside her. Their
bodies linked.

She moved her hips up and down. The strength of

her thighs set the pace for their mutual satisfaction. She dug her fingers into his shoulders. He clutched her hips. Crushing, yet careful. She craved. Lusted. Began to unravel. Their rhythm left her sighing, him moaning. Both panting.

Sensation overtook her. A sexual high. Time went away and her orgasm rose, broke in a sunburst. His muscles bunched, his back arched, and his hips came off the bed. He came a second after her, his expression going from pain to pleasure. Sex defused his anger. Orgasms ended an argument they'd earlier had no idea how to end.

In the aftermath, he rid himself of the condom and came back to bed. They lay facing each other, bodies aligned, forehead to forehead. A light touching of lips. Until his smile broke. "Makeup sex. You're good at it, babe."

He brought out her best. She felt close to him. Reassured in the moment, even if the issue of her connection to Dean wasn't fully resolved. A situation she couldn't push. She crossed her fingers and hoped the two men would come to an understanding. However tenuous. Friendships often formed without conscious thought. Differences and similarities fused. For mutual benefit. Their future might yet come together. Given time.

Shortly thereafter, Joe dragged on his jeans and left her, just long enough to feed Turbo. To let his dog outside. To lead the rottie back to his bedroom and settle him in for the night. Doors opened, then closed, as he cut through their adjoining bath. He arrived with a T-shirt in hand. He held it out to her. "Yours." *Richmond Rogues* appeared on the front. His number, forty-five, on the back. She sat up, knelt on the bed, and tried it on. The XXL dwarfed her, hanging off one shoulder, swaying at her knees. His scent infused the cotton.

He eyed her. "Perfect fit. Wear it."

"To bed. My new pj's."

He shucked his jeans, joined her again, bare-ass naked. He looked good in his skin. He rolled onto his side, curved her into his body, where she felt cocooned and protected. She realized a moment before she closed her eyes that every woman should have a lover like Joe. At least once in her life. As a gold standard for sex.

Sleep tucked them in, and open shutters ushered in sunshine at 6 a.m., fluttering Stevie's eyelids and drawing her yawn. Trapped by Joe's weight, she had no wiggle room. His chest backed her shoulders, his hips bracketed her bottom. Snug. Taking a deep breath, she inched away. At the edge of the bed, she glanced over her shoulder and fell in love with the man.

He remained on his side, arms in the exact position where she'd left him, as if awaiting her return. His hair shadowed his scraped face. He looked battle-worn. She'd applied antiseptic salve to his cuts the night before, and he hadn't grimaced or winced. He had a high tolerance for pain. She herself was shaking after her ministrations. He'd pulled her close, assured her that he was a fast healer. Minor scars would join his twice-broken nose, further hardening his features. She liked him rugged, rough. He emanated strength.

She drew the white cotton sheet over his hip. Admired the sturdy width of his chest, his powerful arms. His flat abdomen. His hellhound tat. Hot. Sunbeams played off his fake gold wedding band, reminding her of their extended honeymoon. Which would eventually end. She just didn't know when. He didn't do monogamy.

She debated getting dressed, then made it easy on herself. Her oversized Rogues T-shirt dragged her knees. She added a pair of black leggings and went to brush her teeth, barefoot. To comb her hair. Then she went to check on Turbo. He lay on the double bed, a scavenger of Joe's pillows. He wagged his greeting, and followed her to the kitchen. Her coffee. His kibble.

The lighting on the staircase was dim, the hallway even darker. The front door creaked, and Lori slipped in. She hit the main light switch, brightening the entrance. Both women startled, blinked. Then came together. Hugged. They smiled knowingly at each other. As close as sisters.

Lori wore her Rebels T-shirt from the exhibition game. Stevie faced her in her Rogues tee.

"I assume you got to Joe," hoped Lori.

"He got me, good."

"How are things?"

"Horizontal."

Lori laughed. "Nice position."

She hesitated, whispered, "How's Dean?"

"I talked him down. He values family. You're important to him. He can live with you seeing Joe. It won't affect his game. But he doesn't want you to get hurt. Joe apparently takes being single to a new level. He's not marriage material."

"I'm not looking to get married." Not at the moment, anyway. Joe's playing groom for an afternoon was as close as she might ever get to wearing a wedding gown. To having a honeymoon. They lived in the real world. "We're just enjoying each other."

"I'm appreciating Dean, too. We're making up for lost time."

The back door lock *click*ed, and Twyla hobbled inside. Her hair was slightly mussed. Her teal wire rims rested low on her nose. She wore a mauve bathrobe belted at the waist. One bedroom slipper and her plaster foot cast.

Lori raised an eyebrow. "Your aunt has that morning-after look."

"Morning after what?"

"Morning after George."

"No way!"

"Way. I passed him leaving in his SUV as I was coming home. He saluted. A definite overnighter."

"George is a nice guy," Stevie said. "My aunt's always been too busy for a relationship."

"Apparently she's not too busy for George."

Stevie embraced the idea of the older couple. In a roundabout way, a torn braided rug had brought them together. Turbo's destruction, followed by Joe's introduction of George to her aunt, had led to a good match. The way they looked at each other promised a future.

Lori sniffed the air. "I smell coffee."

It was always Twyla's first order of business. A rich Colombia blend. Next came Turbo. Afterward, she'd scramble eggs and fry bacon. Heat croissants. For Lori, Stevie, and occasionally Joe. An hour before the doggy day care opened at seven.

"Good night's sleep?" Lori asked Twyla as the girls entered the kitchen.

She eyed both girls. Blushed. Was honest. "Little night's sleep," she said on a yawn.

"Sexual hangover," Lori teased.

Deepening color flushed her aunt's cheeks. "I'll catch a nap later," said Twyla. "You girls will be busy. Unleashed is full today. I interviewed and accepted three new pups Sunday afternoon while you were at the exhibition game. All six to eight months old. Small. Two Maltese and a Yorkshire terrier. Mannered, but playful. They'll need lots of yard time."

Stevie gave her a thumbs-up. "Got it."

"Got what?" came from the doorway. Joe.

"Got puppies today," Stevie told him, as she took him in. He was wearing a worn and torn *Catch Me If You Can* white T-shirt, navy gym shorts. Running shoes. He'd tied back his hair. His face was like a mask, half morning stubble, half bruised and scraped.

"Run?" he asked, tagging Turbo. The rottie made a swift exit, headed for the front door. He nodded to Stevie. "See you before I go." He took off, too.

Lori put her hand on her chest. "Joe makes my heart kick."

He made Stevie's heart quicken, as well—into a rapid pulse felt throughout her body. Echoing in her ears, fluttering at the base of her throat, settling in her belly, a throbbing at her pelvis. She'd never felt this way about any man before. It scared her, excited her, and made her a little crazy.

Joe was difficult to analyze; the outcome of their relationship, unpredictable. Would it develop or end? Either way, she was with him now. Short-lived or long-term, she'd have to take her chances. Let it unfold on its own.

Her aunt soon passed her a plate, and she ate her breakfast, momentarily content. Turbo reappeared before Joe, panting from their jog. He flopped down on the kitchen floor to rest.

Stevie heard Joe head up the steps for a shower and a half-face shave. She finished her breakfast, enjoyed a second cup of coffee, then pushed back her chair. Ready to attack Monday. Twenty minutes before the first dogs arrived.

"We're good to go," she told her aunt. "Time to put up your foot, rest."

Twyla's eyes misted. "You girls are lifesavers. I have a great staff, but I'm not sure I could've managed without you."

Stevie washed off her plate, put it in the dishwasher. Paused by her aunt's chair and gave her a hug. "Family takes care of family. We're here as long as you need us."

"What about your psychology practice?" Twyla asked.

Stevie gave her an extra squeeze around the shoulders. "My degree isn't going anywhere. I've been offered positions at two mental health clinics. The offers are open-ended. I can even hang out my own shingle. I'll make my choice when I return to Roanoke."

"Lori?" Twyla asked.

"No career path yet," she admitted, not the least bit concerned. "I've been bouncing between jobs for three years now. I love Barefoot William. I'm thinking about becoming a beach bum." Big grin.

"You're dating my nephew now?"

Lori finished her eggs, sighed. "I love Dean."

"I know, dear." Twyla patted Lori on the hand. "I've seen how you look at him. How he looks at you. Dean is dedicated to playing pro ball. But he's equally devoted to you."

"Spring training is all-important," said Lori. "Afterward, we'll figure us out."

Stevie waited for Lori to clean up, then the girls took the narrow back kitchen steps to the second floor. They parted ways to dress. Joe heard her bedroom door open, close, and shouted from the bathroom, "Shower's open, babe."

She had little time, so she washed up quickly. Threw on clothes even faster. A yellow *Unleashed* polo, khaki shorts, and brown Keds. She towel-dried her hair. The new short style had its advantages. She left the pretend gold band on her thumb. Silly, but it felt right. For now.

Joe, Lori, and Stevie converged on the front door at the same time, just as the first group of dogs arrived. Turbo awaited Etta. Rylan Cates dropped off his Great Dane, Atlas. Halo Todd came next with pug Quigley, then Will Ridgeway with Chihuahua Cutie Patootie.

Ry spoke to Joe in the entry hall. "Big fund-raiser tomorrow, following practice, at four. Jill wanted me to remind everyone."

"I've already received six texts from her."

"She knows who needs the most reminding."

"I'll be there."

"People-sized wooden board games," Rylan explained, including Lori and Stevie. "The Rogues will split into three teams. Tic-tac-toe, chess, or checkers. My group is checkers. We're human game pieces, playing on enormous boards. We're all wearing black shirts. We need twelve players, but we only have nine. Five Rogues: Halo, Landon, Pax, Joe, and me. My sister Shaye; her husband, Trace. My two brothers: Dune, who's a retired pro-volleyball player, and Zane, a hurricane hunter, who's home on leave. You girls want to join Team Rogue?"

"Yes!" Lori didn't have to think twice.

"I'll inform my aunt, and have the staff close out the day for us," said Stevie. "They're dependable."

Rylan nodded. "Great. We still need one more player."

The front door opened, and Dean Jensen and his bulldog entered. Turbo greeted Etta affectionately. They nuzzled noses, then trotted off together. A furry twosome.

Dean pulled a face. "Of all the dogs here . . ." *Etta chooses Turbo.* His implied insult went unspoken.

Joe set his jaw. His expression reflected Dean's sentiment.

"So . . . one more checker," came from Rylan.

Stevie saw Joe narrow his gaze on his team captain, a *don't-you-dare* stare. Ry ignored him. "Dean, you're aware of the fund-raiser tomorrow afternoon?" he asked.

He gave a short nod. "It's been advertised all over town. I read a flyer. A Rogues/Barefoot William promotion. Fans pay for spots on opposing teams, on all boards. Rogues are showcased, and, win or lose, the challengers exit. Money raised goes to local charities."

"That's right," said Rylan. "I'm in charge of checkers. We're at eleven with Lori and Stevie."

That stunned Dean. "Lori?" He looked at her. Confused.

She responded with, "They need twelve players."

"You'd round off our dozen, if you want," added Ry. "Invitation extended."

Dean swallowed. "To play with the Rogues."

"It's a board game," Joe emphasized. "On the beach, not at the ballpark."

It was clear that Dean was so taken aback, he couldn't speak. Stevie held her breath, hoping he'd accept. Lori nudged him with her elbow, encouragingly.

"I'm there," he agreed.

Stevie caught Joe's eye. His body was tense, his expression resigned. *Thank you*, she tried to convey.

He got her message. His gaze was wicked dark. She received his *thank me later*, as he and his teammates left for practice.

Dean hung back. He curved his arms around the girls' shoulders. Hugged them hard. His grin was explosive. "Damn, I'm a human checker."

Stevie absorbed her cousin's happiness. She appreciated Rylan. Grateful that Joe hadn't objected. She would spread her gratitude all over him later tonight.

Tuesday afternoon came on fast. Rylan appointed Joe chief strategist for Team Rogue. Joe had played checkers as a kid, hustling on street corners for money. He'd refreshed himself on the rules on the Internet. He would call the plays. He presently leaned against the blue metal railing that separated the boardwalk from the beach. He surveyed the setup below. Damn impressive.

Collapsible bleachers enclosed the slightly raised, full-scale game boards. The seating was filled to the max.

Standing room only. Sunshine shimmered off the sugar sand like a mirage. Low tide tugged at the Gulf, widening the coastline. Egrets and heron skimmed the shallow foam for small fish. Pelicans floated in deeper water.

Time closed on four o'clock. He took the short steps down to the beach, where the Rogues were hanging out with fans, providing photo ops and signing autographs. Stevie, Lori, and Dean were last to arrive. It was difficult to maneuver through the thick crowds. Joe greeted Stevie with a casual possessiveness. His arm circled about her waist, cinching her close. Dean eyed them, adjusted to seeing them together. Turned away.

Photographer Eden Cates-Kane walked between the games, her Nikon raised, ready to capture all the excitement of game day. It would be excellent promo for the Rogues' website.

Joe took to the checkerboard and placed the players on their individual black squares. Everyone wore black T-shirts and jeans. Played barefoot. He rolled his eyes when Lori requested to stand near Dean. The two were inseparable. He positioned them in the front row. Sacrifice checkers. Out first and captured. He fit Stevie on the back row, between brothers Rylan and Dune. The guys were friendly, and would put her at ease. He then headed to a border square in the first row. It would be a solid advantage point to view the entire board and call the plays.

The opposing team arrived seconds later. Team Breakers, a local surf club, wearing red shirts and assorted board shorts. All guys. Athletic and deeply tanned. Sunstreaked hair. Each had paid fifty dollars to face off with the Rogues. Nice donation. Shaye Cates-Saunders, CEO of Barefoot William Enterprises, left her square, crossed over, and greeted the guys. Rylan waved to his hometown buddies. He had surfing skills. When not at the ballpark, he could be found on his board.

Shaye returned, walking straight to Joe. She leaned close and whispered, "This is a checker game for charity, Zoo. Don't get crazy-ass aggressive on the locals."

Aggressive? Him?

She poked him in the gut. "Play nice. It doesn't matter whether we win or lose. It's fun in the sun."

Winning was always better.

She motioned to an impartial official who stood in the sand near the edge of the board. Time was now. Megaphone in hand, he welcomed everyone, read the basic rules, then went on to shout, "Play checkers!"

Black shirts moved first. Joe started with Lori, motioning her one diagonal space forward. Red, next. Both sides soon crowded the center rows. Black was first to jump and capture. The Rogues picked the surfers off, checker by checker. Until Shaye loudly cleared her throat, and Joe cut back on his quick captures.

The official moved the game along when the surfers slowed. "No stalling," he called out. "You have to take the jump in front of you."

Which was Rylan Cates. Team Breakers considered him one of their own. They hated knocking him out. With a fist bump and a slap on the back between surfer and Rogue, Ry hopped off the elevated board. He stood among the other eliminated players.

"No jumping Stevie's bones," Joe growled at one of the challengers. "Jumping doesn't include landing on her square and staying. Back it up, man." The guy shrugged, grinned, and moved in another direction. Stevie remained safe.

"Zoo, you're leaving me exposed," Halo called over his shoulder. He stood alone, a stray checker surrounded by red shirts.

Team Breakers was unorganized. They hadn't realized Halo's vulnerability. They were too busy high-fiving, having fun, yet they were losing the game. Joe could've strategized and saved Halo, Landon, and Pax. Instead he let them fall to the surfers. Shaye winked at him, pleased with his decisions.

Joe glanced at his watch. Thirty minutes were allotted per game. There were three further matches scheduled for the afternoon, all needing to be played before dusk. Joe wrapped up play with a triple-jump. A king was crowned. Zane Cates. He got a cardboard gold crown. The fans cheered the hometown hurricane hunter.

Joe kept his eye on Zane and Stevie. Zane paid her attention beyond what Joe felt was warranted. They talked as the surfers left the board and the new challengers took their squares. Stevie smiled over something Zane said. Even touched his arm. Zane seemed taken by her. Too damn taken.

Rylan crossed to him. "Don't death-stare my brother."

Joe turned on Ry. "He's hitting on Stevie."

"Not hitting on her, being nice."

"There's nice, and then there's interested."

"Let it go." Rylan returned to his square.

Joe continued to watch the two. One eye on the game, one eye on them. The next challengers made him smile. Middle-school students from the Checkers Club. Twelve serious boys and girls. The faculty had donated twenty-five dollars per pupil. They were prepared, and they played exceptionally well.

In under twenty minutes, the red players jumped, captured, and blocked the Rogues so they didn't have any more moves. Joe had seen it coming, and let it happen.

Halo held up his hands in defeat. "Trapped."

"I'm backed against the edge," from Pax.

"You kids are good!" Shaye praised.

The students' smiles lit up their faces, and they bounced like pogo sticks. Team Rogue celebrated their win right along with them. The crowd applauded wildly. The board cleared. Parents collected their sons and daughters with big hugs.

Joe hadn't been given the list of challengers. The next opponents from Beachside Memorial totally surprised him. In a good way. Shaye was nearest him, and gave him the rundown: "A doctor, intern, three nurses, and seven children, recently released from the hospital. Administration donated fifteen hundred dollars."

His heart hitched at the sight of nine-year-old Ashley. Small, blond, she'd battled lymphoma and won. He'd planned to visit her one final time before her discharge, but she'd found him first. The doctor lifted her onto the game board. Joe hoped she could identify him without his superhero costume.

She did, running straight to him in her red tee and pink, gold, and brown paisley jeans. Red flip-flops, to keep her feet clean. "Super Z!" she squealed, all happiness and excitement.

He picked her up, spun her around, and hugged her hard. Relieved. "I wasn't sure you'd recognize me."

"I'd know you anywhere, galactic bounty hunter."

His chest warmed. He stared, taking her in. "Look at you, pretty girl."

"Look at you." She touched his scraped cheek. "Owie."

"It doesn't hurt. I'll heal."

"I got all better."

"I knew you would."

She scrunched her nose. "How'd you know?"

"Superpowers."

She angled her head, made Kewpie-doll lips. "You like my hair?" It hung beyond her shoulders. Shiny.

"Beautiful, sweetie. It sure grew fast."

She giggled. "It's a wig, silly."

"It looks real to me," he complimented. "No one ever

wore hair better." He searched out Stevie, found both her and the Rogues watching their reunion.

Kuts for Kids had enabled Ashley to face the world and her peers with confidence. Stevie had provided the gift. He lowered his voice, asked the girl, "Would you like to meet the lady who cut her hair for you?"

Ashley's eyes rounded. "Is she here?"

He set her down. "On the game board."

Ashley targeted Stevie in a heartbeat. She bounced over to her, threw her arms around her waist. "I'm Ashley. I love you." Her voice shook. "Thank you."

Stevie's eyes misted. She choked up, unable to speak. She patted Ashley on the shoulder, finally managed, "I'm Stevie. Love you back." Stevie eased her to arm's length. Admired, "You look better in long hair than I ever did."

"My real hair will grow back," Ashley told her. "But it could take a few months."

"Wear the wig in good health," said Stevie.

Ashley beamed. "I am healthy now."

Joe joined them. He took Ashley's hand as they crossed the board. She skip-stepped beside him. "We played checkers during my recovery," she remembered.

"From what I recall—"

"I won!"

That she had. Legitimately. Joe had gotten distracted and played without paying attention. Once his attention was snagged by a hot nurse taking Ashley's temperature and blood pressure. Second time it was a female volunteer pushing the book cart. She'd reminded him of a sexy librarian with her bun and glasses. She'd helped Ashley select reading material. Joe picked out comic books. While he was preoccupied, Ashley cleaned his clock. Her smile was worth his loss.

He left Ashley on a white square in the last row, between two nurses. The spot protected her from immediate elimination. Whoops and laughter erupted with each move. Joe didn't give a lot of direction. He let Team Rogue jump and capture, then alternately accept their fate and be removed from the game.

Ashley pointed at him as the game board cleared, and only a few human checkers remained on both sides. "Coming after you, Super Zooker," she determinedly announced, spoiling the effect with a giggle.

Soon it came down to the two of them. A checkerboard with a sweet young girl who'd overcome a major illness, and a Rogue who'd cheered her on. They faced off. A move had to be made, diagonally forward. He could avoid her by going left, or land in her path by shifting right.

He rubbed his knuckles over his chin. "What to do?"

Ashley stepped from her white square onto a black, close to him. An illegal move. The crowd went quiet. "We call it a tie." Her expression hopeful. "Like when we had wheelchair races at the hospital, and Batman, Captain America, and you crossed the finish line together. It's come down to you and me, Super Z."

The sideline official lifted his megaphone. "There are no ties."

The fans booed. Long and loud.

The air settled, and Joe informed the man, "Ties are allowed in fund-raiser checkers. Both sides win."

The crowd roared. The right decision had been made. Those on the bleachers stomped their feet in approval. He took Ashley's hand, walked her to the edge of the board. They hugged again. He kissed her on the forehead. She kissed him on his good cheek. Photographer Eden took memorable photos. The doctor soon lifted Ashley down. Her parents were waiting off to the side. Ashley's mom clutched a handful of Kleenex. Her dad was soft-eyed, his chin trembling.

Team Rogue hustled back onto the checkerboard. One

game left to play. Joe raised an eyebrow at Shaye. "Who's next?"

"Take a look over your shoulder," said Shaye. "They signed up for the fund-raiser with the first flyer, a month ago. Weeks before you arrived in town. Sponsored by local bars. They donated ten thousand dollars."

Joe fully turned. Stared. He shifted his jaw. Holy shit. There came his party posse, Team Zoo Squad, shuffling through the sand. Alyssa was leading eleven of the hottest girls on the beach. All in tight red T-shirts and short shorts. Ready to play checkers. Out to win.

Twelve

Woot-*woot* and wolf whistles shrilled the air. Joe's party posse had arrived. The most gorgeous women on the beach took to the checkerboard. Stevie stood off to the side next to Zane Cates, as the women homed in on their main man. Circling and sexual. All hotties with perfect bodies. Coming on to Joe.

Team Rogue stopped talking among themselves. Shaye voiced her unease, muttered, "Kids in the crowd. PG-thirteen, Zoo."

Her concern carried. Joe glanced her way, a man moderately hard of hearing. He grinned. "R-rated, got it."

The guys chuckled.

Shaye rolled her eyes. "Idiot."

Team Rogue listened as the Zoo Squad claimed his attention. "You promised a short weekend break, no longer," a gorgeous brunette reminded him as she got reacquainted. She wrapped her arms about his neck, and her red T-shirt hiked, baring her hip bones and belly. She kissed him full on the mouth. Broke their kiss with, "Missed you, guy."

Stevie's heart lost a beat. Apparently Joe had planned to return to his posse after their wedding shoot. How could he not? The women promised fun and fantasy with their suggestive bodies and sensual smiles. Good times at the bar. Great times in bed.

"That's Alyssa," Zane said, satisfying her curiosity.

"You know her? Them?"

"Not like Zoo knows them. They're all local. They catch fire for athletes."

Joe was a professional ballplayer. A match lit for sex and satisfaction.

A tall redhead patted Joe's butt. "Roz," noted Zane. She soon left Joe for Pax, showing heightened interest in the first baseman.

An athletically toned woman stroked his shoulder and chest, and skimmed his hip. She had incredible legs.

"That's Bo." Again from Zane. "Marathon runner." He quietly filled her in on each one.

Cady, as Stevie learned, led with her chest. The seams on her T-shirt strained, barely containing her large breasts. She hugged Joe with intimate familiarity.

"I've recently seen her with Sam," said Zane. "Holding hands on the boardwalk." He raised an eyebrow. "A few of Zoo's posse seem to be branching out."

Possibly, thought Stevie. Although one woman stuck to Joe like Velcro. Alyssa. She was last to take her square. "Beer later?" she asked him. "Me after midnight."

"We'll see." No commitment. No decline.

Both sides were now positioned to play. Sports-minded Bo directed the Zoo Squad. Joe maneuvered Team Rogue. Stevie admired both teams' strategy. The two were evenly matched. Up until the end. Joe knocked out Bo. Only to have Alyssa come after him. Three checkers remained. Two black, one red. Joe made it to the Squad's back row, was crowned. An about-face, and Alyssa got out of his way. She came after Stevie, who was positioned mid-board.

Stevie was aware that Joe could only move one diagonal space at a time in non-capture mode. Alyssa was on Stevie's ass, about to corner her. Joe managed to keep Stevie two squares beyond Alyssa's capture as he crossed the board to protect her.

He was all strut and checker-attitude when he finagled a backward jump, and took out Alyssa. She'd been concentrating on Stevie, not as a human checker, but as a woman sensing her competition. Now she looked narrow-eyed, pinched-mouth, releasing a forced laugh that he'd gotten the best of her.

Joe and Alyssa hugged it out. He let her go. Alyssa was slower to release him. Her hand lingered on his arm possessively. He crossed four squares to Stevie. Drew her up on tiptoe for a kiss. A claiming kiss that sketched deep lines in Alyssa's frown. Her amber gaze darkened with jealousy.

Dusk dipped the sun beneath the horizon. Neon lights from the boardwalk colored the sand. Music pounded a night rhythm. A flatbed truck came down the beach, bringing workers to dismantle the game boards. Rogues and challengers collected near the pier. There was widespread celebration. The atmosphere vibrated with exuberance and high spirits. Alyssa moved in, beside Joe. She elbowed Stevie. Purposely stepped on her toes. Tossed her hair and grinned. Meanly.

The crush of the crowd separated Stevie and Joe further. She found herself next to Zane. He had a big presence. Stevie felt safe beside him.

"What's next?" Pax called out.

"Beer!" The cry rose, gained momentum.

"Zoo's buying!" someone shouted. "Blue Coconut." Cheers exploded like fireworks. Deafening. A human shift, as partiers left the beach for the bar.

"Where're you headed?" Zane protected Stevie from the onslaught. A wave of humanity. Getting trampled was not her idea of a good time. She'd lost track of Dean and Lori. Joe had been quickly swept away by his party posse and booze fans. Stevie had no chance to catch him. She could only watch him go. With Alyssa. Away from her. Disappointment flooded her.

She shrugged. "I have no idea."

He motioned her to join him. He talked as they walked. "Blue Coconut is a townies' hangout, two blocks off Main Street. The bar can get loud. People talk over each other and the music on the jukebox. No dress code. Baskets of shelled peanuts are served. The shucked shells are tossed on the floor. Crunchy underfoot. A life-size neon Elvis statue leans against one corner of the bar. Dartboards and pool tables draw customers to the back rooms." Pause. "The place will be packed, a bouncer at the door, a line down the sidewalk, sometimes into the parking lot, but I've never been turned away."

He was a Cates—the family owned the town and operated the boardwalk businesses. In a family of five siblings, Zane was the second oldest of the Cates brothers, a year behind Dune. A year ahead of contractor Aidan. Then came Shaye, and lastly, Rylan.

Stevie had gotten to know the hurricane hunter as the afternoon progressed. He flew with the 53rd Weather Reconnaissance Squadron, stationed at Keesler Air Force Base, in Biloxi, Mississippi. Rylan called him "mental" because Zane flew into tropical storms and the eyes of hurricanes. A nice guy from what she could tell. Built like a brick, crew cut, single-dimple smile. Home on a week's leave.

They soon rounded a corner, a half block from the bar. The door stood open, music blasted, and couples danced on the sidewalk to "Ain't Too Proud to Beg" by the Temptations. Free and uninhibited. Stevie slowed near a streetlight. She was curious about the bar. About the party scene. About Joe and his posse. His relationship with Alyssa. Yet a part of her held back.

Zane stopped beside her. "Problem?"

"I'm not sure I want to go inside."

"Second thoughts?"

She twisted the gold band on her thumb. "I've never met Zoo, the hell-raiser. The partier. Downing beers. The most popular guy in the place. The man of many women."

"How *do* you know him?"

"As Joe, a man who loves his dog. Kind. Considerate." She half-smiled. "Persistent." He'd wanted her. Once.

"Avoidance, Stevie?"

"I'm not escaping who he is. Who he might always be. I'm merely protecting my heart."

He eyed her closely. "Sad?"

"Over a man I never had?"

"You may still have him. You just don't realize it."

"Joe is the poster boy of the single life."

"Don't fool yourself." His voice was low. "The right woman wakes up a man. He suddenly finds being a couple more exciting than living alone."

She appreciated his male perspective. "Speaking from experience?"

A self-deprecating grin. "I've loved, lost, and wished things had turned out differently."

She closed her eyes. "I'm wishing right now . . ." Only one man could make that wish come true, and he was in the bar, while she stood on the sidewalk outside. She sighed. "Time to call it a night." She'd ridden to the beach with Dean and Lori, and had no idea where they'd disappeared to. She'd thought to catch a ride back to the house with Joe. No longer a possibility. A cab? Eyes opened, she noticed traffic on the street was bumper to bumper for as far as she could see. Walking was out of the question. Too dark. Too far.

Zane was a mind reader. "Can I give you a lift?"

"I live at a dog day care."

"Rylan mentioned you were Twyla's niece, in town while she recovered from a broken leg." He knuckled his jaw. "Are you hungry?"

She and Lori had split a ham sandwich at lunch. Nothing since. "What did you have in mind?"

"I'd like to decompress after the crowd today. We can pick up a pizza, take it back to Unleashed. Work for you?"

"Sounds good," she agreed.

He had a sudden glint in his eye that hadn't been there moments ago. Not until he'd mentioned pizza. They left the blaring music and the wild crowd, and walked a short distance, soon locating his 1967 Chevy Impala in the employee parking lot behind the boardwalk shops. The muscle car rumbled and growled with the turn of the key. Throbbing metal. Powerful.

"I restore old cars," he told her.

"A mechanic at heart?"

"Antique vehicles pulse with the past."

She liked Zane Cates. She felt comfortable with him. They'd only met that afternoon, yet he had the familiarity of an old friend. He drove to Zinotti's Pizza, located on Commercial Boulevard, alongside other fast food restaurants.

It was a busy place, and parking was tight. He dropped her off at the front door. "Order whatever you like. I'll be in to pay as soon as I find a spot."

As Stevie entered Zinotti's, she was greeted by a red-and-white-checkered floor, red booths packed with customers, enormous photos of pizzas with different toppings, and a short counter for orders. She studied the blackboard menu on the wall near the kitchen.

A striking woman appeared through the swinging doors, stepped behind the counter. She wore a Zinotti's signature T-shirt and black jeans. Her name tag tipped over her left breast. Tori. A pile of auburn hair set off light blue eyes, arched cheekbones, and full lips. Her smile was welcoming. "What can I get for you?" she asked.

Stevie liked the basics, extra cheese and pepperoni. Zane was big, brawny, and appeared like a guy who'd order the works. "Large, the works," she ordered.

"Crust?" Tori asked, her gaze on the computer screen.

Stevie had no idea. She was about to say "plain" when Zane swung through the door. Hearing the question, he went with, "Jalapeño garlic."

Tori's head snapped up. Her jaw clamped shut. A stunned, hurt look flickered in her eyes, followed by the flint of anger. The anger held. Heated.

"What are you doing here?" A low hiss that didn't disturb the diners.

Zane approached the counter, his expression closed. "Picking up a pizza."

"There are four pizza joints on the highway."

"None have your personality."

A dark glare and a harsh word. "Asshole," muttered under Tori's breath. Still audible.

The diners ignored them, as if they'd seen and heard it before. Stevie figured they were residents, not seasonal snowbirds. Locals would recognize Zane Cates. Tori was perhaps a long-term employee.

Silence lengthened, harsh and antagonistic. Stevie stepped aside, out of their line of fire. She eyed them from the far corner of the counter. She sensed a lot of baggage. Hostility or chemistry? Hard to tell. An invisible undercurrent between the two ignited tangible sparks. Tori's features were tight with resentment. Zane's face showed raw control.

Zane finally approached the counter. "Jalapeño garlic crust," he repeated.

Tori's voice sharpened. "I heard you the first time."

Zane reached for his wallet. "How much?"

She deliberately quoted double the cost, according to the pricing on the blackboard menu.

A snicker from a corner booth, covered by a cough. No argument from Zane. He counted out thirty-five dollars, placed the money on the counter. Tori punched his order into the computer, took his cash, and returned to the kitchen.

Stevie watched Zane watch Tori. She disappeared, and his expression slipped for a heartbeat. Indifference fell to pain and disappointment. A moment's vulnerability. He cared.

Zane stared for an inordinately long time at the tip jar between the straw container and napkin holder. Thoughtful. He added a Benjamin Franklin to the singles and change. Stevie's eyes widened at the hundred-dollar tip. For a pizza. Generous man.

He fully detached with Tori's return, pizza box in hand. Tori regarded Stevie and Zane, and Stevie picked up on her look. Her quiet evaluation of their relationship. Were Zane and she a couple? A tinge of hurt appeared in her eyes. Rapid recovery. Back to being mad.

Tori handed the box to Stevie. "Zinotti's thanks you." It was a stiff good-bye. Totally dismissive.

Stevie had the sudden urge to tell the woman that she'd just met Zane, and that they were no more than two new friends sharing a pizza. Zane disrupted her thought, delaying her confession. He curved his hand over her shoulder, nudged her toward the door. "Let's go."

He released his hold in the parking lot. Soon leaned his hip against the rear bumper of his Chevy Impala. He blew out a frustrated breath. Said, "Tori still hates me."

"Who is she to you?"

His pause was so long, she wondered if he'd even tell her. "My ex-wife."

"Oh . . ." Made sense. An explosive history. No surprise, then, to those in the diner. There was a good chance they'd witnessed similar exchanges. Passionate, yet unfriendly.

"An unresolved misunderstanding." He left it at that. He opened the passenger-side door, held the pizza box while she settled on the seat. Told her, "You're taking the first bite. Tori had poison in her eyes."

They arrived at Unleashed as the last pet owner, Livia Taylor, fetched her Brussels griffon, Chester. Stevie found Twyla in the entry hall, leaning heavily on her crutches. She looked tired. There was no one else around. Stevie felt suddenly guilty for taking the time off.

"Where's Dana and Berkley?" she asked her aunt, mentioning their two loyal employees.

"I let the girls leave early," said Twyla. "Several of the owners ran unavoidably late. There was no reason for all of us to wait for them." She pursed her lips. "Dean called, requested an overnight for Etta. I fed Turbo and her. They're out back playing. He chases her. She chases him. They're fun to watch."

She slipped off her glasses, rubbed her eyes. Resettled them low on her nose. Stared at the man beside Stevie. Familiarity lightened her eyes. "Zane Cates, I thought that was you. How are you, son?"

"Well, Twyla, thanks. On leave, home for a week. Catching up with family and friends."

"How're your parents? Your granddad?"

"My folks are on a cruise. Grandpa Frank is living large at the retirement village. He turns ninety this summer."

Twyla smiled. "Good to hear. Did you take part in the game-day fund-raiser?"

Zane nodded. "Rylan recruited me. That's where I met Stevie."

"Two hours of checkers, and he brought me home," Stevie supplied.

"Joe?" her aunt questioned.

"Having a beer with friends."

"You didn't join him?"

No official invitation. She'd stood beside him on the beach until the push, shove, and wave of humanity lifted and landed him at the Blue Coconut. He hadn't missed her. Hadn't come looking for her. She hedged, "I was more hungry than thirsty. You're welcome to join us."

"Appreciated, but I have plans." She turned and hobbled down the hallway ahead of them. She paused at the back door. "George is stopping by later with Chinese. We're both fond of pepper steak."

With one foot out the door, Twyla snapped her fingers, remembering. "There's a message for you on the table. A feature editor from *I Do* magazine would like to stop by late tomorrow afternoon. She'd appreciate an interview to go with the photo shoot."

Stevie held her breath. "Just the bride, or the groom, too?" She'd much prefer to do the interview alone.

Wasn't meant to be. "The couple, if possible," her aunt informed her.

"Might be just me." If Joe declined, preferring to be with Alyssa and his party posse.

Twyla's expression was sympathetic. "You know best, dear." She slipped out.

Did she know best? Stevie wondered. She wasn't so sure. A headache threatened, and her heart hurt.

She walked with Zane into the kitchen. Set the pizza box on the table. Then went to the cupboard and found paper plates. "Forks or fingers?" she asked him.

"Pizza tastes better with fingers."

That it did. Ripped sheets of paper towels became their

napkins. She looked in the refrigerator, asked, "What would you like to drink? Iced tea, Dr Pepper, beer?" Joe's beer.

"Brand of beer?"

"Red Dog."

Zane's brow creased. "I know only one guy who drinks Red Dog."

"Me." Joe now stood in the doorway, his fists clenched. The calmness in his voice was deceptive.

Her breath caught. Stevie turned so quickly, she banged her hip on the refrigerator door. "You're home early."

"Early enough to catch you having pizza with Zane."

"A great pizza with the works," Zane said casually.

Joe widened his stance. He crossed his arms over his chest, hooked his thumbs in his armpits. His *Team Rogue* shirt appeared stretched, as if it had been pulled by fans. He glared at Stevie. "Where did you go?" His tone was low, accusing. "You disappeared. I thought you were behind me as we left the beach. I turned around inside the Coconut and found Alyssa instead." His gaze darkened. "I waited for you. Saved you a seat. You never showed. I left."

Alyssa had taken Stevie out with an elbow to the ribs and a stomp on her toes. Stevie didn't rat her out. Instead, she said, "We got separated with the first crush of the crowd." It had been enormous.

"I came to look for you," he stated. "Too late, apparently. You hooked up with Zane."

Hooked up for supper, nothing more. "I lost—"

"Lost you, found me," said Zane around his first bite of pizza. His tone was intimate. Expectant. Goading.

Stevie started. What was he doing?

Provoking Joe, apparently. The muscles in his jaw flexed hard. Joe's blue eyes turned midnight dark. His temper was barely contained.

She held up a bottle of Red Dog, asked, "Share a beer with Zane?"

"Only my beer."

Sounded ominous. She didn't fully understand. What more could Zane possibly want, that Joe wasn't willing to give?

Something, apparently. Zane looked at Joe. A checkmate stare. Provoking. Intense.

Stevie returned to the table. Set down the beer. Zane pushed back a chair with his foot, offering her a seat. Next to him. "Don't let the pizza get cold, sweetheart."

"She's not your sweetheart."

"The night is young," Zane dared.

Tension vibrated between the two men. The air was thick with testosterone, and escalating rivalry. Spiked irritation.

Stevie sat slowly. Uncertainly. On edge. Zane leaned close, and their shoulders bumped when he scored his second slice. Selecting one piled with more meat than vegetables.

"Join us?" she invited Joe.

"Not sure there's enough to go around." Zane's response shook her. Only two pieces were missing from the large pie. There was plenty left.

Joe's refusal was evident in his silence.

"Try this, Stevie." Zane held his slice near her mouth, offering to feed her. A couple's gesture.

She had no choice but to take a bite. A small bite, otherwise she would've choked. Cheese stuck to one corner of her mouth. Zane thumbed it, pressed it between her lips. Familiar. Overly friendly.

Joe crossed the kitchen in three long strides, before she could even swallow. He flattened his big hands on the table, his fingers curled on the wood. "She can feed herself, and she has her own napkin."

Zane had the balls to touch her mouth a second time. "Missed the sauce." He traced her lower lip.

Stevie was certain there was no sauce. That Zane was merely taunting Joe, for whatever reason.

Joe's growl was guttural. Hellhound-menacing. "Touch her again, and—"

"You'll what?" Zane draped his arm over the back of her chair just to annoy Joe further.

Joe dipped his head, dragged air deep into his lungs. Brought calm to his chaos. "If you weren't Rylan's brother . . ." The threat hung between the men.

"You'd what?" Zane pushed.

"Show you the door. You need to leave."

Zane's grin came slowly, annoyingly. "There's no ring on Stevie's finger. She's free to see whomever she likes."

"Her call." Joe's tone was sharp. "Choose, Stevie. Him or me."

So un-Joe-like. He'd put her on the spot with his seeming jealousy. Demanding a decision. She balked. Said nothing.

"Pick me, and I'll pick you back," Zane said around a mouthful of pizza. Challengingly.

Ludicrous. Stevie recognized a blatant lie when she heard one. Especially from a man who was still hung up on his ex-wife. She realized he was matchmaking. In the most obvious, obnoxious way. Shoving Joe into a corner. Requiring him to commit. Zane's intentions might be good, but it wasn't fair to Joe. She didn't want him to feel trapped.

She held back. She knew Joe liked her; he'd told her so. But did his feelings go deeper? Liking and loving were very different. Joe held his emotions close to his chest. She refused to force his hand.

She placed a piece of pizza on her paper plate. Pushed

off her chair. Took both men in with a glance. "I'm the one leaving. You two need to get along."

Zane's chuckle followed her out.

Along with Joe's, "What the hell?"

"Hell is what women put us through when we love them," was the last thing she heard from Zane, as Stevie climbed the stairs.

"I need a beer," came from Joe.

Men!

Stevie hadn't mentioned the magazine interview to Joe. He'd spotted the message beneath a corner of the pizza box. Read it. He'd done the photo shoot. He was the designated groom. She might not want him answering questions, for fear of what he'd reveal. Too bad. He planned to field at least one or two. Like it or not.

He'd left practice and headed back to Unleashed. His teammates had teased him unmercifully in the locker room about leaving the Blue Coconut before he'd even sat down. He didn't give a damn. They had no complaint. He'd paid for two rounds of drinks, got the party started. Stevie was a no-show. He had missed her. She filled a part of his heart he hadn't realized was empty. It was a scary realization, but worth investigating. He'd cut out, desperate to find her.

Finding her at the dog care with Zane had twisted his nuts. Of all the men on the beach, Zane was a straight shooter. The last to steal another man's woman. Yet Zane had pissed him off. Joe had nearly punched him. Over Stevie. His lady. One minor problem—she didn't know he wanted her in his life permanently. There was always a chance she'd reject him. The interview would tell all.

Joe parked in the circular driveway, exited his Jag, and bounded up the steps. Banged the front door wide.

Closed it more gently. Turbo spotted and greeted him, for all of a second. Only to take off again after Etta. Etta slowed to sniff a male pit bull named Biff. Turbo cut between them, herded Etta out the back door. His boy was territorial.

He glanced in the office, saw Stevie behind the desk. Her blond hair was spiky, as if nervously tugged. Perhaps she'd contemplated telling the truth. That she had no real fiancé. She'd have to face judgment in that case. He didn't want her hurt or embarrassed. A dark-haired woman faced her on a wingback chair. He didn't knock, just entered. His gaze was on Stevie. "Hey, babe."

She straightened, stiffened, unsure of him. They hadn't spoken since the previous night. Her "Hey, yourself," sounded forced. Awkward. "I wasn't sure you'd be here."

A twist to his lips. "Almost didn't make it. The note was under the pizza box. Not in plain view."

He introduced himself to the feature editor. A pretty lady in a red pantsuit with a notepad on her lap. "Joe Zooker."

"Candace Mayne." They shook hands.

He was used to women checking him out. Candy of the light eyes and parted lips openly stared. He was barely presentable. Hair uncombed, unshaved, scraped cheek, scripted T-shirt reading *In My Defense, I Was Left Unsupervised*, ripped jeans. Old, unlaced Adidas sneakers. Nothing much to look at, as far as he was concerned. Still, her gaze held on him. He shrugged. Moved over to Stevie.

Stevie's eyes rounded when he hefted a second wingback over the corner of the desk, jammed it in beside her. Big chair, small space. Tight. He dropped down, hooked his arm about her shoulders, and hugged her close. The moment called for him to kiss her full on the mouth. He went with it. No tongue, but he did nip her bottom lip. Stevie blushed as red as the editor's pantsuit.

Candace smiled approvingly. Stevie was clearly shaken. Unsettled.

He nodded to Candy. "Ask us anything."

"Nothing's off-limits?"

"Your exclusive."

That pleased her. She opened with, "Do you believe in love at first sight?"

Joe didn't miss a beat. "Not before Stevie. We met at the bridal event on the boardwalk. She caught my eye."

"How? Who initiated contact?"

Joe winked at Stevie. "She was trying on a garter. Lady has great legs. I complimented her."

Candace jotted down his reply. She eyed Stevie. "After his compliment?"

Stevie hesitated, slowly said, "I walked away."

"Played hard to get?" asked Candace.

"He . . . caught me."

"That he did," said Candace. "Lucky you."

"Lucky me," Joe added.

Candace tapped her ink pen on her notepad. "So, you haven't known each other long, then."

Stevie faltered, and Joe advanced, "I'm not bound by time. Never have been." He squeezed Stevie close. "I live in the moment. Stevie's more reserved. I told her to flip her calendar ahead a month or more, to whenever she'd be ready for me. She chose June."

Candace laughed. "Summer, Stevie, as in a June wedding?"

"To be determined," Stevie hedged. "Baseball comes first."

"A woman who understands her future husband's career," Candace complimented. She pursed her lips, specifically asked Stevie, "Joe, or Zoo to his fans, has the reputation of being a wild man. Both on and off the field. How do you deal with the fans, the women?"

Stevie owned it. "What fans? What women?" she returned. "When we're together, it's just us."

"So, you're a woman who is secure with her man?"

"Never a doubt." Firm, final.

Joe inwardly smiled, relieved by her answer. Stevie was a psychologist. She didn't analyze him, but she got him. Crazy-ass past and all. She was his present. His future.

Candace further questioned, "Small or large wedding?"

Stevie was thoughtful. "I'd like something similar to the photo shoot. As many dogs in attendance as guests."

"Speaking of the shoot, I have some preliminary pictures." Candace went to her briefcase, removed a file. She spread three photos on the desktop. Two in color. One black-and-white.

Joe studied them alongside Stevie. Her breath caught, her heart in her eyes, and he knew why. His own heart warmed. There was nothing phony or pretend about the pictures. It appeared to be a real-life wedding.

Candace confirmed his thought. "A beautiful bride. A rugged groom. Visible flirting. A sexy happiness. Dogs, a part of the family. One of our best shoots. It'll be the centerfold."

"Publication month?" Stevie softly worried.

"May, both digital and print."

Stevie sank against Joe. "Only two months."

"We could be married by then."

"Or not."

"Where would you honeymoon?" asked Candace.

"Barefoot William is paradise," said Stevie.

"Location is irrelevant," from Joe. "A great bed is all that matters. A big brass bed." As in Stevie's bedroom. "Newlyweds seldom leave their hotel suite, anyway."

Stevie pinched his thigh, indicating *too much information*. Candace smiled, pleased. He was adding zing to her article. She had one final question. "Engagement ring? I don't see one on your finger."

Stevie flinched, but Joe filtered her unease. He laced their fingers, held up their hands. Sunlight split the windowpanes, glancing off the gold bands each of them still wore. "From the *I Do* shoot. Kind of romantic, don't you think? Stevie knows I love her."

Candace sighed. "Beautifully sentimental." She gathered the photos off the desk, returned them to her briefcase. "I'd like to talk with Twyla, get a little background on Unleashed, if she has the time."

"My aunt loves to share the Unleashed story. The dog day care is her first love."

"Maybe her second love," Joe whispered near her ear, as they stood. "George is moving up fast."

They walked Candace to the kitchen, where Twyla was baking organic treats for the dogs. She was ready to get off her feet, and she settled in a chair, willing to answer questions. Stevie stayed behind, waiting for the timer to go off, so the biscuits wouldn't burn.

Joe went in search of Turbo. He found him in the backyard, hiding in the crawl tunnel with Etta. He let them be.

"Hi, groom," Lori called to him. She was playing ball with three collie puppies. She and Twyla were the only two aware of the photo shoot, outside of those from the magazine. They knew the wedding was staged, imaginary, and they were sworn to secrecy. "How was the interview?" she asked.

"We upheld the image."

She threw a handful of rubber balls, and the puppies scampered off. She approached Joe. "For how long?"

"It's up to Stevie. I've no plans to break off our engagement."

Lori gaped. "Reality check. Don't lead her on."

"I'm not."

"Oh..." Her smile was dazzling. "Dean and I might have news soon, too. Based on this week's outcome."

Triple-A cuts. Dean had lived up to the coaches' expectations. But was he ready for the major leagues? The final roster would soon be announced. There was a team meeting scheduled for late Friday. Kason Rhodes had an appointment to speak to the team.

The back door opened, and Stevie called out, "Pickup time. Gather the pups. The owner's waiting."

Lori whistled, and two of the three collies listened. The third ran away from her. Lori looked at Joe, who took the hint and chased down the little guy. As he carried the pup inside, he noticed the name on his collar, Dash. He lived up to his name.

Joe cornered Stevie. "Is she gone?" he asked, referring to the feature editor.

"Candace just left. She and Twyla had a nice chat."

"We need to talk," he pointedly said.

"I know." She sounded defeated. She expected him to dump her. Not his intention.

"Your bedroom, in an hour."

His chosen location surprised her. She slowly nodded.

He slipped his car keys from his jeans pocket. "I've got an errand to run. Back shortly."

Fifty minutes later, he returned to an empty foyer, carrying a bakery box. No sign of Stevie. Or Turbo. Twyla poked her head out from the kitchen. "Quiet night. Your boy's with me."

Joe was appreciative. He took the stairs two at a time. Knocked once on Stevie's bedroom door, warning her of his arrival, then entered. He found her looking out the window. Her back was to him. Sunlight kissed her hair, one side of her face. His heart swelled, warmed, just looking at her. He didn't fight the feeling. He let it spread. It felt amazingly good.

He set the bakery box on the table, then went to her. Separated from Stevie by inches, he'd yet to touch her.

She dipped her head, and her shoulders sagged. "I'm listening, Joe," she said, requesting that he speak first.

He did so. "Good dialogue with the feature editor."

She started. "You thought the interview went well?"

"We gave her what she wanted."

"A notepad of untruths."

"Who's to say what's real, what's not?"

"We know better."

"I want what's best for us."

She turned slightly. "And that would be . . . ?"

"Whatever you want."

"I got us into this—I'll get us out."

"You breaking off our engagement?"

"We were never really engaged."

"We convinced people we were," he reminded her. "We shared a photo spread."

"Couples part ways, without explanation."

"You'd need a damn good reason for dumping me."

"You're not the marrying type."

"You don't know that."

She faced him fully. "Prove me wrong."

"A cupcake will set you straight." He guided her to the table. "For you."

She eyed the box, uncertain. Her hand shook as she lifted the lid. A peek inside, and she gasped. Could barely catch her breath. "What does this mean?"

He collected the gourmet treat. The wrapper was swirled in silver and gold with a lacy white bow. "That I like jumbo cupcakes. Vanilla cake, whipped vanilla frosting."

"The topper?" Her eyes were overly bright.

It was a plastic bride and groom. "Us, our future. Marry me, Stevie."

Tears escaped, and she cried. Not quite the reaction he'd expected. "Is that a yes?" he asked, seeking assurance.

She nodded against his chest.

"Happy tears?" he assumed.

She only wept harder. He could live with happy tears. She was *really* happy. He held the cupcake in one hand, eased her close with the other. He comforted her. She wrapped her arms about his waist. Held him tight. Sobbed out her soul. For minutes. Finally she was able to say, "I love you."

He spoke his heart. "I love you, too."

She sniffed, reached around him for a Kleenex from the table next to the bakery box. Wiped her eyes, blew her nose. Managed a watery smile. "A cupcake proposal."

"Best I could do on short notice."

"It looks delicious."

They tasted the cupcake—and each other.

And were very satisfied.

The week progressed in a blur. Days of spring training. Nights with Stevie. Twyla and Lori cried over their engagement. Joe figured tears were a woman's thing. He'd passed the Kleenex around.

The Rogues' locker room went silent when he told his teammates he'd be getting married. No one believed him at first. The boozer with the party posse had finally found his woman. Stevie did it for him. She calmed him. Settled his soul. Married player Brody Jones was the first to congratulate him. Their fist-bump sent a tremor up Brody's arm. He winced. Odd. His buddies came around. Joking, offering marital advice, happy for him.

Later that afternoon Kason Rhodes and the coaches conducted a meeting first with the Rebels, then with the

Rogues. It was a sober moment when the minor leaguers exited the conference room, shouldering their disappointment at not landing on the seasonal roster. The guys shook hands with the pros, followed by a few slaps on the back. They next hefted their athletic gear and duffel bags and boarded the Greyhound bus. Back to Roanoke.

Joe was quick to note that Dean Jensen and pitcher Noah Scanlon were not in line for the bus. What the hell? The Rogues were soon called to the meeting room. Brody hung back, didn't attend.

The room was large, yet Joe immediately spotted the two Rebels in the back row, on the far side. Taking in the meeting with the team. That did not bode well for Joe. He and Dean had both fought for left field. His gut tightened. He'd know his fate soon enough.

The remaining Rogues crowded in, found seats. Kason surveyed the room. He congratulated the team on a strong spring training. And he was proud to announce the addition of Jensen and Scanlon to the roster. Scanlon would close for starting pitcher, Will Ridgeway. Nods all around. He had a hell of a fastball. Didn't rattle easily. He was ready for the majors.

Kason read off the infield starters, no big surprises. Until he got to shortstop. "Brody Jones won't be returning this season," he said solemnly. Silence settled heavily over the room. "Because of a recurring shoulder injury, he's decided to retire."

Brody was older than the other players, often quiet. He came to work and did his job. No complaints. He'd covered short as if his life depended on it. He would head back to Plain, West Virginia, with his wife and kids. He would be missed.

Kason called off names in the outfield next. He stopped at left. His gaze shifted between Joe and Dean. "There's been stiff competition for left field. Joe's got longevity.

Dean's coming on fast." There was a prolonged pause. "Execs and coaches feel that Dean deserves a chance this year."

A chance at left field . . . Where did that leave Joe?

An unnerving silence until Rylan stood, his shoulders squared. An unprecedented moment. "Team captain objection, with all due respect. I want to speak on Zoo's behalf. No offense to Dean, but Zoo's proved himself over five seasons. He's solid in left. The man face-smashed the cement post to catch your fly ball. Let the roster stand."

Halo Todd pushed to his feet next. "Zoo throws dead-on from left to home. We don't need a relay third baseman. No offense, Landon."

"None taken." Landon rose and said, "Zoo's difficult, hard-core, but he always has our back, on and off the field. I vote for him."

Pax, Sam, and Will added their endorsements. Catcher Hank Jacoby reiterated the strength and alignment of each outfield throw. It was a humbling moment. Joe was part of the team, but not until that moment did he truly feel the brotherhood. Eight players stood by him. Their opinions mattered. Even if they didn't sit well with Kason.

Joe glanced over his shoulder at Dean. He sat slumped on his chair. Unhappy. Uneasy. Unwelcome. Joe felt an honest sympathy for the man. Whatever the ultimate result would be, his teammates had stuck by him. He exhaled his hatred for the minor leaguer. Breathed in hope.

"Done, guys?" Kason appeared more amused than annoyed. There was no further opposition. "Had you let me finish . . ."

Kason's "*finish*" stayed with Joe on the drive back to Unleashed. He couldn't believe the outcome. Dean pulled in behind him at the doggy day care. Both men climbed from their vehicles. Neither tried to trip up or shove the other off the stairs. It was six fifteen, and Unleashed was closed for the day. All the dogs had been picked up. Stevie and Lori huddled in the entry hall. Twyla and George in the background. All awaiting their news.

Each man embraced his woman. Shaking and scared, Lori spoke first. "What happened?"

Stevie clutched his arms, whispered, "Joe?"

He eased her mind. "I'm still playing left."

Relief from Stevie, followed by concern for her cousin. Her gaze clouded. She bit down on her bottom lip. "Oh . . . Dean."

Lori closed her eyes, disappointed.

Joe held up his hand. "Don't feel bad for the Rogue."

Both girls startled. Lori's eyes snapped wide. "The *Rogue*?"

Seconds of suspense passed before Dean grinned, told them, "Brody Jones is retiring. Shoulder damage. Kason Rhodes went back through my college records, noticed I'd played shortstop for two years before moving to outfield. That I'd won the Brooks Wallace Award, Shortstop of the Year, determined by the College Baseball Foundation." A release of breath. "I always liked short. The spine of infield action. I'm fast. Good arm. Kason offered me the position. I'm suiting up in the majors."

Lori whooped, jumped on Dean, wrapping her legs around his hips. Relieved laughter and lots of kisses. They slowly broke apart. Dean received heartfelt congratulations from Stevie, Twyla, and George. Joe gave him a short nod of approval, then stepped back.

He went in search of his rottie. He found Turbo and Etta in the Toy Room, surrounded by tennis balls, Kongs, Nylabones, Frisbees, and stuffed socks. They chewed together on opposite ends of a tug rope. Etta had brought him to heel. His once-manic dog was now mannered. Tamed. Content.

Stevie came up behind him. Curved her arm about his waist. Leaned into his side. "Turbo will be glad Dean made the team."

"My boy would've missed Etta if Dean had returned to Roanoke."

"The dogs will continue to see each other here, and then back in Richmond. A happy ending. Not only for them, but for Lori and Dean, too."

"Dean." He ran his hand down his face. "A Rogue. Blows my mind. A total mental explosion."

"It's been a life-changing couple of weeks. Twyla and George. You and me."

"Meant to be is meant to be."

"I think so, too."

Turbo yawned, nudged Etta. The two dogs left the Toy Room for the kitchen. Joe grinned. "Inner clocks. It's dinnertime."

"I thought to make tacos for us," Stevie offered. "Cupcakes for dessert."

"Can we start with dessert?"

"If you like."

"I like."

He kissed her then, tasted her sweetness long before the cupcake. Dessert had nothing on Stevie. She was his favorite flavor. Forever.

Connect with Us

Visit us online at
KensingtonBooks.com
to read more from your favorite authors, see books
by series, view reading group guides, and more.

Join us on social media

for sneak peeks, chances to win books and prize packs,
and to share your thoughts with other readers.

facebook.com/kensingtonpublishing
twitter.com/kensingtonbooks

Tell us what you think!

To share your thoughts, submit a review,
or sign up for our eNewsletters, please visit:
KensingtonBooks.com/TellUs.